# WIRED ROGUE

PARADISE CRIME THRILLERS BOOK 2

TOBY NEAL

Cover Design: Jun Ares aresjun@gmail.com
Formatting: Jamie Davis

*"Unraveling external selves and coming home to our real identity is the true meaning of soul* work." ~ Sue Monk Kidd

# CHAPTER ONE

CHILDREN SHOULDN'T BE TREATED like slaves. Anger tightened Special Agent Sophie Ang's hands as she adjusted the binoculars a little more to focus in on ten kids of various ages, bent over in a water-filled patch of land planted in the deep green, heart-shaped leaves of the Hawaiian *kalo*. They wore bathing suits and palm frond hats as they worked in the hot sun, an adult supervising from the shade of a nearby palm tree.

Taro farming was backbreaking work, and it looked like the Society of Light cult was using their smallest members to work with the submerged tubers, a staple of the Hawaiian diet. Sophie's partner in the operation, Ken Yamada, shifted restlessly beside her in the camouflage surveillance tent on a rise of ground across the river from the compound. "Ten is more children than we were told about," he murmured.

"We have to locate the two targets," Sophie said, for the benefit of their SAC, Waxman, monitoring through their comms. "Can't identify the children positively yet." The homemade hats hid the red blond hair the children's mother had told the agents to look for. Sophie widened her scan, and took in the rest of the cult's property.

A high wooden wall provided cover and security for the

compound deep in the Waipio Valley on Hawaii. Surrounding their location were the vast, steep, green-jungled walls of the largest, deepest valley on the Big Island. Rising to breathless heights, bisected by a giant waterfall at the end, Waipio was a beautiful and untamed place where wild horses roamed and people lived as they had a hundred years ago. Midday sun overhead increased steamy humidity, and gnats and mosquitoes buzzed over the FBI's pop-up cover in a noxious cloud. Coconut palms and tropical trees broke up a sweep of pastureland before the compound, dotted with live-stock grazing beside the wide, jade-green river.

The site seemed to have been chosen for maximum defensibil-ity. Set deep in a valley that was accessible only through a single steep one-lane road, the complex was walled in wood and topped with razor wire. From their vantage point, they could look down into the grounds. Yurts were clustered like chicks around the hen of a big, metal, barn-like structure, probably where the cult met as a group. Its functions would be revealed as their surveillance progressed. "See any armaments?" Sophie whispered.

"Yeah. Nine o'clock. Sniper tower disguised as a tree," Yamada said.

Sophie's earbud crackled with their Special Agent in Charge's cool voice. "Get me eyes."

"Roger that, sir." Sophie turned and opened a plastic case. She took out the small, high-powered video camera with its instant wireless streaming abilities. The reverse camera showed Sophie's image as she screwed the camera onto a tripod and aimed it at the area Ken had identified. Her golden skin looked sallow in the little square, her large brown eyes haunted—but at least her cropped hair was too short to be any different than usual. Sophie applied her eye to the viewfinder and adjusted the high-powered lens.

A small platform, camouflaged with branches, was built into the tall avocado tree in the far corner of the compound. A man wearing green camo gear sat in the lookout, a rifle resting on the narrow parapet around the nest.

"Seems pretty extreme. Why would a peaceful cult out in the boondocks of this valley need to be walled and guarded with fire-power?" Ken said.

"And yet here we are, surveilling them," Sophie muttered.

"Right. Just because you're paranoid, it doesn't mean they aren't watching you." Ken's severely handsome face was unforgettable when he smiled. *Good thing he was gay.* The last thing she needed was to be attracted to a partner. A devastating breakup with her almost-boyfriend Alika six months ago had left Sophie lonely, prone to wondering if she'd always be that way.

"Stay focused. How many unsubs?" Waxman's crisp voice brought her back on task.

They continued to gather data all day, counting thirty adults, mostly white, in the twenty to forty-year-old age range. They tracked the flow of behavior patterns: children, supervised by a single adult, worked the taro fields in the morning while adults did other tasks among animals and gardens. A noon meal was held all together in the main building. Another shift of afternoon work by adults in fields, gardens, and outbuildings went on as the children were seated in a circle for some kind of instruction, in the shade of the sniper tree.

The cult leader, Sandoval Jackson, distinctive in orange robes trimmed in gold, walked the grounds, trailed by a woman attendant. Flowing silver hair and a full beard distinguished him from the severely buzz cut hairstyles of the other adults, all wearing various shades of orange robing.

"What does this cult believe in?" Ken kept his binoculars to his eyes as Sophie filmed the children, holding small whiteboards, participating in school-type instruction.

"The Society of Light promotes a blend of Sufism and Hindu beliefs." Sophie had put together a quick case file before they took the chopper out of Honolulu that morning. "Jackson apparently had a revelation that led to his development of the Society. He's been recruiting members of the well-heeled yoga set."

Sharon Blumfield, mother of two, a Society member that had "escaped," had initiated a case against the cult to get her children returned to her. It had come to the FBI after the Big Island PD had asked for their help in investigating the child kidnapping complaint.

"I don't see any abuse happening from the data you sent, or from the visual surveillance." Waxman's voice sounded tinny and detached. "Where is the father of the children?"

"They were fathered by Sandoval Jackson, the cult leader." Sophie's throat tightened on her reluctance to speak the words. *She wanted this case.* She'd pushed to get out from her computer lab and into the field to check out the complaint. The endless series of computer file reviews and hard drive reconstructions that made up the bulk of her work had been hard to concentrate on and find fulfilling, after the drama of her last case.

For the first time in her life, Sophie felt restless 'wired in' to her computers. She wasn't allowed to use DAVID, her data analysis program. She missed Alika and worried over his recovery from injuries, even though they weren't a couple and she was having no luck locating the enigmatic online vigilante, the Ghost, whom she'd uncovered on that last big case, though they continued to chat and flirt online.

Going to the Big Island to help some children be reunited with their mother had been a welcome change of pace.

"The cult leader is the father?" Waxman's voice was sharp. "We have no grounds for her kidnapping case, then. They are with a parent."

"Sir. They are being prevented from joining their mother," Sophie argued. "That's parental kidnapping."

"This is an armed compound filled with crazy religious civilians. Ever heard of Waco? We have no grounds to confront these people. Pull back. Let's discuss at headquarters."

Sophie bit her lip. "The children are being made to work long hours of manual labor. They aren't in school."

"Yes, and you see that with our migrant farm workers all over this nation," Waxman snapped. "Also, I notice on the video that they're being instructed and getting some kind of education, even if it's not the kind you or I might choose. No laws are being broken here. This is a custody issue between parents. Once the mother has an injunction from family court returning custody of the children to her, local PD can show up with a custody order and get them out and return them to her."

Disappointment curdled Sophie's stomach. "There must be something illegal going on there, or why would they have defensive capabilities?"

"I gave you an order, Special Agent. Stand down, pack up, and report to HQ for a team meeting review." A decisive click in her earbud made her wince as Waxman disconnected.

Ken was already stowing his binoculars in their molded plastic case. "You pissed him off."

*"Son of a goat herder's pox-ridden three-eyed cousin,"* Sophie muttered in Thai. *"I know. I hate that."*

"Well, he always goes easier on you than the rest of us." Ken slanted her a glance. "You're his pet."

Sophie didn't reply. That Waxman favored her was a fact—this investigation wouldn't have gotten even this far without that factor.

Her heart sank for the woman who'd escaped from the Society of Light and brought the case to their office via Big Island PD. A slim, narrow-hipped blonde with the kind of leathery skin that came from too much time outdoors, Sharon Blumfield had never stopped crying as she shared a story of recruitment, inclusion, virtual slavery, and degradation.

"I stayed in so much longer than I wanted to," Blumfield told them via Skype as they considered the case. "I didn't want to leave without my children. Jackson replaced me long ago in his bed, and I began to fear for my life. The other mothers of his children have all left the Society, never to be heard of again—I think something happened to his other women." She'd made ridiculous accusations at that point: that the women might have been sold into sex slavery, or become human sacrifices to enrich the crops. The cult believed in "aggressive reincarnation," a process by which people could advance further in the wheel of reincarnation through serving Jackson and sacrifice. Blumfield claimed this had led to "terrible acts by people high up in the leadership."

Captain Ohale, commanding officer of Hilo PD, sitting in on the video meeting, shook his head at that point. "Ma`am. You have no evidence whatsoever of any of these claims. We do take your complaint seriously, but without evidence of a crime…"

"My children are kidnapped and being held against their will," Blumfield insisted. Sophie couldn't stand it any longer, and had spoken up for their team, assuring the woman that they would check out the situation.

*And now they were pulled off the case, just that easily.*

Sophie looked back toward the walled compound as she and Ken folded the camo-printed pop-up surveillance cover. *"I'll get you out of there,"* she murmured to the children in Thai. *"I will find a way."*

Sophie had more ways than most to get things done.

# CHAPTER TWO

Sophie strode back to her office in the Information and Technology lab. She needed to work out—she felt hot, grubby, and highly irritable from the recent rehash of Waxman's rationale on the situation, and his final word nixing the Society of Light case.

She barely paused as she passed through the quiet, sound-proofed lab, cool as a subterranean cave. Dimly lit computer work bays glowed in the light of monitors, and dense, insulated carpeting absorbed her footfalls. Sophie's fellow agents, headsets on, eyes and fingers busy as they worked at the myriad tasks associated with computer and online investigation, barely looked up at her passage.

That was IT. Everyone was in his own little world that connected to a much bigger cyber world, and preferred it that way.

Sophie stopped at her own bay, quickly activating her faithful computers Amara, Janjai, and Ying, and setting up the video camera's data from the case to download. She grabbed a weighted jump rope and large exercise ball out from under her desk and took the items to the carpeted "lounge" area in the corner of the room, with its floor-to-ceiling tinted windows. Sophie always wore stretchy black pants, athletic shoes, and a tank shirt under her regular button-down so she could really move; now she stripped off her regulation shirt and got going on the rope.

Used to Sophie's exercise breaks, no one so much as looked up as she jumped, the whirl and slap of the rope on the padded, tight-napped carpet the only sound besides her even breathing.

Gradually the frustrated whirl of her thoughts calmed like a shaken snow globe settling. The rhythm of the rope, her breathing and heartbeat brought a temporary peace that she couldn't access any other way.

The lab began to empty out as six p.m. passed, but Sophie continued, finishing half an hour on the rope and switching to a workout using the large rubber exercise ball, as she mentally ticked over the steps of the case.

They'd taken the FBI chopper, painted in low-key matte camo paint, back out of the valley and stopped in at the South Hilo Station to speak to Captain Ohale, letting him know that the FBI had declined the case. Sophie had given the captain a copy of the video footage and surveillance data they had collected.

"I'm not sure if there's grounds for a child abuse or neglect case," Sophie said. "But our SAC recommends Ms. Blumfield pursue her concern through family court."

"Back on us, then." Ohale rubbed his chin with a thick finger. "You say the place is armed?"

"Yes." She'd described the sniper nest and security enclosure. "Can't tell if the wall is to keep people in, or out."

"Blumfield says both." Ohale had scrawled the woman's name, email address, and number on a memo pad from the Hilo PD. He handed it to Sophie. "You get to talk to her and tell her the bad news."

Sharon Blumfield was not going to take it well. Upon their return to the office in the chopper, the team meeting hadn't yielded anything but more frustration as they reviewed why this wasn't an FBI case, and she and Ken got a lecture from Waxman on unnecessary investigative expenditures, such as pilot time and helicopter fuel.

Sophie shut her eyes and speeded up her sit-ups on the ball in annoyance. Ohale wasn't going to do anything more than he absolutely had to, and she really didn't blame him. She couldn't use DAVID, her rogue data-mining program, at work to dig up anything else actionable on the cult. But when she got home, she could access it from her replica work lab...

"Sophie." Waxman's voice was right above her, and she almost fell off the big plastic ball in surprise.

"Sir." Sophie managed to turn the slide into standing, bouncing to her feet. She glanced around. The lab had emptied as everyone else left and she stood facing her boss alone.

"Leave off the 'sir.' It's Ben, remember?" Waxman reminded Sophie of Anderson Cooper, the journalist, with his prematurely silver hair and steel-blue eyes. He was always immaculately turned out, and today's mist gray suit fitted his well-maintained body flawlessly.

"Ben." Sophie set her hands on her hips and didn't soften her tone. "What can I do for you? I thought the meeting was pretty thorough."

"I came down to speak to you privately. I know you didn't like the outcome of today's investigation."

"I'm not sure what talking about it will achieve, sir."

Waxman slid his hands into his pockets and jingled some change there. "I've noticed you get emotionally involved in cases regarding children," he said mildly.

"Is that a problem?" Sophie widened her stance and crossed her arms, tightening her biceps. She'd practiced this pose for her MMA fights, to maximize her physical presence. "I notice you get particularly agitated whenever we have cases involving—oh. *Wait.* You never get agitated. The perfect wax man." She was being insubordinate, but he'd invited her to call him *Ben*, and right now she was past caring if she got written up. Waxman's brows rose in surprise as Sophie forged on. "I care about children. Nothing is going to happen for those kids now that we won't take the case."

"You don't know that. Ohale could still do something through Child Welfare or the mother's appeal to family court."

"You and I both know he's not going to take on that sniper tower."

"Well. Be that as it may, I won't reiterate the reasons this is not our case. I actually came down to tell you something else you won't like." Waxman folded his arms, imitating her posture, so Sophie dropped them. She wasn't falling for his matching body language mind games. "Remember I was going to get back to you about the presentation to the bureau chiefs about DAVID?"

Sophie nodded. In a final attempt to get Bureau approval, she'd put together a PowerPoint on the Data Analysis Victim Information Database, and how the program worked by searching law enforcement information data storage using keywords and a probability algorithm to predict outcomes of case hypotheses.

"They reviewed the information we provided and the cases in which the program was used. I'm sorry to tell you, the program was disapproved for use by the Bureau. Permanently. Furthermore, it's being confiscated as a security and liability risk." Waxman's jaw bunched.

"You can't do that." Sophie'd had these arguments with the Bureau already, and not that long ago. Her voice rose. "My patent application is pending. I own that program. You can't take it from me."

"Sophie." Waxman shook his head. "It's not me taking anything. I am in favor of DAVID, you know that. These decisions are being made above my head."

"Doesn't matter. DAVID doesn't belong to the FBI. And I don't either." The frustration boiling in Sophie's chest spilled over. "I won't work for an agency that doesn't see a good thing when it punches them in the nose."

Waxman froze, eyes widening. "We can work this out, I'm sure of it."

"I don't think so." Sophie paced back and forth in front of Waxman, hands on her hips. "Confiscated as a security and liability risk sounds pretty final to me. And I'm tired of these short-sighted restrictions and limitations. Like the case today."

"Those two things are completely different issues."

"That's undoubtedly true, but both of them illustrate the FBI's tendency to lose sight of the forest for the trees." She was proud of how calm her voice was, how adeptly she'd worked in that American idiom. "I'm sure there are plenty of security firms in the private sector that would be happy to have my talent on their team." Sophie refused to meet Waxman's eyes. He'd been more than a boss to her, and this conversation was painful—she didn't want to see in his face how it was for him. She bent and retrieved the jump rope and the ball. "I'm sure you'll need to have my resignation in writing. I'll have it on your desk by the morning, and given the hostile circumstances of the FBI's confiscation of my program, I'm sure you'll forego my two weeks' notice."

She walked back to her workstation and sat down, refusing to look at Waxman as he followed her.

"Sophie. Please." He set his hand on her shoulder but she shrugged away from his touch. Waxman spoke to the back of her head as she shut down her computer rigs. "I'll appeal this decision about DAVID. I will do everything I can to get it turned around."

Sophie blinked several times, hard, before slanting a glance up at Waxman. His cool blue eyes were sincere, his mouth pinched. "This team needs you, Sophie. *I* need you." Waxman took a breath, blew it out. "I'm sure I'm not that good at hiding how I feel."

Sophie pushed the wheeled chair out from her desk and stood to face him, apprehension tightening her chest. "What do you mean?"

"I mean that I care about you. I…" Waxman ran a hand through his immaculately barbered hair. "I don't want you to leave. Please stay."

Sophie backed up a step. "All the more reason, then, that I need to leave." She softened her tone. "Ben. I don't feel the same. And I never could."

Silence drew out for several long moments as they gazed at each other. The warm light in Waxman's eyes died out, leaving them an ashy gray.

"I understand. I'll look for your resignation in the morning." Waxman drew himself upright and walked out, shoulders squared. The light over the doorway lit his silver hair briefly.

Regret twisted Sophie's gut. He'd been a good boss, a great mentor, and a sometime friend—but she wasn't attracted to him that way.

The long-simmering situation with DAVID and the hidebound attitude of the FBI had finally brought things to a head. She found a box and packed her few personal items.

Just like that, her time at the FBI was over.

# CHAPTER THREE

GINGER, Sophie's yellow Lab, leapt out to give her an ecstatic greeting as Sophie unlocked the red lacquered door of the penthouse apartment owned by her ambassador father. Ginger had been at doggie daycare all day with plenty of exercise and company—but the dog never failed to act as if they'd been parted for weeks any time Sophie returned.

Ginger's slobbery affection was a balm. Sophie dropped to her knees in the doorway and embraced the dog's sturdy neck. "Oh, hey, girl. I need a hug today."

She fetched the dog's leash off the hook beside the door and they rode the elevator down to the ground floor as Sophie called her best friend, fellow agent Marcella Scott, to tell her the news.

"I'm quitting the Bureau," she said baldly when Marcella answered. She endured the shriek of negation and the peppering of questions. Sophie took Ginger outside to do her business on the scrap of lawn beside the elegant edifice as they talked. She was still on the phone when Jenns Rudinoff, head of building security, contacted her. She ended the call with Marcella to take the call.

"Ms. Ang, there's a detail from the FBI here with a search warrant."

"What?" The sentence wouldn't compute. Sophie yanked Ginger's leash and sprinted back toward the entrance. "Where are they?"

"At the check-in desk."

Sophie strode through the double doors into the elegant lobby, Ginger tight to her side. Fellow IT operative Special Agent Bateman, doughy and pale, and Ken Yamada stood at the security desk. "What the hell is this?"

"Let's speak privately." Ken's austere face was pale with strain. Bateman carried a black briefcase of tech tools and looked shifty-eyed.

"I hear you have a search warrant."

"I would prefer we spoke privately," Ken repeated. Sophie walked to the elevator and stabbed the button. They got on, Ginger panting and wagging with excitement to see her mistress's friends. As the doors closed, Sophie pointed to the dome of the security camera in the corner, so they rode up to her apartment in tense silence. Arriving at the small square foyer area with two doors to the penthouse apartments, Sophie whirled on them. "Ken! What the hell!"

"Waxman called me back in to work. Said you'd quit and that I was to serve you with a warrant for the retrieval and removal of company property. Namely, your DAVID program."

"I've been through this already." Six months before, Bateman had verified that DAVID was removed from Sophie's home rigs; she'd offloaded it to the Cloud for safekeeping and retrieval. With this latest development, Sophie hadn't had time to even take a shower let alone prepare for the swiftness of Waxman's response.

"Then you have nothing to worry about." Bateman's face was blank.

"Show me the warrant."

Ken produced it and handed it to her, his eyes downcast and movements slow. "Waxman told me you quit. Please tell me it's not true."

"True. And with this *monkey shit* going down, I'm obviously making the right decision." Sophie's hands shook so badly that she couldn't get the door keys into the lock. Ken took them from her and opened the door. Sophie deactivated the alarm as Ken gestured with his chin to Bateman.

"Go. Do what you have to do and don't take a minute longer."

Bateman headed for Sophie's bedroom with its triple bank of computers, set up to mirror her FBI workstation.

"Bateman won't be able to get in without this." Sophie pressed a button on her key fob that activated the triple-protected workstation. She turned away, facing the grand sweep of windows that was one of the nicest features of her father's swanky apartment. Tears pressed against the back of her eyes as she balled her fists at her sides. "This is so wrong. I own that program."

"I'm sorry this happened. I was in shock when Waxman called me to come in and serve this on you. What happened between the team meeting and now?" Ken's voice was soft with compassion.

"Waxman told me DAVID was denied for use by the FBI and was being 'confiscated.'" Sophie made air quotes with her fingers. "A security and liability risk. On top of today's fiasco with the Society of Light case, I'd had enough."

"I'm surprised Waxman let you resign." Ken's straight brows had drawn together in concern.

Sophie covered her face with her hands. "Like he can stop me. To top it off, Waxman apparently has…feelings for me. I told him they weren't reciprocated. I had to leave, with all of that." Sophie stuck one of her fists in her mouth and bit down on her thumb to keep the pain inside. "Everything I worked for. Everything I built…"

"Waxman's always been a straight-up guy—a bit of a prick, as we all knew. But going after you personally? No. He wouldn't do that. This warrant is simply shutting a door you left open on your way out. And I'm damn sorry about it all." Ken shook his head. "I hate to say it, but ultimately you might be happier in the private sector. Your skills will be in huge demand in the general marketplace, even if you can't use DAVID."

Bateman reappeared, case in hand. "Removed and saved one copy of the DAVID software to backup hard drive. Computer's clean. Cloud access to Bureau files is shut down. Security clearances are revoked." Bateman raised round, pale blue eyes to meet Sophie's. "I'm sorry. This hella sucks. We're going to miss you bad in the IT lab."

Sophie couldn't bring herself to speak. It was all she could do to keep the tears from falling. Bateman headed for the door and shut it.

Ken knew she didn't like a lot of touching, but he folded strong arms around Sophie, pulling her close. She rested her head on his shoulder briefly as he squeezed her tight. "You're going to be okay. I know you are, partner," he said softly. "You're going to come back from this stronger than ever. The FBI's lost the best agent I've ever known today."

Sophie let out a sob she'd held locked in her throat, but stood rigid, trapped in her feelings of grief and loss, unwilling to cry on the shoulder Yamada offered. Ken crushed her close for a long moment, then held her away, gazing into her eyes with his best samurai stare. "Don't let this get you down. You're better than all of us combined." Ken walked out and shut the door behind him.

Sophie made it to her bedroom on shaky legs and sat down at her computers. Her brain felt spongy as the depression, always waiting for her, rolled in like a damp and sticky fog. She had a few things to do before she took to her bed.

Sophie composed her resignation letter carefully. She stated her reasons for resignation to go on record for any future litigation, and emailed it to Waxman. She wrapped up the Society of Light case by emailing Sharon Blumfield the Bureau's decision, but adding that private security firms were available to assist in either getting the children out or collecting data for her family court case. She listed several, including Security Solutions, the one she'd investigated some months before.

There were good people at Security Solutions, including the CEO, Todd Remarkian, who had become something of a friend. They'd gone on a couple of hike-runs together, and she liked the upbeat, hardworking Aussie. Ginger adored Anubis, the dignified Doberman Todd had inherited from his partner who'd gone overseas.

And that partner was someone Sophie kept in touch with. She opened the private chat room contact she maintained with the man calling himself the Ghost. Logging in under her username of MMA Fighter, she typed out a note:

*"Thought I'd let you know I resigned from the Bureau. I won't be hunting you on their behalf anymore. Not that I ever got close enough to catch you. Still, it was fun to try."*

Sophie paused, fingers poised above the keys.

There was always the chance the Ghost was logged in and would see her note in real time. The hope that he was online mattered enough to frighten her. They exchanged messages several times a week, and Sophie had come to anticipate the flirty, sharp-edged, bantering exchanges with the man she suspected was Sheldon Hamilton, an eccentric billionaire and former CEO of Security Solutions, now living abroad at an unknown location.

As minutes went by, the heartbeat pulsing of the green cursor on the black background of the chat box gave her a lonely, vulnerable feeling.

*Here I am,* it seemed to say. *Here I am. Please hear me. Please answer me.*

And as usual, no one responded.

Sophie killed the window and pushed back from the desk. She shut down the rigs with a push of the key fob. She closed the heavy blackout drapes she needed to sleep, turned off her phone, stripped off her clothes, and crumpled into bed. She let Ginger come up on the jade-green silk comforter, and she embraced the warm, hairy, loving dog.

The Labrador licked the tears that flowed down Sophie's cheeks as she finally wept for all she'd lost.

# CHAPTER FOUR

MORNING WAS DISTINGUISHED from night by Ginger licking her face again—the drapes cut the light so completely there was no way to distinguish the two. Sophie rolled to look at the glowing red numbers of her bedside digital clock: 10:00 a.m.

"Oh, girl." She tossed the covers aside. "You need to go out." Ginger whined in agreement.

The depression she'd struggled with on and off since her late teens had swept Sophie under. Every movement felt forced and sluggish, like swimming through tar. Sophie walked through the apartment naked, as was her habit. She put the teapot on to boil water and took out a ceramic teapot, her body remembering the habitual movements of the morning ritual.

She would take one day to indulge in the depression. *Really wallow.*

After all, she didn't have anywhere to be today.

*Or any day.*

She was unemployed.

The thought made Sophie bow inward, hunching around the pain. The kettle dropped from her nerveless fingers into the elegant oval steel sink.

Tea wouldn't help. Nothing would help. She just needed to take the dog out. Then she could go back to bed and stay there until she felt better. *If she felt better.* The murk was so thick that ever feeling different seemed impossible.

Sophie dressed in running clothes and took Ginger outside into a bright Honolulu day. Mynahs chattered in the blooming rainbow shower trees on her block, colored petals fell like confetti in the warm breeze. Doves cooed and danced courtship to each other on the sidewalk as Ginger did her business on the scrap of lawn. Sophie's eyes registered it all, unseeing.

Ginger tugged and whined, looking down the sunny street with its swishing traffic, waving palms, and busy walkers. Sophie usually ran with the dog on her days off. Ginger wanted to do what they usually did, and bathe in all the glorious smells.

"No." Sophie twitched the leash and headed back into her building.

Ginger frolicked in the lobby, bouncing and cheerful and way too energetic without exercise. Possessed by that deep exhaustion, Sophie walked Ginger to security and left her there to be picked up by the Doggie Daycare service that usually took care of her during the day.

She was too flattened even to feel guilty about neglecting her dog as she got back into bed and shut herself into the dark.

Dealing with Ginger and her needs were the only activities Sophie engaged in for the next two days.

Sophie slept, or she simply lay in her room staring at the ceiling.

*Hello, darkness, my old friend.*

She reviewed her life, hopelessness sapping her energy as her thoughts cycled through negative, repetitive patterns. She'd fought hard to escape from the disastrous marriage to sadistic businessman Assan Ang. She'd also fought hard to build her career in the FBI. She'd created DAVID and tried to make the world a better place.

*All for nothing.*

Of course she still had a copy of DAVID's software, stored on a hard drive in a safe hidden in the apartment—she was too smart to let the FBI take it from her. But the fight ahead just felt too difficult right now.

She should get up. Exercise. Call her father, or her friend Lei on Maui, or Marcella. Eat. But she did none of those things.

The depression wasn't passive. It felt powerful and destructive, a fierce predator that held her in its jaws, shaking the very life out of her.

Sophie stared at the blackness of the bedroom ceiling, her eyes wide open. They were dry and unseeing as desert stones. It felt like if she waited long enough, her body would just cease. Turn off. Begin crumbling away as if she'd never been.

*A pounding at the door.*

The pounding stopped.

Started again.

Stopped.

If she ignored it long enough, whoever it was would eventually go away.

The alarm system activating was a shrill throbbing electronic tone that demanded a response. After the apartment was breached six months ago, Sophie'd had it tied straight into the building's security. Now, if she didn't deactivate it, police would be on their way.

Sophie groaned and threw on her sleep tee, walking with an effort to the panel by the front door. She deactivated the alarm.

"Sophie! Open up right now or I'm breaking in!"

*Marcella.* Her friend's voice was loud but muffled by the solid door. She might have known Marcella would persist. Sophie opened the door. "I'm okay."

"No, you're not." Marcella's cheeks were flushed with the effort of pounding on the front door to the point that the alarm was triggered. Wisps of sleek, chocolate-brown hair had escaped from the chignon she'd nicknamed the FBI Twist. There was no hiding her gorgeous, curvy figure, but Marcella played it down in a plain white blouse and gray slacks. "You look like hell. When did you eat last?"

Sophie shrugged and let go of the doorframe. Marcella followed her in as Sophie pressed the intercom button on the blinking alarm panel. "This is Sophie Ang." She spoke the all-clear code and let go of the button. "Marcella, I know you mean well. But please. Leave me alone."

"Of course not. Clearly you don't know what friends are for." Marcella set her hands on her hips. "What the hell did you quit for? You're going to win this DAVID thing. You need to stay in the fight and stick to your guns!"

Sophie turned and walked away. She flopped face down on her bed.

"Sophie, I'm fixing you something to eat. Go get in the shower. You smell disgusting." Marcella headed for the kitchen. "Get to it, or I'll call Marcus to come over and help me put you in the shower whether you like it or not."

*Marcus Kamuela.* Marcella's intimidating Hawaiian HPD detective fiancé tolerated Sophie for Marcella's sake, but they weren't friends. The thought of that burly man hauling her by the scruff of the neck to the shower was humiliating, and Marcella would follow through on that kind of threat. Sophie was too depressed to be embarrassed, but that next phase of shame wasn't far off—she could smell a whiff of it like smoke in the air.

She got to her feet, shuffling to the bathroom. She could hear Marcella talking on the phone in the kitchen, probably discussing her with Lei Texeira, their mutual friend. Sophie groaned aloud. *"Daughter of a stillborn water buffalo!"* Cursing in Thai just didn't feel satisfying enough so she tried a string of English cusswords.

Those didn't work either.

Sophie turned on the water. She avoided looking in the mirror.

22

She'd just see her skin gone sallow, purple circles under her eyes, her cheekbones jutting.

At least her cropped hair was too short to give her any trouble.

Under the flow of water, the smell of coconut soap brought her beautiful mother Pim Wat Smithson back. *This was the cycle that her mother went through.* Sophie had her to thank for this 'sickness of the soul' as her father called it.

Mama had been depressed as long as Sophie could remember: withdrawn, lethargic, prone to tears, and unresponsive to her daughter's needs, with rare times when she came out from beneath the disease to bloom like a flower. To reach adulthood and fall prey to the same affliction Sophie had struggled against with her parent felt like one more rock in the bag of them around her neck.

Marcella opened the door, letting steam out. "Hurry up in there. Food is almost ready."

The door shut with a bang.

*"Ugly sister of a poxy whore."*

"I heard that!" Marcella bellowed from the kitchen. "And I can't understand it, but I know it's not nice. I'll kick your ass in the ring, 'cause that's where we're going next."

Sophie snapped off the water and shook the extra water off her hair. Her brain sloshed in her skull with the abrupt head movement. She just needed to comply long enough to get Marcella off her back and then she could go back to bed.

Several hours later, Marcella said goodbye and left Sophie at the building after a thorough trouncing at Fight Club, the gym where they both practiced MMA fighting. The Doggie Daycare had dropped Ginger off, and she waited at the security station. Heading back up to the apartment holding the dog's leash, Sophie had to admit she felt better.

She still had DAVID, even if the program was mothballed. She had friends. She had a dog that loved her. She just needed to beat the depression back enough to get ahead of it.

The elevator doors opened.

A tall, well-built, dark-haired man stood outside of her apartment, his hand raised to knock on the red lacquered door. He turned, raked her with a glance, and broke into a grin.

"Sophie Ang? Just the woman I came to see."

# CHAPTER FIVE

SOPHIE EXAMINED the man's ID, presented in the kind of leather cred wallet she'd once carried with the FBI. *Jake Dunn, Extraction and Security Specialist*, was six foot three inches, one hundred ninety-five pounds, with brown hair and blue eyes.

Only his eyes weren't really blue. They were gunmetal gray, with a blue ring around the iris, and quite arresting. Dunn wore black cargo pants and a tight ribbed tee that left little of his well-defined torso to the imagination. His belt was loaded with holstered weapons and he wore the kind of laced-up combat boots that meant business.

The Security Solutions operative shifted from foot to foot in front of her. His ID photo didn't capture the sense of crackling energy that surrounded him.

Sophie took her time to examine his credentials and call them in to Security Solutions.

"Satisfied? My boss, Todd Remarkian, sent me here to recruit you." Dunn's tone was impatient. "He said he had an offer for you as a tech agent, and a case he knew you'd be interested in. It's on the Big Island."

Interest, flickering into life through the muffling deadness that surrounded Sophie, felt like the prickling of a frozen limb awakening to warmth.

"Where on the Big Island?"

"Waipio Valley. A cult. The Society of Light. I can't tell you more until you sign the offer. Can we get out of this damn hallway and talk privately?"

Sophie unlocked her apartment. "Wait here five minutes. I need to get cleaned up." She wasn't about to shower with this G.I. Joe action figure of a man sitting in her front room. Ginger was useless as a guard dog, already fawning over Dunn and rubbing herself lasciviously against the man's leg.

Sophie tweaked the dog's leash, hauled her inside, and shut the door soundly. She heard a deep-voiced curse through the door as she headed for the bathroom.

Sophie smiled. Beating Dunn in the ring, or on a computer, or perhaps at shooting—was going to be fun. She enjoyed besting testosterone-driven males.

She took exactly five minutes to shower and change into a pair of yoga pants and a slim-fitting, ruby-red top. She opened the door. "Come in."

Dunn swept her with an assessing glance. "Todd didn't tell me you were hot."

"I fail to see how that's relevant." Sophie's neck heated with annoyance. "And if we're ever going to work together you should keep those thoughts to yourself." She sounded fussy and prim as she folded her arms over her chest.

"Got a stick up your butt. I can dig it." Dunn sat down on the low Danish-style couch, his thick legs sprawled, arms stretched out along the low back. "Nice place."

"My father's. Where's this contract? Unless you just came to waste my time with Neanderthal insults."

"Oh, when I insult you, you'll know it." Dunn unbuttoned one of the cargo pockets on his leg and extracted several folded pages. "Here."

Sophie took the papers and went to a nearby desk. She sat on the sleek chair, flicked on the lamp and began to read. Dunn got up and paced back and forth in front of the floor-to-ceiling windows. Sitting clearly wasn't something he did well, but he moved gracefully for such a big man. "Frickin' awesome view. What does your father do?"

Sophie didn't take her eyes off the contract. Looked like a terrific package; the pay was close to twice what she'd earned as an agent. "Curb your language, *foul-mouthed son of a yak.*"

"What language is that you're speaking?" Dunn stopped in front of her, legs planted like tree trunks, arms crossed on his chest. Hawaiian tribal tattoos of interlocking triangles banded sinewy forearms. Dunn was clearly used to getting whatever he wanted with a minimum of time and effort. Women probably rolled over and spread their legs for him as easily as Ginger, currently lying on her back, wriggling in ecstasy as he scratched her belly with the toe of his boot. "You look ethnic. What kind of ethnic are you? Balinese? Black and Balinese?"

He wasn't far wrong. Sophie's black and Thai heritage was usually hard to pinpoint. Perhaps Dunn was sharper than he first appeared. "What kind of ethnic? Who asks questions like that? Clearly you're overdue for some sensitivity training."

Dunn tipped his head back and laughed. He had the kind of laugh that made babies giggle and female toes curl. Sophie tried not to smile as she looked down at the contract.

"Okay. Good behavior starts now. I can take instruction." Dunn spun and began his pacing again. "Todd said you're one of the best operatives at tech he's ever encountered. High praise from a man who helped start a security firm whose main product is an artificially intelligent home security system."

"Todd exaggerates." Sophie reached the end of the contract. "This seems in order, but I'd like to speak to Mr. Remarkian myself before making any decisions."

"Fine. Dick around with it all you want. But don't waste my

time. You want in on this case? 'Cause I can't talk to you about it without more, and actually I need your intel from the FBI recon before I go over to the Big Island." Dunn sat back down, but she felt his presence and will pressing on her like a bulldozer blade.

"I'm interested. But I'm not talking to you tonight about this. Or anything." Sophie stood. "Thank you for bringing the contract by, Mr. Dunn."

Dunn stared at her for a long moment, then laughed again. "Hard to get, are you? I can dig that too."

Sophie kept her face blank with an effort—but she had years of hiding her emotions, thanks to Assan Ang.

"I like you, Ang. I think we'll get along fine." Dunn strode to the door and pulled it open. "Your dog likes me. That oughta mean something. Here's my number. Let me know what you decide." He set a card on the shiny black lacquer table beside the front door and shut the door behind him.

Sophie let out a breath she hadn't known she was holding. Dunn seemed to have sucked all the life out of the room and taken it with him. Ginger appeared to agree, as the dog sat and stared at the closed door, whining mournfully.

TODD REMARKIAN ANSWERED her call on the second ring. "G'day, Sophie! Thought I might hear from you." The Australian's tone was upbeat, as usual. "I take it *Get 'Er Dunn* hit your doorstep."

Sophie snorted a laugh. "The man has the manners of a tank."

"Jake's a diamond in the rough. So I take it you got the contract? Calling with questions?"

"I want to know why you reached out to me with employment at this time."

Remarkian sounded surprised. "Security Solutions got this Waipio case, apparently on your referral. I thought it was high time I tried to steal you from the FBI."

"Oh." No one but her immediate FBI team knew she'd quit the FBI. She smoothed the contract on the desk before her. "I'm not sure I'm ready to make a commitment as an employee. But I'd like to work this case. Can we work out a temporary contract to start?"

"Sure. I'll have Human Resources work up a private contractor contract. We do that all the time, actually." A long pause. "So, Dunn is primary on this case. He has a number of useful skills, but he needs a partner, someone with communication and tech skills who can also work out in the field if need be. Think you can work with him? I know he's a little crude…"

"I can handle him." Sophie folded the contract decisively and slid it into the drawer of the desk. "Shall I come down to your office tomorrow to take care of the paperwork?"

"What about the FBI?"

"I resigned. Irreconcilable differences." The trite phrase was all she planned to say to anyone about it.

"Their loss is our gain." Remarkian sounded delighted. "Meet me at nine a.m. at our downtown office. I'll have the contract for you, and you and Dunn can plan the op."

"Sounds good. Thanks for thinking of me." Sophie ended the call.

The depression was back in its box, banished by Marcella and the whirlwind that was Dunn and this new job opportunity. Sophie sat down at her computers. She emailed the lawyer she had filing the patent on DAVID, asking for some kind of motion to keep the FBI from claiming it as work product and explaining what had happened. *Could she sue for damages?* She inquired.

It was worth a try. And now it was time to see if the Ghost had checked their chatbox.

He had.

*"I'm sorry to hear you won't be chasing me anymore. I enjoyed our little games. You deserve to work for someone who appreciates your talents. Please don't hesitate to contact me and let me know how I can help you. A word in the right ear could open doors."*

*Sophie wrote back. "Thanks, but it's under control. Know anything about the Society of Light cult on the Big Island? About to figure out what life is like in the private security sector in a case involving children held against their mother's will in a compound in the Waipio Valley."*

She paused, fingers poised above the keyboard. She wasn't sure what she wanted from this man.

The Ghost was someone who killed—indirectly, through manipulation, it was true—but killed nonetheless, by using information he'd stolen to turn unsavory criminals against each other. She'd uncovered this using DAVID, and now that the program was shut down, there was no way to track if the Ghost was still up to his tricks.

*"Until next time, I'll be adjusting to civilian life."*

Sophie shut the chat window and got up. Time to organize herself for the first morning of the rest of her life.

TODD REMARKIAN GREETED HER, walking forward for a brief hug. He smelled of sandalwood aftershave and the hair gel spiking his dark blond hair. His blue eyes were bright with pleasure to see her. "Sophie! You're looking terrific."

"Thanks." She'd got up early and put on makeup, which she seldom used—but something had to be done about the circles under her eyes. She'd dressed for the meeting in her standard FBI "uniform" of a crisp white button-down with a tank shirt underneath, stretchy black pants, and athletic shoes. The shoulder holster holding her Glock rubbed a little against her elbow through the gray blazer she wore to conceal it. "I'm excited to get those kids out of the Waipio Valley."

"Hey." Jake Dunn had been leaning on Todd's desk, and the man pushed off, striding forward to engulf her hand in his. "Glad you're coming on board."

"Just a trial run." Sophie addressed her comment to Remarkian. "Thanks for the opportunity. I have a vested interest in this case. I'm sure you heard from the children's mother that my SAC pulled the case and punted it back to Hilo PD."

"Yeah. And they aren't doing anything until the mother has a custody order. So what can you tell us about what we're getting into?" Dunn was dressed for action as he'd been the previous day, and looked ready for action.

Sophie took a step back to get more personal space. "I turned over all the video and surveillance to Hilo PD, but I can give you a verbal recap of the intel we collected."

"Before you get into all that, let's dispense with the contract formalities. Jake, can you give us a moment in private?" Remarkian asked.

"Sure. I'll see you at my office, Ang, and we can get started planning the op." Dunn lifted a hand and exited. Sophie was left with the sense of a dust devil passing, leaving a whirl of energy settling in its wake.

Todd's eyes crinkled. "He's a piece of work. But gets the job done, Dunn, as it were."

"Lots of puns to be had with his name," Sophie said. "I'm sorry. I'm not quick with those. I'm bilingual, but didn't move to the US until around five years ago. At least I can catch them now."

"You don't need to be funny. You're intelligent and talented, not to mention beautiful." Todd's voice was warm, and Sophie glanced at him. His expression was guileless and bland, his smile neutral. Sometimes she had the feeling he was interested in her in a romantic way, but he'd never asked her out beyond their shared interest in hike-running with their dogs. She wasn't sure how she'd respond if he did make a move.

"You had a contract for me to look over?"

"Of course." Remarkian handed it to her, mounted on a clip-board with a silver pen attached.

Sophie sat on one of the chairs in his seating area, a fluid arc of poured wine-red plastic that was surprisingly comfortable. "Looks in order." She was shocked at the high hourly pay, which she was to log and submit an invoice for. All expenses were covered, and additional "bodily hazard insurance" was offered. She initialed, accepting the insurance, and signed the paper. She handed it back to Remarkian.

"Good." He took the contract and walked around to his desk, another red poured plastic form which somehow looked right in the modern minimalist décor. The downtown Honolulu view made a tropical backdrop, framed by huge windows. "Now that this is in order, you can get started. I have an office assigned to you temporarily, next to Jake's. Down a floor, and to the left. You two will be reporting to Kendall Bix, VP of Operations. I don't usually work with individual service providers, but I wanted to grease the wheels to get you on this case as fast as possible."

"Thank you, Todd." Sophie held the man's gaze and spoke with sincerity. "This offer came at the perfect time."

"My close friends call me Connor. It's my middle name. Glad we could find a way to make it work." Remarkian's tone was a little over-hearty, the Aussie accent broader than usual.

Somehow his comment reminded Sophie of Waxman's insistence that she "call me Ben."

"I'm not sure that's a good idea. You're kind of my boss now." Sophie frowned.

"You're a short-term contract employee and you answer to a distant department head. What, we can't be friends now?" Remarkian's chuckle sounded forced. "I would rather have you for a friend than an employee, much as I value your skills."

Sophie looked at the floor. *Friend she could do.* She wasn't ready to be more with Remarkian. "Okay, Connor."

"Let's run this weekend if you're free. Dead Man's Catwalk?" Remarkian named an off-limits but famous hike that ended at a spectacular tongue of concrete protruding from a giant cliff over the ocean. "Anubis needs a workout."

"Ginger does too. Excellent." Sophie gave a mock salute. "Thanks. I'm ready to get to work."

LOOKING AROUND HER NEW OFFICE, Sophie battled a sense of unreality.

Just days ago she'd been in her haven, her cave: the FBI's IT lab, with its cool dark bays and humming, quiet energy.

Now the light of a bright Honolulu day blazed through tinted windows, illuminating a large desk, sleek computer console, phone, and round-tabled seating area with a large smartboard mounted on the wall. She was going to be out in the field, not behind a computer, most of the time.

"Nice, right?" Dunn thumbed to his office next door, identical to hers right down to a green-shaded lamp on the desk. "Come check out this topographical map of Waipio that I've got set up. The company helicopter's reserved to take us to the Big Island in two hours, so we need to get to it."

"I see why Remarkian calls you *Get 'Er Dunn*." Sophie followed the big man into the next office.

Dunn grinned at her. "I'll answer to that. Now gimme all the intel you picked up over there, and let's get over to the Big Island."

# CHAPTER SIX

THE HELICOPTER they took into Waipio was a Bell Jet painted in camouflage colors, every bit as fast as the FBI one she'd taken there just a few days earlier. They'd timed the flight for late evening—a popular time for helicopter tours, frequent in the big valley with its spectacular waterfall and soaring, ridged green walls.

Sophie leaned her forehead against the curved Plexiglas window, watching the ripple of the ocean pass beneath them, cobalt blue and crinkled as a crumpled piece of aluminum foil. "No whales this time of year," she commented to Dunn, sitting up front with the pilot.

He nodded. "Lived in Alaska for a few years. Amazing how far the whales are willing to come to play in the warm water here. No food for six months either. That's commitment."

They flew past the variegated hump of Maui, crowned in clouds. The Big Island loomed ahead, blue-purple in a haze of "vog," volcanic emissions from Kilauea's ongoing eruption. The rugged golden slopes of the dry side of the island soon gave way to the lush green of the eastern side, where rain clouds were captured by the prevailing height of the dormant Mauna Loa volcano.

Waipio Valley appeared as a vast rift in the island, a primordial layering of shades of green. Even having been there recently, Sophie half expected dinosaurs to appear among the spreading albizia trees along the velvet pastureland and olive satin of the river.

"Fly along the valley walls and set us down at least a mile from the compound," Dunn directed. "Don't want to spook the target."

"Roger that." The pilot kept them at a typical tourist viewing height, then swooped swiftly down to land in an open area on the top of one of the ridges. Sophie hopped out of the chopper, lug-soled boots sinking into soft mud.

She and Dunn unloaded their surveillance and extraction equipment and waved off the chopper, with orders to come in and pick them up out of sniper range from the compound's tower when they called for it.

Sophie slung on the lightweight backpack packed with everything they had anticipated needing to extract two potentially unwilling children from a hostile, armed compound.

Her heart thudded in the cage of her ribs. Was she really up for this kind of work? No way to know but to get in and find out.

Jake handed her a shallow tin of camouflage paint. "Do your face and hands. We can't be identified. This isn't the FBI, where you have the weight of law on your side. It's get in, nail the objective, get out. They're justified in shooting at us if they catch us."

*Not like the FBI at all.* She'd always been protected by her position as a federal cop before. Now, the law was on the other side. The shift felt surreal, especially since what they were doing was the ethical thing.

Sophie rubbed the thick, gooey paint onto her face. "I don't need as much as you, white boy." Teasing him for the first time felt like taking a risk.

"Yeah, I'll give you that." Dunn's grin was a flash in the gloom of approaching dark. He wasn't offended. "Let's get the night vision goggles out for when we need them."

They'd chosen evening for the flight and nightfall for the raid. Sophie checked her weapons, loaded with nonlethal ammo, and hung the NV goggles on their adjustable strap around her neck.

"Ready?" Dunn cinched down his loaded pack.

"Ready."

Dunn took off at a rapid walk, finding a goat trail down the side of the ridge. Sophie was glad of all the hours she spent at her favorite hobby, hike-running rough trails, as they navigated the slender track in near dark at a fast clip. She dogged Dunn's heels, pushing him faster.

Once they were off the ridge, Dunn used a GPS to navigate toward the compound's coordinates. They moved as fast as they could through long grass and tangled brush. Sophie was glad Hawaii had none of the poisonous snakes or hazards of the jungle in Thailand, though they ran into a stand of "cat's claw" vine with huge thorns and had to navigate around it. They were able to make better time once Dunn found a cattle track heading in the general direction of the compound.

"Let's set up a surveillance node within a klick of the compound," Dunn said. "Raised ground would be ideal. Let's go in slow in case any guards are posted outside."

The landscape was rendered in glowing green through the NV goggles and depth was hard to judge. The coordinates glowed from Dunn's handheld GPS as they slowed to a stealthy walk, pausing to check for movement. Sophie's senses felt heightened: every touch of leaf, the smell of dry grass and mulch, the rustle of wind in the trees—all of it was magnified by the surge of blood through her veins.

*Adrenaline was a great antidote to depression.*

They found a slight rise but no handy vantage points to see into the compound. "Gonna have to climb trees," Dunn muttered. "Hate climbing trees."

"I don't mind." Sophie clipped the climbing spikes they'd brought onto her boots and in moments she was up in the spreading limbs of an albizia, NV binoculars held to her eyes as she tracked movements inside the compound and relayed the information to Dunn.

Sophie watched for an hour before climbing down. "The children are all together in one yurt and in bed already. Identifying our targets in the dark is going to be an issue. That and the dogs." They had a photo of each of the children, but how would they find the ones they were after? They each had copies of the photos in their pockets and they'd have to try to keep the kids quiet while they found the targets. Sophie hadn't spotted any more guards patrolling besides the manned sniper tree—but that was because two large black German Shepherds were wandering loose. "Got those tranquilizer darts handy? We need to take out the dogs and the sniper, too."

"Hate dogs," Dunn said. "Unpredictable."

"Kind of a baby, aren't you?" Sophie said, beginning to enjoy needling him.

"Yeah." Dunn grinned with the easy good humor that seemed to be part of his personality. "Want to kiss it and make it better?"

She had no comeback for that.

"The tricky thing is going to be getting close enough and high enough to tranquilize the dogs without them raising the alarm," Dunn said. "You're good at climbing. I want you to get up the wall and take them out with the rifle. Then cut the razor wire. I'll be right behind you and we'll go over and penetrate the sleeping area."

Dunn was testing her. He knew Sophie had been mostly backup support at the FBI, insulated from front-line activity by her tech role. Now she was leading a dangerous civilian raid. She'd never felt more vulnerable, more uncertain—and yet more alive. After the lethargy of the last few days, the acuteness and energy felt like a drug.

"Roger that." Sophie wasn't about to let her lack of confidence show. Dunn handed her the silenced rifle, already fitted with a NV scope and loaded with tranq darts. He gave her a belt and a climbing rope. She bent and attached the spikes to her boots, then donned heavy leather gloves.

The ten-foot wall of the compound rose dead ahead, a dark monolith, the razor wire topping it a lacy scrim against the faint glow of yellowish security lights that stayed on even though everyone in the compound had gone to bed. Sophie made sure that wire snips were in her cargo pocket and patted her Glock for luck. She approached the wall at the farthest corner, partially out of view of the sniper tower and behind one of the taller tents.

Making a cradle for her boot, Dunn boosted her higher up the wall than she would have believed—the man was strong. She caught the top of the heavy wood, careful to grab between the coils of razor wire. Using upper arm strength, she hauled herself high and dug the spikes at the toes of her boots into the wood of the fence.

The razor wire caught the heavy ripstop sleeve of her black jacket and sliced it like butter. *"Maggots writhing in rotting deer meat,"* Sophie cursed softly.

"What's that?" Dunn's voice sounded tinny in her earbud.

"I'm going to have to cut some of this wire before I can do anything else." Sophie set a metal piton into the top of the fence. She ran the rope through her belt and the piton, dropping the loose end to Dunn on the ground. Once he held the rope, anchoring her with the piton to the top of the fence, she was able to use both hands to cut a section of the razor wire, working with quick, quiet movements.

A low growl from below the fence froze Sophie as she dropped the large section of wire to the ground.

"Get him before he barks!" Dunn's harsh whisper reverberated in her earbud. Sophie let go of the fence, relying entirely on the spikes in her boots and the rope at her waist to hold her upright. She unslung the rifle, and scanned the ground through the NV scope.

The dark shape directly below her stalked forward, stiff-legged and snarling. Its behavior had attracted its partner, a streak of moving canine menace headed for their corner.

Sophie shot the nearest dog in the neck and the running one in the side. Without waiting to see if they'd collapsed, she brought the rifle up and trained it at the sniper tree.

The watchman was slumped against the trunk, sleeping.

She nailed him twice in the chest, then looked back down at the dogs.

They'd collapsed, silent black mounds of fur. She shot each of them again, not in the mood to be bit as they passed by with the children they were taking. "All clear."

"Good work. Drop the ladder." Dunn handed her up a rolled bundle. Sophie tossed one side of the slender black nylon rope ladder over into the compound, and dropped the other back down to Dunn.

"Move out," Dunn ordered. Sophie could feel Dunn's leashed power behind her as her partner climbed the flimsy but strong ladder behind her, the wall thumping slightly as his weight swung against the wood. Sophie angled her body through the opening in the razor wire and slung a leg over, finding the ladder with her boot, trying not to snag the spikes on it. She only used a couple of the ladder's supports before jumping backwards to land on her feet. She bent and unclipped the spikes, stowing them in a pocket, the rifle cradled in her arms as she scanned the compound.

Speed and silence were of the essence.

Dunn took the lead as they moved out of the relative cover of the yurt that visually blocked their penetration point. Sophie stayed close to his imposing bulk as he trotted from cover spot to cover spot until they arrived at the raised tent Sophie had identified as the children's sleeping quarters. They avoided the entrance, marked by a yellow security light.

He signaled her, covering them as Sophie located a sharp cutting tool in her pack. It slid through the heavy tent material, zipping through the weave with a low hissing sound. Dunn went through the slit first.

They were going to appear so frightening to the children. She pulled the tranq pistol packed for human dosage but dreaded having to use it. Hopefully they could find the kids in their beds using the NV goggles and the photographs—but how to convince them to come without raising an alarm? She hoped the picture they'd brought of Blumfield would help.

Sophie took a deep breath and plunged after Dunn into the yurt.

The interior was pitch black and smelled of warm bodies—but not the muskiness of adults. The sweetness of this smell was innocence, sleeping. Through the glowing green of the NV goggles, Sophie saw Dunn already working his way around the series of bunk beds, holding the photo up next to each face.

Sophie turned to the bunk nearest her.

A boy was on the bottom, his long legs and large feet showing he was too old to be the child she was looking for. Another large boy's feet protruded from the top bunk.

She moved on. A shock of blond hair on a smaller boy looked pale green. On the top bunk, a girl around the right age rested. Hair that would be red in daylight was a darker green than the boy's.

"Possible targets located," Sophie whispered. "Need to make positive ID."

Dunn moved silently to her side. Sophie lifted the NV goggles and flashed the penlight she carried in the boy's face.

"Target identified." Sophie paused, unsure how to proceed.

A weight landed on her back and a scream filled her ears. Sophie grunted, dropping to her knees as the heavy adolescent's momentum carried her forward to hit the floor. Her attacker must be the boy from the top bunk beside them. She heard the muffled spit of the tranq gun in Dunn's hand and abruptly the weight crushing her disappeared.

But all around her, the tent rustled with the sounds of waking children.

Dunn spoke low but definite. "Stay in your beds and you won't get hurt. We are here to take two children, Lono and Pele, to their mother, Sharon Blumfield. Keep quiet, understand? This kid on the floor is just sleeping, he's not hurt. I don't want to have to tranq anyone else, though, ok?"

Silence.

Sophie hated that Dunn was frightening the kids, but it seemed to be working as the total stillness of held breaths continued. She tugged the girl down from the bunk.

"Pele?" The girl nodded. "Your mom sent us. My name is Sophie." Sophie lit the photo of Blumfield with her penlight, and then bent to show it to the boy, still in his bunk. "We need you to come with us. Quick and quiet, now."

The girl nodded, reaching for her brother. "Let's go, Lono," she said.

Sophie took the girl's hand as she grasped her brother's, and they ran across the room and out through the slit in the tent. She could hear Dunn's breath behind her, the thud of his boots. The dogs she'd tranquilized were motionless black blots on the ground that made the kids turn their heads curiously.

The most challenging part still lay ahead: the wall, the flimsy ladder, and the escape.

"I'll go over first and help them down on the other side," Dunn whispered, reminding Sophie of the plan they'd discussed if the children couldn't be retrieved without being knocked out.

Dunn surged up the ladder as Sophie turned, her tranq gun ready, to surveille the compound.

No one moved. The children in the tent had not given the alarm after that first cry.

"Where are we going?" Pele asked.

"To a helicopter that will take you to your mom."

"Ready," Dunn said, from the opposite side of the fence.

Sophie lifted the boy to grasp the ladder. He was a solid sixty pounds or so, and she steadied him and helped the girl up next, grateful for all her exercising, and feeling a target between her shoulder blades with her back turned to the compound.

The kids made it to the top and Dunn was helping them over as Sophie took a quick look around through the NV goggles. The sniper was still snoozing in the tree. The children's tent was silent. Guilt stabbed Sophie—she hoped they hadn't scared the poor kids out of their minds.

She jumped up and climbed, the tranq rifle banging on her back by its strap. She followed them through the gap in the razor wire, slinging a leg over, taking a step down on the ladder, and jumping back to land on the earth in a crouch.

"Chopper will meet us by the river. Gonna make some noise so let's move out before we call for it."

Sophie took the girl's hand as she held her brother's, and they followed at a trot into the deep grass. The bulletproof vest Sophie wore prickled with sweat and apprehension as they tried to get some distance from the compound.

The kids weren't as fast as Sophie would have liked as they hurried down the cattle trail. Suddenly the lights came on in the compound, throwing the NV goggles into a whiteout glare as the place lit up behind them.

Dunn reached the relative cover of the albizia tree they'd climbed for their original surveillance of the compound, and Sophie and the kids were right on his heels as he used the walkie-talkie to call for the helicopter. "Five minutes," the pilot said.

They moved out from under the tree, hearing yelling and shouts from the compound—and striking further dread into Sophie's heart, the deep bark of the dogs. "They must have woken up!"

"Move, move!" Dunn rasped. They ran, reaching the open area near the river that they'd chosen as a rendezvous since it was out of sniper range but open enough for the chopper to land.

They could hear the chopper, but it wasn't yet in sight.

Even in the dim light Sophie saw Dunn's eyes widen. "Shit. Here they come."

Sophie spun. A gate in the wall had retracted. They heard the roar of a four-wheeled ATV coming their way, along with the bark of dogs.

# CHAPTER SEVEN

"FALL BACK TO RENDEZVOUS TWO!" Dunn barked in her earbud, both to her and to the chopper, whose noise they could hear approaching, but not fast enough—not nearly fast enough.

Dunn spun and broke into a lope down the cattle path, sweeping the small boy up into his arms. Sophie ran after him, Pele's hand held hot and tight in her own. Surely these people wouldn't shoot at them with the children? But who knew what they believed. With 'aggressive reincarnation'…perhaps human life wasn't even valuable.

As if to punctuate her thoughts, the blast of a shotgun rained leaves from a nearby tree down on her. "Stop! Stop right where you are!" She heard the shout over the rumble of the quad and the barking of the dogs.

They were parallel to the river. "Ditch the packs so we can move faster," Dunn said. "They'll sink in the water."

Sophie stripped off her heavy pack, tossing it into the nearby water, black and slick as tar in the faint light of the moon. Their packs splashed and sank, bubbling.

"Can you run faster?" she asked Pele. The girl shook her head, wheezing—apparently she had asthma. "Okay. Jump on my back."

She picked the girl up, and ran after Dunn's already retreating form.

The dogs were gaining.

Sophie could hear the barking getting louder as they headed back up the rugged goat track. They couldn't follow on the quad on this rough ground with its rapid elevation, but it slowed her and Dunn too.

The chopper was directly overhead, settling down lower.

*If she could just make it to the rendezvous point...*

Her whole focus narrowed to the path in front of her, steep, rough with stones and protruding branches, rendered in shades of shallow green by the NV goggles. Her arms ached with the weight of the little girl, seventy pounds at least. Her legs burned. She breathed in hot, rending gasps that left the taste of blood at the back of her throat.

But she was keeping up with Dunn. They were going to make it.

The dog caught her from behind by the pants, his teeth leaving a fiery pinch. Sophie fell with a cry, rolling desperately to the side to try to protect the child. Pele shrieked with fright as she hit the ground. "Run!" Sophie screamed. Pele scrambled to her feet and ran up the trail.

The dog didn't let go of Sophie. It dragged at her by the leg, shaking her, growling—and he was big enough that she slid backward down the steep, rough path. "Jake!" Sophie yelled.

Dunn appeared through the otherworldly green of the NV vision like a demon rising from hell, a knife in one fist and a gun in the other. He kicked the Shepherd and caught it in the side, lifting it off Sophie with a yelp as he tranqed it—just in time for the second dog to leap at him from the trail. Sophie scrambled to her feet and ran. She didn't have time to see if Dunn was going to be okay—she had to make sure the children got to safety.

The chopper had landed, and the side doors were already open. The children squatted in the open doorway, their eyes huge—but they were in the chopper and safe. Sophie whirled back around as Dunn ran toward her. "Let's move out!"

Sophie jumped into the chopper. "Get into the seats and get your belts on, kids."

Dunn jumped into the chopper right behind her, slamming the door. "Get us the hell out of here!" he yelled to the pilot.

The chopper rose, weaving slightly. Sophie helped the kids fasten their four-point harnesses and finally put on her own. She slipped her helmet on as the chopper leveled out and sped up, banking to head back toward Oahu.

"This what it's like every day?" She asked Dunn, seated beside the pilot in front.

He turned to look at her, gray eyes bright in his painted face, and grinned. "Only the best days are like this."

OVERHEAD LIGHT BATHED Sharon Blumfield and her children through the Security Solutions medical clinic's window. It had been a long night, but a good one.

A bubble of satisfaction swelled Sophie's chest as she and Dunn stood in the doorway watching the tender reunion. The company's on-call doctor had met them on the helipad to assess the children, and he'd taken the kids down to the clinic area to meet their mother.

Sharon Blumfield's sunken eyes overflowed as she embraced her children, and both of them embraced her too, everyone crying. "We missed you so much, Mom! Why did you leave us?" Pele exclaimed.

"I had to. But I sent Sophie and Jake to get you. It was the best I could do," Blumfield said.

"But what about our brothers and sisters? Where are their moms? Did they run away too?"

*Where, indeed?* That question was really beginning to bother Sophie.

Blumfield made soothing noises, and Dr. Kinoshita, Security Solutions' psychologist, came forward. "You kids seem to have some questions. Come sit with your mom and me, and let's talk."

The doctor, with a nod to Dunn and Sophie, shut the clinic door to give the family privacy.

"You must be Sophie Ang. I've heard so much about you."

Sophie turned to face the male voice at her elbow.

"Sophie, this is Kendall Bix, our immediate supervisor in charge of operations," Dunn said as Sophie shook Bix's hand. The man's grip was light but strong, and he looked her over with sharp brown eyes. Razor-cut black hair and an upright bearing showed a military influence. "Pleased to meet you," Sophie said. "I thought I'd meet you yesterday, when we were planning the op, but Dunn said you were busy."

"Not that busy." Bix's smile was a baring of teeth. "Let's debrief upstairs." He spun on a heel.

Sophie followed Dunn and Bix down the hall. They took the elevator in silence to the third floor. The whole five-story building on a quiet Honolulu side street was given over to the private security firm's operations. The high-rise building Sophie had visited during a previous case she'd been on was only a small portion of the company's holdings.

Bix waited until they entered a conference room before he lit into Dunn. "Dunn, you took a completely untested short-term contractor on a dangerous op with possible impact to human lives—children's lives! Without even a heads-up to me! And no backup!"

"I knew what I was doing."

Bix and Dunn faced off, bristling.

Apparently the FBI wasn't the only workplace with protocols that Sophie already wasn't following—not that she was taking any responsibility for this. She exhaled a long slow breath. "Mind if I sit?"

Neither man responded, so she sat.

"I had total confidence in Ang. And as you can see, she pulled it off," Dunn leaned into his superior's face. "We're damn lucky she came on board. She can work a lot more than computers, it turns out."

"That's not the point. You had no experience working with her! We always rehearse, do a dry run. The case wasn't time-sensitive. There was no reason to go all Rambo out there, making it up as you went along!"

"Worked out, didn't it?" Dunn wasn't backing down.

Sophie cleared her throat. "I apologize. If I was in violation of protocol, it wasn't intentional."

Bix's brows went up. "I'm not blaming you." He seemed a little mollified. "I'm sure this won't happen again."

"I can't speak for Dunn, sir. Just let me know your standard operating procedure and I'll do my best to follow it." Sophie leaned in Dunn's direction, conciliatory. "And Jake, it was a pleasure working with you. I wouldn't have made it out if you hadn't got that dog off me."

Dunn gave her a brief glance of gratitude before resuming the stare down with his boss.

"Why didn't you submit an operation plan and run this whole thing by me?" Bix said, raising his hands. "Including hiring Ang? I should have been in the loop."

"I had orders to recruit Sophie from Remarkian himself, and even the case we were working. I think it was part of Remarkian's effort to recruit Sophie—give her something he knew she wanted in on. I assumed you knew all about it, because orders came from over your head. So if you have a problem with this, Remarkian is the one to speak to."

Bix breathed heavily through his nose a moment.

"Wait here." He left.

"I pity Remarkian right now." Dunn flopped into a molded plastic chair beside her.

"Remarkian did tell me we reported to Bix," Sophie said mildly. "I wondered why we didn't have a sit-down with him before going in." She longed for a shower. The dog bite, a bruise on the back of her calf, ached. "You should have checked the op with him, and I think you know it."

*"Et tu, Brute?"* Dunn's gray eyes crinkled with humor. "Thought you wanted to go get those kids."

"Et tu, Brute? Some kind of slang?" Sophie still ran into phrases she wasn't familiar with, after being born in Thailand, educated in Switzerland, and living in Hong Kong.

"Too obscure to explain. Google it." Dunn extended long legs in muddy black trousers. His huge lug-soled boots had already marked the shiny floor. He stretched thick, ropy arms overhead and gave a jaw-cracking yawn. "Bix is just sore we didn't get his rubber stamp of approval."

"I don't blame him," Sophie murmured. "I would be angry too. After all, we plunged right in after a brief planning session with a topographical map and consult with the pilot. I was surprised we didn't do more prep and rehearsal. So many things could have gone wrong."

"But they didn't." Dunn surged up and began his restless pacing, back and forth in front of the windows. Dawn was sharpening the silhouette of Diamond Head, just visible between nearby skyscrapers. It was a familiar view, but from a different, unfamiliar angle.

Sophie missed her cool dim computer lab with a sudden fierceness. She missed the quiet, the corner where she liked to exercise and watch the sky, the private feeling of each computer bay, the way the tech agents left each other alone to chase perps down cyber-pathways.

This place, this way of working, this team were all so new and different. She wasn't used to so much ad-libbing, to so few procedural safeguards. Dunn had none of Waxman's objectivity, Ken Yamada's detached professionalism, nor even Marcella's quick sophistication.

Jake Dunn was competent, all right—but his style was raw and edgy, his modus operandi improvisational, his physicality intrusive.

Bix reappeared and addressed Dunn. "Todd explained the situation. He apologized but also told me he informed you of the chain of command."

"I guess he did, Boss." Dunn turned from the window with an unrepentant grin. "You gonna smack my wrist?"

"We'll talk later, Jake. In private." Bix turned to Sophie with a deliberate smile. "Let's start over. Hi, Ms. Ang. I'm Kendall Bix, VP of Operations. All ops come through me, and go through me. You come to me for planning, approval, budgeting, and quality assurance."

"Great to meet you." Sophie stood, shaking his hand with a smile. "I'm happy to hear that you're running a professional organization here, and it's not just Dunn running around, playing commando."

"Hey!" Dunn threw himself into the chair next to Sophie, mock-pouting. His ebullient personality was one of the things she was coming to like about him—he never stayed down or angry for long. "We planned. We had a topo map and everything."

"Well, better late than never. Take me through all the steps of the op." Bix sat and opened the laptop he'd carried in. "We need to log it and write it up for liability purposes. We might well be facing a lawsuit from that cult—if Sandoval Jackson is the children's father, he'll be justified in bringing one."

"Possession is nine-tenths of the law in child custody cases," Dunn said. "Mother has them now, and he can try to get them back —but I doubt he will. Didn't you see that happy reunion scene?"

"I'm all about the professional objective. Did you get a deposit from the mother? You know our standard retrieval contract terms, and they aren't cheap."

"Ah. No." Dunn cleared his throat, displaying the first embarrassment Sophie had seen, a redness along his cheekbones. "She said she had rich relatives who would pay."

Bix gave Dunn a long stare. "You better hope she was telling the truth. Now, step-by-step. Take me through it."

# CHAPTER EIGHT

SOPHIE MADE her strong Thai tea, and sat down in her home yoga corner the next morning. Cradling her mug, she called Marcella at her friend's FBI office. "Got a minute? I want to catch you up on some things."

"I sure do. Let me just close the office door." Sophie heard the sound of the door closing, the rattle of the door's blind being lowered and rotated. "Waxman's on a rampage since you left. He's ordered a top to bottom self-audit of all our cases, and Internal Affairs is sniffing around. I suspect they are auditing every case you ever worked."

"What?" Sophie's throat tightened. "Waxman's looking for some wrongdoing? It wasn't enough that he took DAVID?"

"I don't know what Waxman's doing besides being in a total snit over you quitting. We've got a shit-ton of extra work, and IA is all over the place. If they're looking into you, it spills onto all of us since you did tech work on virtually all of our cases. I think it's something to do with DAVID."

*"Monstrous offspring of a three-headed buffalo,"* Sophie cursed. "Like it wasn't enough for the Bureau to try to steal DAVID from me!"

"Just thought I'd give you a heads-up. I don't think the shit is done rolling your way. So what're you calling to tell me? Besides that, you're out of that dark bedroom, which I'm glad to hear."

Sophie filled her in on her first contract job for Security Solutions. "Jake Dunn is an interesting phenomenon."

"He sounds hot," Marcella said. "Is he hot?"

"Um. Yes. He is very physically attractive." Sophie sipped her tea, seated herself in lotus position on the carpet in front of the floor-to-ceiling picture window that made her father's penthouse her favorite place to watch the sky. "But I don't like him like that. He's my partner."

"I smell a rat. You *are* into him."

"No. He's…kind of devastating in a way. You can't ignore Jake Dunn. He's bigger than life. And really very brave and competent. But a loose cannon. Not my style at all. I can't imagine relaxing around him, and I don't think he knows how to."

"Fun, though." Marcella was sipping something too, probably one of her many daily cups of black coffee.

"Fun, yes. And he likes to flirt."

"So I take it you're going to accept the job."

"I'm seriously considering it."

"You should. The pay alone blows the Bureau out of the water. But how did it feel being on the other side of legal?"

"Not good. I did not enjoy it at all. I felt guilty, and I still do. Especially about the children we left inside the cult." Sophie filled in some more details. "It couldn't have been more different from how the FBI would have gone about getting them out. Except the FBI decided it's not a real case." She heard the bitterness in her tone and modified it for her friend's sake. "I never expected this, Marcella. I thought I would be in the FBI for the rest of my life." Unexpected tears pricked her eyes and her throat closed. "I didn't want to quit. But I couldn't let them take DAVID from me."

"That damn computer program. It's been as much a curse as a blessing to you!"

"It's a tool. Nothing more. But it's a good tool, and I shouldn't be punished for all I put into developing it." Sophie's resolve strengthened as she remembered the humiliation and frustration of the last couple of years as the FBI wrangled over what to do with her program. "I should go. I have to check in with my lawyer."

"Come to dinner with Marcus and me. This weekend?"

"Maybe. I might be hike-running Dead Man's Catwalk with Todd Remarkian."

"The head of Security Solutions?" Marcella whistled. "You didn't tell me you guys were hanging out. Talk about hot!"

"Remarkian is a friend," Sophie said with dignity.

"Those eyes, those abs—and that accent! Mmmm." Marcella gave an exaggerated moan. "I'm betting he'd like to be more than a friend."

"You are incorrigible."

"And Italian. I tell it like I see it." Marcella ended the call.

Sophie was still smiling as she went into her morning yoga routine—but she hadn't been at it more than a half hour when the doorbell rang.

Two agents showed at the peephole, holding up cred wallets. Her stomach dropped. She schooled her features into the compliant and neutral mask her ex had taught her with his fists. She opened the door. "Yes?"

"Sophie Ang, I'm Special Agent Pillman and this is Special Agent Rapozo from FBI Internal Affairs. We have some questions for you regarding the use of your data mining program known as DAVID."

Sophie examined their cred wallets for form's sake, but she recognized Pillman as the chilly-eyed agent who'd gone after her friend Lei Texeira on a case a few years ago. The man was a pit bull, relentless and cruel. That debilitating investigation had definitely had something to do with her friend leaving the FBI to return to local law enforcement on Maui. "I don't believe you get to investigate me as I'm no longer with the FBI."

Pillman seemed prepared for this. "All federal officers are subject to examination before and after working for the Bureau. You should have read the fine print of the contract. Now, may we come in?"

Sophie stood aside and they stepped into the shining foyer area. Pillman's sharp eyes tracked the luxurious surroundings, and she felt his judgment as he turned to face her. Her heart thudded. "What is this regarding?"

"We'd like to ask you some questions. Beginning with how you afford this penthouse."

"The apartment belongs to my father, Ambassador Smithson. Perhaps you'd like to contact him in Washington for verification? He can be reached at the White House." Sophie held Pillman's gaze. She had done nothing wrong, and was not without resources. "What legal counsel am I entitled to?"

"You may no longer use FBI union representation, of course, but you are free to employ private counsel." Rapozo was a short, dark-complexioned man who reminded her of a pigeon, with a puffed-out chest and short, bandy legs that seemed to tip him forward.

"You gentlemen have come far enough into my father's apartment. I will be obtaining legal counsel for any further meetings." Sophie stood tall and gripped the doorframe so tightly that it hurt. "Thank you for stopping by."

Pillman held his ground for a long moment, pale eyes scanning the apartment and returning to her, sweeping her body with a contemptuous stare that took in her cropped hair, exercise bra, and yoga pants—and stripped her naked. "We'll be in touch."

"So be it." Sophie closed the door softly behind them, to compensate for the urge to slam it. Ginger, who had been unusually quiet through the proceedings, padded up and leaned against Sophie's leg, whining.

"It's okay, girl." Sophie leaned her head on the door, stroking the dog's ears and feeling a wave of panic sweep over her.

She felt blind and cut off without DAVID, and she was under attack. Her enemies, and even the Ghost, knew where she lived, how to get to her.

She had to get off the grid and figure out how to go on the offensive. She'd never be able to relax here now, knowing someone she needed to defend herself from could show up at the door anytime.

The apartment that had been such a haven didn't feel safe anymore.

Sophie breathed through the panic, calming herself by making a quick mental list of tasks. She booted up her rigs with the key fob as she placed a series of calls and packed a bag.

# CHAPTER NINE

THE CASH-ONLY RENTAL apartment had what Sophie needed: an internet cable already installed and a wheezing window air conditioner. It was a corner unit five floors up with good visibility from a sun-battered deck. Sophie wore a ball cap, sunglasses, and a white eyelet sundress, the furthest thing she could find in her limited wardrobe from her usual clothing.

"I'll take it." Sophie handed an envelope of cash, enough for a deposit and three months' rent, to the manager. The sun gleamed on the greasy strands of the man's comb-over as he licked a thumb and counted the money.

"Making sure you have the dog deposit in here," he muttered.

"Of course," she said politely, Ginger's leash tight in her hand, the bag over her shoulder heavy with computer gear. "What kind of security does the building have?"

"What? You get sometin' fo' hide?" The man's pidgin was thick as he looked up at her with beady brown eyes.

"No. Just a woman alone. I have to make sure my home is safe." Sophie smiled.

The landlord thawed visibly, caterpillar brows bouncing. "Oh, you safe heah. I keep an eye on you."

"No, that's fine. I just wondered if there was any—video surveillance? Alarm systems?" Sophie kept the smile pasted on though her cheeks ached.

"What you need all that foah? Get gold in that bag?"

"Ha ha. I'll take my key now." Sophie put out her hand and the man slapped the key into it, then clasped it between calloused, sweaty palms. "Don't you worry 'bout nothing, pretty girl. I watch out for you."

Sophie pulled her hand away and wiped it on her skirt. "Thank you."

Sophie blew out a breath as she left, and tugged Ginger inside the apartment.

There was no furniture, and the linoleum floor was stained. The walls had been so freshly painted that the place still reeked of it. A contact she'd met through the Bureau had provided her a new ID. Sophie still had to bring up her other bag, a duffel of clothing, from the beater white Ford truck she'd bought for cash and registered in the name she was using, Mary Watson. Her pearl-colored Lexus SUV was parked in a long-term rental lot, and her ID, credit cards, and everything else that identified her as Sophie Ang was now in the secret safe deposit box where she'd kept a copy of the DAVID software.

She couldn't wait to get DAVID set up again, but worried about detection without the elaborate firewalls she'd used at the FBI and her father's apartment to screen the program's location. She let go of the leash and Ginger quested about the barren space as Sophie headed for the rickety Formica table with a couple of metal-tubing chairs set up in the kitchen area.

She opened her gear bag and plugged in the high-powered laptop that was the only thing she really cared about that she'd brought from the apartment. She booted it up and plugged in the small, square, boxy shape of the hard drive that held DAVID, and plugged in a second monitor—one screen was never enough.

While the system was loading, she went out to the truck and

retrieved her second bag and a metal toolbox. At the door, she installed a lock bar, a deadbolt, and a small surveillance camera over the door that fed remotely into her laptop.

Security measures established, she set her hands on her hips. "Guess we need a few things to make this a home, Ginger."

Ginger wagged her tail in agreement.

She'd left her regular cell phone in the safe deposit box with the battery unplugged...but she'd called everyone she wanted to have her number with the burner she'd purchased before she deactivated it.

Now that phone buzzed and bounced on the table. She glanced at the contact and picked it up. "Hello, Jake Dunn."

"Why the change of number?" Dunn asked by way of greeting.

"None of your business." She wasn't ready to disclose anything about her situation to him. "Got another job for me?"

"Just the salaried offer Remarkian already made you. Was wondering when you'd be able to give us an answer."

Sophie blew out a breath. She didn't want to commit yet—her life felt too upside down. "I need another week to think about it."

A long pause as Dunn breathed loudly through his nostrils in annoyance. "I want you as my partner and we have some other ops coming up. Remarkian said I could offer you a bonus from the first job."

"Oh really?" A bonus would come in handy. Sophie had savings, but executing her disappearance plan had cost a chunk of money. "I take it Sharon Blumfield came through with paying her bill?"

"Yeah, she did. Thank God." Dunn gave a theatrical sigh. "My ass would have been grass if she hadn't. Now she wants us to investigate what happened to the other children's mothers. Hilo PD already told her that without evidence of a crime, without a body, there's no case. But she thinks the women were murdered. There were three others, besides her."

"I remember her saying that." Sophie felt her interest quicken.

This was a meaty case involving things that mattered to her. "So four women gave birth to ten children, total?"

"Two of the women had three each, and one other besides our client had two." Dunn sounded disgusted.

"So what has Jackson's response been to his children being taken from the compound?"

"Nothing, as far as we can tell. Our client's hiding out in a hotel with the kids. We have an operative on her, keeping an eye out, and she's still working with our psychologist—but she's leaving tomorrow to take the children to her family in Oregon, where she hopes they'll be far enough away from Jackson that he will give up pursuing custody. So what's it gonna be, Ang? Want to go back to the cult and dig up some evidence, spring the rest of the kids?"

Sophie looked over at her laptop. It had been frustrating her to no end not to be able to use DAVID on the cult investigation. Now she could.

"I'll be in tomorrow." She ended the call on Dunn's whoop of triumph.

SOPHIE TOOK several hours to go to Target and buy the bare necessities, including more sundresses and a floppy-brimmed straw beach hat. Paying cash for her wagonload of purchases, including a blow-up mattress, she felt the claws of depression reaching for her again.

Going off the grid like this was paranoid. There was no real threat against her that justified it, and not going to Fight Club to work out had a price tag—she needed the endorphins to battle the depression.

But she wanted to gain control of her life, and she couldn't do it in her father's place since the apartment had been breached and bugged in recent months. The Ghost, the man who'd done it, seemed positively inclined toward her—but he knew where she lived, he had surveilled her using video. And IA and the FBI were liable to pop in at any time and strip her computers.

No. *She had to do this.* She could resume her real identity for work, and disappear into Mary Watson at the end of each day.

She had to at least try this, and see if it helped.

Sophie ate a simple meal of stir-fried tofu and veggies at the apartment and then took Ginger out for a run. She ran down the cracked sidewalk in the warm, exhaust-smelling Honolulu evening, Ginger trotting at her side. Inserting a Bluetooth into her ear and slipping her phone into her pocket, she called Marcella.

"What's with this new number?" Marcella asked.

"Burner phone. I'm off the grid." Sophie filled her friend in on the overview of the steps she'd taken. "I'm taking the job with Security Solutions. But I need to stay under the radar for a while."

"What are you hiding from? Anything IA does you'll see coming from a mile away."

"That's just it. I didn't see it coming." Sophie described the agents' visit. "I felt really—ambushed, even though you alerted me."

"You just want to be able to use DAVID and not get busted."

Sophie smiled. "You know me so well. But I never agreed with that statement, for the record—if you're ever called to testify against me."

"You think it's going to get that bad?"

"Agent Pillman came to my door. He's the one that went after Lei a few years ago."

"Ugh. He reminds me of Agent Smith in the Matrix movies." Sophie could almost see Marcella's shudder. "I'd drop off the map too if he were after me. Well, I assume you won't be going to Fight Club?"

"Not for a while." Sophie hated to say the words. "Security Solutions has a state of the art gym. I'll be using that for now. But let's meet for a run or something, and you have my private number."

"And you have mine. Check in with me every day. If I don't hear from you, I'll assume you're in the closet in a fetal position and hunt you down."

"You can try to find me." Sophie gave a hollow laugh. "But I'm feeling better. I promise."

It was a lie. The depression beat its black wings around the edges of her vision. She just hoped to stay ahead of it by disappearing, by exercising, by getting DAVID working.

And by finding out what happened to the mothers of Sandoval Jackson's children.

# CHAPTER TEN

SITTING in her new Security Solutions office with DAVID booting up on her laptop and a mug of strong Thai tea at her elbow, Sophie decided she'd done the right thing by choosing to take the job. She badly needed somewhere to be, things to do. Sitting alone in that ugly apartment was not a good thing.

Dunn blew in. "I thought we'd begin our case by building profiles of the missing cult mothers. Our client arrives in half an hour, to give us their names and as much background as she knows."

"Good. That's how we'd do it in the FBI," Sophie said. The laptop's screen was too small, so she'd hooked up to the monitor Security Solutions had provided.

"What've you got back there?" Dunn loomed over her desk. He smelled of something lemony and masculine, and the tiny hairs on her arms lifted in awareness.

She didn't take her eyes off her screen. "Remarkian didn't hire me for my skills in the field. I come with some extras."

Dunn grinned. "I can make that happen for you, I guarantee it."

"Inappropriate, Dunn." Sophie slanted a glance at him. "As if

I'd ever sleep with a partner. I can't work with you if you keep up the sexual harassment."

"Hey. Can't blame a guy for trying." Dunn blinked his pretty eyes and shrugged his big shoulders. "Gotcha. Platonic and professional. That's how you want it, that's how it will be."

"Good." Sophie felt better for smacking him down. Dunn struck her as the "give an inch and he'll take a mile" type. She turned the monitor so Dunn could see the data on the screen and the program's process results cache box. It was time to share the program with him—he had to know how it worked if they were going to use it on cases. "This is DAVID. The reason I left the FBI. DAVID stands for Data Analysis Victim Information Database. It's a data-mining program that can penetrate law enforcement information storage and sift through cases and aggregate results. It seeks information using keywords, and then uses a confidence ratio to assess results. I've entered everything I know about the Society of Light and the situation at the cult: the compound, the number of people there, the children, and the background of Jackson. I asked DAVID how likely it is that the children's mothers were murdered. You can see the result here."

Dunn leaned in close, squinting. "What am I looking at?"

"A sixty-two percent confidence ratio that the women were murdered. Which is very strong. These confidence ratios are seldom that high because they can only work off of known data that's been inputted, and a lot of case information never makes it into the electronic databases." Sophie swiveled the monitor back. "The other thing DAVID can do is retrieve data from confidential sites based on keywords. I'm going to have it sift for everything to do with the cult's finances. I want to know where Jackson gets his money and if there's any financial motive for the women's deaths."

Dunn straightened up and whistled low through his teeth. "You're even better than I thought."

"None of it would be admissible in court, though." Sophie said as she stood. She straightened the same white button-down blouse and smoothed the loose-fitting black Lycra work pants she'd worn at the FBI. She'd brought gym clothes and her "disguise" outfit to change back into when she left Security Solutions for the day. "But we can use it to get evidence that can be."

"That's the thing about private contracting. We don't have to worry about a court case unless it's what the client wants or our investigation uncovers a bigger crime. Of course, if we find any evidence of murder, we'll want to turn that over to Hilo PD. Follow me. Let's go meet the client."

Sophie unplugged her laptop and tucked it under her arm, walking to the conference room behind Dunn.

Too bad she couldn't just sleep with him. A few orgasms would probably help her depression, help her get over the heartbreak of her breakup with Alika Wolcott, brutally injured in her last case and now relocated permanently back to Kauai. Yes, sleeping with Dunn would be a terrible idea. Really bad. But she could still admire how he looked from behind. Even if that made her a hypocrite...

As if detecting her thoughts, Dunn winked at her as he opened the conference door. "After you."

Sophie preceded Dunn into a well-appointed room with a long, gleaming conference table and whiteboard on one wall. A bank of windows framed the Honolulu skyline on the other wall. Two women sat at one end of the table—the washed-out, leathery blonde Sophie recognized as the client, and a striking Asian woman wearing a fitted sheath dress. Both stood to greet them as they entered.

"Sophie, meet Sharon Blumfield, the client whose interests we're representing. And this is Dr. Helen Kinoshita." Dunn made a little bow to the psychologist. "She's the best in the shrink business."

Dr. Kinoshita actually blushed. Sophie was relieved that she wasn't the only woman working with Dunn that was susceptible to his charms.

"Pleased to meet you," Sophie stepped forward and shook the client's hand, smiling at Blumfield. "I am so glad we were able to get your children back to you. They look lovely. Are they doing all right?"

"They're fine, thank you! Really, I can't thank you enough." Blumfield's eyes filled. "My mother flew out and she's with them at the hotel now."

"They're adjusting well," Kinoshita said. "Considering they were woken up by two armed operatives."

"That was the best possible extraction we could come up with," Dunn said. They all sat around one end of the table as Sophie opened her laptop. "Something you may not know is that Ms. Ang recently joined us from the FBI. She's very familiar with investigative techniques and has some unique tools to help us find answers regarding the women you are concerned are missing."

"I do have some unique tools. But we always begin basic." Sophie smiled at the women. "I'm going to type as we talk, and begin building a case file. Tell me the names of the missing women, and a brief physical description. Any details you can recall will be helpful."

She built three separate files, one for each woman.

Mandy Jones, brunette, long brown hair, curvy build, glasses, age thirty-four, had three children, Odin, Freya, and Thor, with Jackson, and disappeared five years ago.

Jennifer Roberts, tall slim blonde, age thirty-five, had two children, Zeus and Hera, with Jackson, and disappeared four years ago.

Amy Fillmore: disappeared two years ago. Curvy redhead. Had three children, Horus, Isis, and Osiris, with Jackson.

"Interesting." Dunn was taking notes on a yellow legal pad. "What's the significance of the god names?"

"Jackson believes the children are reincarnated beings, and that giving them the names of gods captures some of the gods' power."

"Jackson doesn't seem to have one certain physical type he's attracted to," Sophie observed.

"We're chosen for him by his Council of Elders." Blumfield looked down, working a pleat of fabric between her fingers. "We were nominated. Interviewed by the Elders. Inspected physically to make sure we were healthy and fertile."

"What criteria were used to determine…" Sophie groped for a word. "Eligibility?"

"Well, as I said, health and fertility were factors." Blumfield drew a breath, blew it out. Kinoshita patted her arm encouragingly. "Our duty was to bring forth reincarnated Elders, which his children are believed to be. Are you familiar with the Society of Light's beliefs?"

"Just a little. I reviewed the website," Sophie said.

"Jackson calls it enhanced reincarnation. By performing deeds for the Society, further levels of advancement can be achieved. When you return in the next life it's to be in a better body, in a better position to do the work of the Society." Blumfield pulled a tissue from the box on the table and dabbed her eyes. "I'm sorry. I can't believe I was so deep in it. It wasn't until I saw how the elders took over my children, how they were brainwashing them and using them for slave labor, basically—that I realized what a lie I'd swallowed—and had to keep on swallowing."

"Do you think the children's mothers might have been promised some advanced 'reincarnation position' in return for dying for the cause?" Sophie made air quotes with her fingers. "Was anything like that ever proposed to you?"

"It's possible. But I never heard anything like that. I wasn't Jackson's favorite, though. He spent more time with all of the other women than he did with me. He visited me strictly to get me pregnant." Blumfield's face twisted with old pain. "Not that I minded. I wasn't into him that way either, after the first time or two."

"So with you gone, and these others gone—does he have a new woman?" Dunn asked.

"Two. Jessie Sparks is pregnant, and Petra Perkins is new. Not yet pregnant."

Sophie felt revulsion rise up, an acid taste at the back of her throat. "Do you have any information on those two? And please tell us anything you can about the missing women. Anything about their families, where they came from—anything you can remember."

Sophie steadily built the files as Blumfield responded to their questions and gentle prompting from Kinoshita. Finally, Blumfield seemed to hit a wall. "I think I've told you everything I can think of."

Dunn fetched them all a tray of coffee and they took a break as Sophie finished typing up her notes.

"I have enough for us to try to find these women's families, perhaps see what the custody situation would be for the children if we can get them out of the cult," Sophie picked up her tea, gone cold—and Dunn pushed a fresh mug over to her, which she accepted gratefully.

"Sharon, I think we should start at the beginning," Dunn said. "Help us understand how you were recruited to the cult in the first place. How it operates."

Sophie shot Dunn a glance. His sensitivity was surprising, and their different styles complemented each other.

"Okay. I was in college, and didn't have much direction—I come from a family with money, as you're already aware." Blumfield started her story in halting sentences, but as she got going, the words flowed more easily.

She'd been an aimless young woman attending UCLA and going to yoga classes on campus. Sandoval Jackson had come to town to do an advanced teaching seminar. Blumfield had attended and "fallen under his spell."

"He was so much more than a yoga teacher. His very presence was both calming and energizing. He made me feel like I could do anything. Be anything. Like I had a special purpose, and I badly needed one." She explained how her involvement with the Society was engineered in stages until she was living in the compound in Waipio, an idyllic setting that was presented on social media as the pinnacle of healthy, beautiful living out in nature. "It's like the rules that guide the rest of the world are left at the door of the compound. Sandoval is…god there." She shook her head. "I fought for the chance to be one of his consorts, as we were called. I was thrilled when I made it through all the examinations and evaluations to be his bedmate."

"And…did you get pregnant right away?"

"I did." She nodded. "The other consorts and I all got along. We took turns in his bed and waited on him at his yurt. We got to have the children at our breast until they were one year old, then they went to the children's care run by women elders. But we got to be with them every day when we had free time."

"So no one else in the cult had children?"

"No one else was allowed to."

"That seems tough to enforce." Dunn flipped a sleek metal pen that looked like it could double as an assassination device between his fingers.

"Only single people are allowed at the compound, and sex is allowed as part of certain rites—but life at Waipio is a spiritual path. If people wanted to pair up or have children, they had to leave and go to one of the lesser group living situations. Sandoval's compound was considered the apex of the Society. A utopia of sorts." Blumfield's mouth twisted.

"But what makes you think foul play befell these women?" Sophie asked. "Perhaps they simply left and went to these other compounds."

Blumfield shook her head. "I guess it's possible, but they were very devoted to Jackson, and their children were at the compound." She licked thin lips. "There's a ritual called the *rooska*. It is a voluntary suicide to help the group in some way. I believe they were asked to *rooska*. Maybe they agreed to it, maybe they were forced."

"What does *rooska* involve?" Sophie typed as she talked, capturing Blumfield's words for later analysis by DAVID.

"Poison. With oleander. Accompanied by some opiates to make you sleepy."

"So have you witnessed it?" Dunn asked.

"Yes." Blumfield looked down, fiddled with the tulsi bead bracelet on one wrist. "One of the people who did taxes for the Society had taken money from the group. There was a ceremony where he renounced his wrong, and we were all sworn to secrecy —a blood vow—and he took the oleander and died. He was buried in the garden to enrich it."

"Is there a certain burial area?" Dunn pushed his legal pad toward Blumfield. "Draw us where it is within the compound. Being able to search for the body would really help us."

"Bodies are buried right in the garden. We all come from the earth, and return to the earth." Blumfield's eyes gleamed with a strange light for a moment.

"We will need to go over all of this and form a plan," Sophie said. "I hope you're prepared for it to take some time and expense."

"I am. Jake has provided me with a preliminary contract. I'm pledging a portion of my trust fund to stop Jackson's activities," Blumfield said. "I want my children's siblings to have a future beyond those walls—and for my sister consorts to have some justice."

# CHAPTER ELEVEN

Sophie's burner phone buzzed with an incoming text as she headed back to her office. It was a texting phone with a flip-open case, and she read the message. *"This is Connor. Still up for a hike-run day after tomorrow?"*

She already badly needed some sort of physical outlet. *"Wish I could go today,"* she texted back, reaching her office and shutting the door. *"But Dunn has me working hard on the cult case. We are investigating three missing consorts of the cult leader on behalf of our client."*

*"Sounds more fun than what I'm doing. Quarterly shareholder reports. Just kill me now."*

Sophie smiled as she read. Connor had been left in charge of the growing security company by its departed CEO Sheldon Hamilton, and clearly some parts of the CEO job suited the breezy Australian better than others.

She plugged her laptop back in and was organizing her notes and files when Dunn reappeared from escorting the women to the elevator. "So. We gonna do some investigating today?"

"Yes. Let's divide up some of the tasks. I want to run a deep background on Sandoval Jackson using DAVID. I no longer have official access to VICAP and the other FBI databases, but I can still get into them using DAVID and search keywords. I will also build a background as much as possible on these victims. But we can find their parents easily enough. Why don't you do phone interviews with the parents, find out their attitudes about their daughters' involvement with the cult, and what they know about the women's whereabouts?"

Dunn gave her a level look out of those gray eyes. "You trying to give me orders?" He quirked a brow. "You know I'm in charge of this case, right?"

"Really?" The back of Sophie's neck got hot. "You can't have a simple talk about who's doing what without throwing your weight around?"

Dunn lifted his hands. "Hey. We're new at working together. I just thought I'd remind you of the lay of the land. And it so happens I agree with your plan. What I don't like is this separate office deal. If I could make these phone calls in here, you could listen to them and I wouldn't have to recap everything I just said."

"And if you think I can do highly complicated computer inputting and calculations with you talking in the background, putting your feet on my desk and thinking I'm hanging on your every word, you're unfamiliar with tech work. I need cool. Quiet. Dim light. No ambient noise but my music." Sophie lowered the shiny metal blind to shut out the bright Honolulu day. She rotated the blind and the room plunged into twilight. "So no. I don't think sharing an office would work."

Dunn stood up, offense in every line of his big body. "Sorry to cramp your style." He took three long strides and was out the door, shutting it hard enough to rattle the blinds.

Sophie blew out a breath. Clearly neither of them was used to having a partner. At least they'd worked well together on the raid and the interview.

She checked the thermostat on the wall and turned it down to sixty, then took her headphones out of her bag and plugged them in. She put on a padded Bose headset, settled back in her chair, and sank into the oblivion of being wired in.

SOME HOURS later her phone buzzed again, interrupting the spell of her background building with DAVID. She picked it up and read a text from Dunn. *"Sorry I was an ass. I haven't worked with a partner before, only a unit I commanded. So we're going to have a few adjustments. Can we confab?"*

Sophie stored her latest input and texted back. *"Yes. You can come in now."*

She hardly had time to take off her headphones when Dunn appeared at the door. "Got some good stuff from the parents. Mind if I hit the light?"

"I prefer natural light if at all possible." Sophie swiveled the blinds halfway open.

"You really are a delicate flower, aren't you? Brr. It's cold in here." Dunn's buoyancy was back.

"I'm more like a finely calibrated machine that needs certain conditions for optimal performance," Sophie said stiffly. His energy might just be a good balance for her, especially when the depression was bad.

"Whatever." Dunn flopped in the chair next to the table that he seemed to have chosen. "So. All the parents have concerns about how long their daughters have been missing, and about not being allowed to see their grandchildren. Jennifer Roberts's parents hadn't heard from their daughter in ten years and didn't know where she was at all. The grandchildren and the cult were news to them. We may get more contributions to this op than just Blumfield and her money. The women's parents who knew about it hated the Society of Light." Dunn had brought in two water bottles along with his legal pad, and he tossed her one. "You need to hydrate, for that finely tuned brain to be properly calibrated."

Sophie took the lid off the bottle and drank deep as he continued. "So Mandy Newburt's parents, the first woman who disappeared, have been the most active. They filed a missing person report, but they did that in their hometown in California, not with Hilo PD. So it seems that the message never got through to Hilo. Amy Fillmore's parents are also concerned that they hadn't heard from their daughter, but chalked it up to her being 'so involved with that sick guru of hers.'" He air quoted his words. "And as I said, Jennifer's parents hadn't heard from her in ten years, but they were estranged from their daughter."

"Did anyone suspect foul play?" Sophie got up and came around the desk. "We need to get a murder board going. Okay if we do it in my office? That way if we need something on the computer I can pop over and look it up."

"Fine. Use the whiteboard on the wall."

Sophie began a timeline at the top of the board with the month and year of each woman's disappearance, according to Blumfield. She turned to Dunn, frowning. "Is it possible that any of these women might have fled, like Sharon did, and just be hiding?"

"Blumfield didn't think so, if you recall. But I suppose that's a possibility. I bet that's what Jackson will say if we confront him about these disappearances."

"And that brings up an interesting question." Sophie capped her marker. "Is it murder if the victim voluntarily committed suicide?"

"How voluntary could it be in a setting like that?" Dunn said. His sleek metal pen had reappeared. He spun it helicopter-style around his fingers. "I'd say it's inherently coercive, but we don't have to determine that—we can let the district attorney and Hilo PD figure that out. At the very least they have an illegally buried body under the vegetables, the accountant whose *rooska* suicide was witnessed by the cult. We find that body, and we can boost it as evidence to Hilo PD. Once they have a search warrant, they could bring in ground-penetrating radar and scent dogs and look for the other bodies."

"But how are we going to get back in there and look for the body?"

"You leave that to me." Dunn winked. "Now, what did you come up with on Jackson?"

"Interesting background. He is the son of a pair of medical doctors who spent their lives overseas, working in hot spots doing humanitarian aid. They were killed during a coup in Africa when he was twelve. An impressionable age, it turns out. He was shipped back to the United States to an aunt and uncle, where he had his revelation about accelerated reincarnation and began his spiritual quest." Sophie went back behind her computer and read off her notes. "Jackson studied in ashrams in India and Nepal. He mastered many forms of yoga and other spiritual practice, and began to gain followers. He has a group of six "elders," and they seem to do the main running of the Society of Light empire— which is quite lucrative." She read off some statistics. "Their tax return revenue last year as a nonprofit was ten million."

Dunn whistled. "And where does that money come from?"

"Franchises of his Society of Light yoga studios, curriculum, workshops, swag, and merchandise—and from donations from the Society's members. All members living in the group settings turn over their income to the cult for the duration."

"Any malcontents out there we can talk to? Preferably in Hawaii?"

"As a matter of fact, there are. Several members who left Waipio have started blogs. There's one here in Honolulu. Peter Corbett." Sophie swung her monitor, and Dunn got up to lean in and look. "Seems a bit angry."

"I'll say." The website featured a pulsing skull and a rambling rant against both the Society of Light and law enforcement, for not taking Corbett's numerous complaints seriously.

"Seems like someone we can talk to in person. Ready for a field trip?"

Sophie stood. Stretched. Locked eyes with Dunn. "What I really need is an exercise break. Ever done any mixed martial arts?"

# CHAPTER TWELVE

THE GYM at Security Solutions was state-of-the-art. Nautilus machines lined the walls along with treadmills, stairclimbers, ellipticals, and bikes. A free weights section filled one corner, and in the middle of the room was a roped-off sparring ring. The space was empty in the late afternoon, sunlight pouring in through the windows.

Sophie came out of the women's locker room in her fight gear: tight-fitting shorts, an exercise bra, a padded helmet similar to what bikers wear, and split-fingered, padded gloves.

Dunn was already up in the ring, jumping to loosen his muscles and moving with nervous energy. He was an impressive sight in a tight tank and loose nylon shorts, his chiseled frame moving with the restless grace that was such a part of him.

"I don't want to hurt you." His gunmetal eyes were worried and sincere as Sophie climbed into the ring.

Sophie smiled. "You don't have to worry about that." If he hadn't heard about her fighting, she wasn't about to tell him. She'd have the women's middleweight MMA title for Oahu right now if the FBI had allowed her to compete, having trounced the champion several times in non-competition bouts.

"Well, like I said, I haven't done MMA officially. But I've done some jiu-jitsu and boxing. And of course, hand-to-hand."

"We'll use all that. Basically, you want to get me on the mat and hold me there until I thump. And vice versa. Ready?" Sophie bent her knees, smiling, her arms loosely spread.

"Ready." And he came at her like a hurricane.

Sophie dodged, getting a sense of his style, which was much like his personality: a lot of force upfront, easy to see coming. She bobbed and weaved as he continued to swing and try to grab, while she sneaked in body blows that stole his breath and turned him red with unspent frustration.

Done toying with him, Sophie swept his legs out from under him and straddled him from the side, her powerful thighs twisting back his arm. He writhed and cursed in impotent fury, trying to get loose, but she tightened her grip, going very still.

She could keep this up all day while he burned energy. He thrashed and struggled, but contorted on the padded mat in a hold he couldn't break, he eventually thumped.

Sophie immediately let him up and sprang to her feet, and it was a good thing because he lashed out a kick from the mat right where her head would have been, catching her hard in the side. She flew backward as he shot to his feet and followed up with a series of jabs. She evaded them and sneaked in another kick to the back of his knee, knocking him to a kneeling position—and then she jumped on his back and slammed him face-first into the mat.

Dunn filled the room with a rich stream of creative curses, and dug his fingers into her thigh. "Let me up, woman, damn it!"

"Not until you thump."

He punched her thigh, hard. It was going to leave a bruise. "Unacceptable, Dunn." She wrenched his arms harder, and twisted. He yelled, an inarticulate howl of pain, and she let go and leapt back out of range.

Dunn didn't get up this time, though. He just lay there, face down, arms twisted in the position she'd left him in. His muscled back heaved with his hard breathing. *Had she hurt him?* It should have been painful—that arms-back restraint hold was a bitch—but not injuring. Not tearing anything essential.

"Jake." Sophie bent over, touched his shoulder. "You okay?"

She didn't even have time to suck a breath before she was slammed onto her back. He jumped up and came down above her, his bent arm at her throat.

"Do you give?" Dunn rasped, his face red. His gray eyes glowed with fury. Sophie nodded, and touched her throat reflexively as her diaphragm got going.

Dunn was a dirty fighter, and he didn't like losing. It was something to keep in mind.

PULLING up in front of cult malcontent Peter Corbett's address the next morning in the tan Security Solutions SUV, Dunn slanted Sophie a glance. "You sore today? Cause I sure as hell am."

"A little." Sophie smiled. "Especially where you punched me in the thigh. Not a gentleman move, Dunn."

"You could have warned me you were one of the top MMA fighters in the state, which I found out when I searched you and found out you're the reigning champ at Fight Club. Not a gentle-woman, Ang. I needed every sneaky trick I could come up with just to reclaim my manhood." Dunn's dark mood was gone—in fact, it had been gone within minutes of their bout in the ring. He was like weather in Hawaii—blowing in fierce at times, but usually sunny.

"Like it would have mattered. I'd have beat you the same."

"But I wouldn't have been as surprised at how good you are. Or as pissed off when I lost." Dunn grinned. "I totally get why Remarkian pounced on you the minute he heard you left the FBI."

"Took you long enough to appreciate my skills."

"That's not the only thing I appreciate." Dunn kept his eyes front as he put the SUV in park in front of a beige apartment building on a seedy street in west Honolulu. Last night's rainfall had knocked plumerias off the trees at the entrance, and flowers dotted the damp asphalt, browning pinwheels that scented the air. "I've never seen you so much as glance at yourself in the mirror, let alone fuss with lipstick like a normal woman—and you always look amazing."

"I thought I told you no more of that kind of talk," Sophie said.

"What, now I can't even give my partner an honest compliment?" Dunn threw up his hands. "Fine. I'll never say another nice thing to you. Wart-ridden hag."

Sophie laughed and got out of her side of the vehicle.

Corbett's building had a trashed-looking old elevator so they took the stairs. Sophie followed Dunn. She could have reciprocated the compliment he'd given her: Dunn looked incredible too, and while aware of his charm, didn't seem vain. She certainly didn't mind the view ahead as she followed him up the stairs.

She'd slept wonderfully well the night before, the depression beaten further back by an exchange with the Ghost.

He'd sent an encrypted email. *"Hear you're no longer with the FBI. Dare I hope you join me someday in dealing justice to those who won't ever be caught by normal means? I'll be on at the usual place at nine p.m. your time."*

She'd felt a noticeable mood lift as she logged into the anonymous chat room at nine p.m., relieved to be distracted from how bare and ugly her new apartment was even after her trip to Target. Ginger, curled at her feet, was the best thing about it.

*"You making me a job offer?"* Sophie typed, smiling. The sunset was long gone, but ambient light from the city lit the sky with a warm glow, her only illumination besides the glowing screen.

*"Ha. This is strictly pro bono volunteer stuff."* His answer unspooled rapidly, appearing in old-school green DOS letters against a black screen.

*"I was just going to look into your activities, but you saved me the trouble. Still up to your old tricks? Getting stockbrokers to roll on each other and gangsters to off each other?"* Those were only a few of the creative ways the Ghost had used to deal out his brand of "justice."

*"Always looking for new creative challenges. I have to say, I'm relieved to hear you are no longer at the FBI. You might have caught me eventually."*

*"I am still planning to."*

*"I hope you will. But for a different purpose, entirely. We could be something to each other."*

Sophie sucked at a swelling the bout with Dunn had left on her lip. The tiny pain felt like pleasure. The flirty warmth of her fascinating adversary's words spread through her, enhancing the sensation. *"Dare I ask what you mean?"*

*"I can't tip my hand just yet. But let's just say—I'd like to see a lot more of the view I had in your apartment."*

Sophie gasped. The view he had in her apartment! He'd bugged her, and watched her do yoga—naked. She'd tried to forget that ever happened.

*"I told you before and I'll tell you again—I never meant to see what I did. But some things are not meant to be unseen."*

*"That's creeper talk. And it's not exactly fair, you know. I never bugged your place and watched you walk around naked."*

*"I could fix that situation. Just say the word and I'll hook something up for you. What's your pleasure? I'm guessing the gym. I have my own private one. I could do some back extensions for you. Overhead presses? Whatever it would take to impress you. I'm told I'm not unappealing, and I take my fitness as seriously as you do."*

Sophie felt a curling of heat deep in her gut. She really did want to see what Sheldon Hamilton looked like naked and flexing. She sat chewing her bruise, unsure what to say.

*He must have thought he overstepped, because after a few*

minutes he continued. *"I'm sorry. You're not ready for that. I understand. But I might just send you something on email so you know I'm not just a pervy troll with a potbelly who gets his jollies spying on women. I'm serious about knowing you better, meeting IRL someday. Anyway, glad you left the FBI. That box couldn't handle a woman of your talents."*

*"It was a very good box. I miss it. And my friends there."* Staying distracted was the best way to deal with second-guessing her decision to quit the career she'd been sure would be for life. Busyness was the only way to mitigate the ache of loss and grief she still felt—and apprehension about the legal confrontations that lay still ahead.

*"You have other friends."*

*"Oh, so you're a friend now? Shouldn't I be worried about a 'friend' who's seen me naked and routinely uses technology to get people to eliminate each other?"*

*"You never have to worry about harm from me. Haven't I proved that to you yet?"*

He had. The Ghost had done what no one else could do: helped her abusive ex's teenaged bride escape a gilded cage that Sophie was all too familiar with. She considered carefully before she replied.

*"I will always worry about someone like you being free to decide right from wrong, and having the means to execute those decisions. No one should be both judge and jury."* Sophie typed slowly, almost unwilling to state her truth so baldly—but there it was. She didn't, couldn't support his vigilantism, while wishing she could. The ambivalence sawed at her nerves. *"But I'm a hypocrite. Because I also appreciate that you do things that could be done no other way. Things that make the world a better place."*

The period at the end of her sentence pulsed at her. Finally, he responded. *"Then I will just have to let that be enough."*

And he was gone.

No one in her life made her feel quite like he did. But how

could anything ever come of it? And why did he want to show her he wasn't a "pervy troll with a potbelly?" He must know she was onto the Ghost's real identity as Sheldon Hamilton. He was always at least two steps ahead of her, damn his cleverness.

They'd reached the door of Corbett's apartment with no more time for musings. Dunn knocked on the sun-bleached door decorated with a Buddha statue and pot of purple basil.

"Peter Corbett?" They held up ID wallets to the cadaverously thin, tall, bald man who opened the door. Dunn gave his most charming smile. "We're investigators working for a client who has left the Society of Light. We found your writings on the internet and wondered if you'd have a few minutes to talk with us."

Corbett took both of their wallets, looked at them closely. "Not cops?"

"No. Law enforcement currently has no interest in the Society, as you mentioned on your blog," Sophie said.

"I need a minute to verify your identities. I hope you don't mind if I make a few phone calls. Can't be too careful." Corbett withdrew inside, shutting the door.

"Huh. Dude is paranoid," Dunn said.

"I would be too. He's been vocal about his complaints about the cult. And if we could find him, others can too." Corbett's name and address had been masked, but it had been child's play for Sophie to trace him.

Five minutes went by before Corbett returned to the door. "I called Security Solutions and verified that you are employees. Come in. Have a seat."

The room smelled faintly of unknown herbs, and was furnished sparely with lauhala matting on the floor, and a daybed in carved wood. Pillows surrounded a low coffee table. A wall hanging in beautiful painted silk covered one wall with a scene of the Na Pali Coast on Kauai.

Sophie and Dunn perched on the daybed. Corbett folded

himself up gracefully for one so tall and sat on one of the floor cushions. "How can I help?"

"Why don't you tell us, off the top of your head, what you are most concerned about regarding the Society of Light. You seem older than the usual people involved with the group," Dunn said. He took out his phone. "I'd like to record you, if I may."

"You may not record me," Corbett said with dignity. "But you can take notes. And I'm older because I was one of Sandoval Jackson's Elders."

Dunn replaced his phone. Sophie never carried pen or paper, and wished she did in this instance. Clearly Dunn did too, as he made a writing gesture with his hand, his brows raised.

Corbett shook his head. "Really? You don't even have a pad of paper?" He gestured to the kitchen. "Left drawer next to the sink." Dunn rose and retrieved a small tablet of hotel stationery from the drawer. He resumed his seat, withdrawing the steel pen he favored from a pocket.

"An Elder," Sophie read. "I read that there are five. And they basically run the financial and business end of the Society."

"We do." Corbett cleared his throat, a hollow rattling sound. "Or did, I should say." He took a breath, pinned Sophie with calm blue eyes. "I am ill. Cancer. When I began not feeling well, the doctor that lives at Waipio told Sandoval that she suspected I had cancer. He told me to make my peace, and that I had earned a place returning next time in the body of one of his children." Corbett looked away, out the sliding glass door to a view of distant high rises and the sea. "Jackson asked me to consider *rooska*, to accelerate the process of my reincarnation. I had a crisis of faith when I realized I didn't want to die…and because I knew he just wanted to replace me as an Elder. I had been one of the few who expressed opinions he didn't like. He said he appreciated my gift for truth, but I knew that the minute he had a chance to replace me, I'd be gone." Corbett coughed. Sophie got up and filled a water glass for him from the minimally appointed kitchen. The man sipped, nodding in thanks.

"How did you get out?" Dunn asked.

"I had business for the Society in Hilo. I simply didn't return to the compound when it was completed. As Elders, we had a degree of trust and freedom that others did not."

"So in your time there, did you see and experience things that concerned you?" Dunn asked.

Corbett raised tufted blond brows. "Really? You are asking me this. And here I sit, someone who has continued to speak out about the Society. Haven't you read my blog?"

"We need your direct testimony, if you're willing," Sophie said.

Sophie listened while Dunn took notes on the things Corbett had seen and been a part of—activities that, if verified, would put Jackson away for a long time.

"Can I ask you something?" Sophie said. "Do you think the cult might try to silence you?"

"I think they're waiting for the cancer to do that. They have a PR department that has painted me as a malcontent with a screw loose." Corbett sipped his water, and his hand trembled.

"Would you consider discontinuing the agitation? The blogging? We'd like to bring this man to justice. If we find hard evidence, we can turn it over to law enforcement, and you'd be a key witness. We want you safe," Sophie said.

"Young lady. I appreciate what you're saying. But those are a lot of ifs, and the cancer is not an 'if.' The cancer is now, and if something I say or do can keep one person from joining the Society *now*, then it's worth my last breath to speak."

SOPHIE AND DUNN were silent on the drive back to the office. "I think it's time we updated Bix," Sophie said as Dunn navigated the company SUV into the secure garage.

"I agree. I don't want another spanking from him, and this thing is snowballing," Dunn said.

Sophie gave him a little punch to the shoulder. "What? Jake Dunn reporting to a superior?"

"I know when to cover my ass, believe it or not, and I'm getting pretty concerned about what we're uncovering here." Dunn's blue-and-gray eyes were grave as he looked at her. "This cult is bad news."

"I wish Waxman had let us investigate a little further. If we'd uncovered all of this, talked with Blumfield more..."

"But there's still no case from a law enforcement perspective. It's still all hearsay, the reports of disenchanted former cult members." Dunn put the vehicle in gear and turned it off. "I'll text you when Bix can fit us in. I have an idea about how to get into the cult."

SOME HOURS LATER, Kendall Bix leaned back in the office chair in the conference room. He pushed a hand through hair marked by wings of silver at his temples, brown eyes coolly intent. "So what I hear you asking in all this is for me to authorize you to go back into the cult, poke around, and look for evidence of these alleged bodies."

"Yes. And I have a plan to get Sophie in," Dunn said. They'd been back at the office for a few hours, during which time Dunn had closeted himself in his office and Sophie had been working DAVID. They'd just presented the results of their last couple of days of investigations to the VP. "It's not a full frontal attack. Sophie is going to go in undercover to an upcoming yoga retreat at the Waipio compound, and gather what she can. The retreat begins next Tuesday. I already have a spot reserved for a very dedicated yoga practitioner named Mary Watson."

# CHAPTER THIRTEEN

DUNN STUCK his head in the door of Sophie's office. "Seriously. I'm going to request that we get a door put in this wall over here so I can just yell over at you when I need to. Since you don't want me to move in here."

Sophie looked up from the glowing screen before her, slightly disoriented from being sunk deep in DAVID's data stream. "What?"

"Never mind—it's just that it's Friday evening, and unlike the FBI, no work until Monday. Don't stay late. You'll make me look bad."

Sophie leaned back and rubbed her eyes. "This is all going to take some getting used to. I slept in the lab sometimes when I was on a case. We all did."

"It's comforting to know how seriously you feds take your jobs. This is private sector and there are no current emergencies on this case. Whoever's dead is already dead. Pack up and go home. Unless you'd like to join me for a 'pau hana' drink?" Dunn wiggled his brows.

"No thanks, Dunn. I'll wrap up when I reach a stopping point."

"Whatcha working on?" Dunn pushed his big body away from

the doorjamb and entered. Being relentlessly curious was a good quality in an investigator, if a little annoying in a person.

"Just tracking the cult's money stream. You wouldn't understand it."

Dunn narrowed his eyes. "Try me." He came around the desk and leaned on his fists, looking over her shoulder.

She should have known he would take that as a challenge.

"These coded numbers are bank accounts. These are balances. When I get into each account I can see the direct deposits and amounts. Some are passive income that I can track to find what that money was. This one, for instance." She clicked on one of the numbered deposits. "This goes to a big trust account at a bank in California. The name on the account is one of the missing women. I don't think these brides were chosen for Jackson based on looks, fertility, and dedication. I think they were chosen for having the right background to feed money into his machine."

Dunn straightened up. "Sweet. We have motive, times three. I bet these women changed their estates to benefit the Society."

"Well, the tricky thing is that their estates wouldn't come to the cult until they are declared legally dead, which takes seven years from time of disappearance. But each of these women was on a trust fund income, which was transferred to feed directly into the cult's accounts. I was going to tell you all this, to follow up with on Monday morning after a restful weekend doing whatever it is you do."

Dunn leaned a hip on her desk. "Want to find out what I do on the weekend?"

"No. Thank you. I've had quite enough togetherness with my partner for the moment. No offense."

Dunn was opening his mouth for a rejoinder when a knock came from the doorway. "Sophie Ang?"

They both looked up. A pimply-faced young man stood in the doorway holding an envelope.

"Yes?"

"Delivery for you."

Dunn pushed off of the desk as the young man approached and handed her an envelope. "You have been served."

Sophie's mouth, opened to thank the kid, stayed that way as the young man turned and strode out.

"Hey!" Dunn roared out from behind her desk and took off after the kid. She heard the rumbling interrogation in the hallway as he captured his prey.

Questioning the messenger wasn't going to change whatever was in her hand.

She looked down at it. An FBI logo and Quantico address decorated one corner, with LEGAL DEPARTMENT underneath. Her name, c/o Security Solutions, and the business address of this building marked the front of the envelope.

At least they didn't currently know where she lived. That was something she'd taken a lot of time, effort, and cash to ensure. But it was too much to hope that the FBI wouldn't find her here, of course.

Sophie slid a finger under the flap of the envelope and loosened it.

Dunn reappeared, shaking his head. "Messenger service. Kid doesn't know anything."

"I know what this is." Sophie removed the folded paper and opened it.

*SUMMONS TO APPEAR IN FEDERAL COURT* blared at her from the top line.

Sophie skimmed, feeling the heat of Dunn's presence as he came around to read over her shoulder.

A court date one month from today had been set *"in the matter of the legal ownership of the program known as Data Assessment Victim Information Database."* The Honorable Judge Reimbold would be presiding. Sophie's patent was still under review, and until it was awarded, she was vulnerable.

"Those fuckers." Dunn's big hand squeezed her shoulder.

"They've been taking more than they're entitled to since J. Edgar Hoover."

Sophie blinked. The letters on the paper had just disintegrated into meaningless gibberish. "Why don't you take off, Dunn. I have some phone calls I have to make."

"No. Let me help. I can…"

"No, Jake!" Sophie snarled. "This is my private business, started before I came to work here. I'm handling it. Now get out of my office and give me some space!"

Dunn drew himself upright, gray eyes hurt. "If that's how you want it." He strode out, shutting the door hard.

Sophie looked back down at the letter again and swore long and fluently in Thai, then folded it neatly and replaced it in the envelope. She picked up the handset of the office phone and called her lawyer, Bettina Smithers, and apprised her of the court date and the situation.

"I knew this was coming, but it's still a shock to see it in black and white. They really think they can steal my work from me."

"Well, you have work logs on the hard drive of the computer you used while you were creating DAVID, right? And it wasn't an FBI computer?" Bettina Smithers was a stylish forty-something black woman based out of Los Angeles. Smithers loved patents and inventions and the hapless people who always seemed to fall prey to those trying to steal them. The Smithers contact had come from her father, whose diplomatic job helped him cross paths with professionals in many different positions. "Let's have a Skype meeting tomorrow and revisit our strategy and I'll see what I can come up with. For now, I'll file a stay-put motion so you can keep using DAVID legally up until the court decision."

They set up a time for their conference the next day.

Sophie sagged in her chair as she hung up. She had to call her father and tell him all that had gone on, including her departure from his apartment, but she didn't feel strong enough for that conversation just yet. He was going to be worried and upset that she'd left.

Right now, she needed to pick Ginger up from doggie daycare.

Sophie shut down DAVID, saving all the data she'd collected on the case to the cloud, and unplugged the laptop.

The heaviness of depression sucked at Sophie, deadening her energy as she stood, flicked off the lights, walked out of the office and took the stairs down to the secure garage.

The depression rose around her like a dark greasy fog, engulfing her as she drove the Lexus to the public parking garage where she stored it, only a few blocks from the doggie daycare. She parked the Lexus and changed inside it into Mary Watson's flowing sundress, sandals, and pretty straw hat.

Collecting her backpack filled with everything that mattered to her from the back seat, she beeped the SUV locked for the weekend and went two floors down in the garage to Mary Watson's beater truck. She drove the truck out of the garage, the hat down to shield her face from any cameras, turning out onto busy Kalakaua Avenue.

She picked up Ginger and headed home.

The dog, sitting on the battered, sandy passenger seat beside her, sensed her mood and whined, thick tail lashing. "Yeah, you want a beach walk, don't you? It's 'pau hana' Friday, as Jake reminded me. We might as well stop at the beach on the way home."

Maybe a beach walk at sunset in Honolulu, a gorgeous event any day of the week, would head off the crippling malaise swamping her brain.

Driving on autopilot took her to Ala Moana Park. The sunset was indeed a glorious sight, painting the sea and sky with scarlet and gold, touching poufy cumulus clouds with Maxfield Parrish glory.

But walking in sand warm from the day, little waves curling around her feet, Mary's soft rayon dress blowing around her legs, just emphasized her isolation. Her loneliness. Her emptiness. The futility of all she'd tried to rebuild of her life after Assan Ang—now in prison, but likely to be extradited to Hong Kong for trial if he hadn't been already.

Assan had judges on speed dial in Hong Kong. But never mind. He, at least, was no longer her problem. She'd paid a high price to make sure of that.

Sophie walked the length of the beach and back. Ginger panted happily as they climbed back in the car and drove "home" to the awful little apartment.

What was she going to do with herself for a whole weekend?

Oh yes. She had a phone conference with her lawyer tomorrow.

And she had a hike-run with Connor Remarkian in the morning.

If she could find the energy for it, which was unlikely. *Better to cancel now.* The thought of interacting with Connor's upbeat personality, dragging herself on a strenuous run-hike was almost as repellent an idea as having to see Jake Dunn again any time soon.

Sophie narrowed her eyes at Ginger, currently rolling on her feet, whimpering in bliss that she'd had a walk and was now home with her mistress. *Life is good when you're a dog.*

Sophie composed a text to Connor from her burner phone, canceling the hike because she was sick. In a way she was: sick the way that her mother had been. Sick at the heart. Sick to the core. Sick of the fight that was living.

But she didn't send it. *Not yet.* Maybe she would feel better in the morning, and exercise always helped her dig out from under the boulder. No. She couldn't cancel. It would be good for her. Medicinal, like castor oil, or the herbs her aunt used to dose her with in Thailand.

She fed Ginger.

In the shower, she stroked the tattoos in Thai that were a part of her new life, a reminder of what she sought: the inside of one arm reminded her, *hope* and *respect*. The other, *power* and *truth*. On the exterior of one thigh, *freedom*. On the other *courage*. Circling her navel in tiny writing, were *love, joy* and *bliss*.

*Maybe someday she'd have some semblance of any of those.*

Sophie dried off and walked naked into her tiny bedroom. She drew the blackout drapes she'd bought at Target. She fell onto her blow-up mattress, drew up her blanket, and sank into the oblivion of sleep.

*Stars spun in her vision, obscuring the man's face as she tried to break his hold with her good hand, writhing beneath him. He'd landed on top of her, sour breath inches from her face, his fingers squeezing her throat. The razor sliced down toward her, and she squeezed her eyes shut.*

*"Sophie." He breathed her name in the voice of nightmare. She opened her eyes. She was looking into her ex Assan Ang's face, congested with rage and adrenaline, his panting breaths burning her skin, his bloodshot eyes inches from hers.*

*His hand tightened and her breath shut off. His weight on her body and his practiced grasp on her throat were as effective as ever. A slow grin twisted his full lips.*

*"My Sophie." The razor caressed her cheek. "I didn't dare hope it would be you coming after me. This is just too good."*

*Sophie felt blackness closing in. A sense of hopelessness and inevitability rose up and swamped her. It was as if the whole five years between her escape and this moment had never happened.*

*"You're mine until I'm done with you," he breathed into her ear. Goose bumps erupted as she shuddered, gasping in vain for breath. One arm was trapped beneath him, one raised beside her head but still nerveless from the blow. Her heart lurched as his big hand depressed the nerves and veins in her neck, just as he'd done a hundred times in the past.*

*She was disappearing, conditioned by his assault and smothered by his weight.*

*He was going to kill her this time. She'd seen that in the exul-*

*tant certainty in his eyes as he recognized her. Her heart felt like it was bursting. Her vision dimmed as he raised the razor.*

Sophie thrashed, and her arm connecting with Ginger's furry bulk woke her up. She sat upright, bathed in sweat, panting.

She'd survived. He couldn't hurt her anymore.

She lay back down, and Ginger snuggled close. She draped an arm over the warm, smelly dog.

It was a long time before she fell asleep again.

# CHAPTER FOURTEEN

CONNOR REMARKIAN STRODE up to Sophie in the parking lot the next morning. Ginger slavishly groveled and wagged at the sight of Anubis, his stately Doberman. The only indication of Anubis's excitement was the swiveling of his pricked, cropped ears.

"G'day!" Connor's voice was irritatingly cheerful, as she'd known it would be. Sophie leaned over, tightening the laces of her running shoes. The smell of rain was a metallic tease on the air, along with a faint mustiness from the thick pili grass surrounding the off-limits trail area, clearly marked NO TRESPASSING. "I thought of a perk to your leaving the FBI—you're just a regular citizen now, if we get popped for trespassing." He pointed to the sign, smiling.

Connor had dressed for movement in running shorts and a mesh shirt that showed off a near-perfect physique. None of it did a thing for Sophie. He was as annoying as Jake Dunn, and the ragged bits of nightmare still clouded her vision.

She wasn't in the mood to pretend this morning. The only way she could handle being with him during the hike was to shut him up. Her days of being a quiet, compliant woman were over, and if that left her alone, there were worse things.

"Listen, Connor. I'm only here because I think a run out in nature might be good for me right now. So I'll take the lead. Not in the mood to chat." Sophie slipped into a thin nylon daypack holding water for her and Ginger. "Let's go."

Connor's face went still. He gave a stiff nod and tweaked Anubis's leash. Sophie jumped Ginger over the large cement blocks beside the gate that supposedly kept hikers out, and hit the ground running.

The Catwalk was not a strenuous hike, fairly flat although winding through long, choking grass. At one point they had to crawl through a hole in the fence to run along a closed-off road. Sophie didn't begin to feel a slight loosening of the darkness on her mind until they crested a rise, and the soaring view of the ocean from thousands of feet up on the ridge broke into her view. She stopped to take it in, hands on her hips. Connor came to stand beside her but said nothing.

Whatever pique he might have initially felt at her brusque words seemed to have gone, and frankly, she didn't much care. They continued on in silence, and the famous tongue of concrete known as Dead Man's Catwalk came too soon.

Why was she here on this hike? *With him?*

Because he'd asked her on the hike, and she needed to get out, interact, exercise—even if that was the last thing she wanted to do.

Because she felt a mild tingle of attraction to him now and again—objectively, he was a very attractive man—and because he was a connection to Sheldon Hamilton.

But the Ghost, Sheldon, was who she really wanted to have a connection with.

Sophie dropped Ginger's leash at their destination. She took off her pack and poured water into a portable bowl for Ginger, who flopped in a bit of shade under the long grass around the area as Connor did the same for Anubis. Sophie removed her own water bottle and walked out onto the end of the cement tongue, the stunning backdrop of thousands of social media posts and selfies. She sat on the end, her legs dangling into the vastness of space over-looking a multi-hued sea far below. Connor joined her there, and mercifully, still didn't speak.

Sophie let the vista, a grand swath of wild blue ocean, turquoise reefs, and steep green cliffs, fill and calm her mind with beauty.

When would she accept her lot in life and not let it get her down? She had done all she could to better her situation. She'd grown up with a clinically depressed mother and a loving but distant diplomat father. She'd had an early and disastrous marriage to a sadistic businessman. She'd had a brief but solid career in the FBI.

Her goal, to hunt down those who would harm others, remained unchanged. Even though she'd had to leave the FBI, she was still hunting perpetrators—just in another way.

A way with fewer restrictions.

A way that had some room to color outside the lines.

She'd win this fight with the FBI over DAVID. And if she didn't, she'd just build an even better program.

*No one could keep her down. Not even Assan Ang.*

Sophie turned her head to look at Connor. He didn't meet her eyes—his gaze was on the far horizon. He had a face like a profile on a coin, timeless and handsome. She liked the sun on his tanned, muscular shoulders. She liked his silence.

"Sorry I'm so negative."

"Nothing to do with work, I hope?" His glance was reserved. His eyes were more turquoise than blue.

"No. Other things. Personal things." Sophie shut her eyes a moment, enjoying the swish of the breeze, soaring up from the sea to dry the sweat from her body.

"Anything I can help with?"

"Afraid not. But I really like working for Security Solutions. You're doing a good thing, with the company. We can help people law enforcement cannot, and I like that."

"That's good to hear."

"Do you ever—have contact with Sheldon?" Sophie couldn't resist asking about the Ghost.

Connor raised his brows in surprise. "You know I do. Why?"

"I just...wonder how he's doing." She gestured to Anubis, sitting sphinxlike beside Ginger at the base of the concrete ledge. "He must miss his dog."

"Yeah, he does." Connor looked back at Anubis too. "But Sheldon seems happy enough. He's chasing new endeavors."

"Like what? Women?" She turned to gaze at the lines of white foam marking wave action over the reef far below.

"I'm sure there's some of that," Connor said slowly. "But Sheldon's a loner, for the most part. I, on the other hand, enjoy female company. Even the negative kind."

Sophie smiled at him. "Thanks for not talking. I'm working with Jake Dunn, and that man never shuts up."

Connor laughed. "Jake's like a rubber ball. You can't keep him down and he's liable to bounce in any direction."

"We're figuring out how to work together. It's an adjustment for both of us."

"Well. I just thought I'd tell you—people care. If you're going through a hard time, sometimes it helps to talk about it."

Sophie glanced at him. He was looking away at the horizon. Was he offering friendship? A shoulder to cry on? Connor sounded sincere with his offer, but she couldn't talk to him. She had Marcella and Lei, and she wasn't sure she needed any more friends. Friends were a lot of work and often confusing—and in fact, Connor's behavior was a little confusing, too. She could tell he was attracted to her, but he'd never made a move or asked her out besides these runs. She wasn't sure how she'd react if he did.

"Thanks, but sometimes it's just better to keep quiet and wait until things get better." Sophie stood, walked back to the dogs and prodded Ginger, sprawled and panting, with her toe. "Let's take the long way back. I need more exercise." What she needed was more endorphins to fight the depression.

They took the abandoned road back, which led for miles through a residential area. Sophie enjoyed Connor's silent company. The sound of their shoes on the pavement became a metronome that both soothed and energized her—and slowly, slowly, it pushed the darkness away. By the time they reached the cars again, Sophie felt better—almost back to normal. She'd be able to deal with the call with her lawyer more positively now.

"Thanks for the exercise." Sophie unlocked the battered Ford.

Connor quirked a brow at her. "What happened to your Lexus?"

"In the shop." She'd come up with a better story eventually. She put on Mary Watson's floppy hat.

Connor's brows rose further. "New look for you." Sophie filled Ginger's water bowl, and as the dog lapped, he went on. "Do this again next week? I was thinking maybe really push ourselves and try the Stairway to Heaven."

She looked up at him with a smile—another famous, illegal hike with stunning views. "Sounds excellent. I've been wanting to do that one for a while."

Connor stepped a little closer as Ginger hopped up into the truck and over to the passenger seat. "I wanted to say something about Sheldon. There are people looking for him. In Hong Kong, and elsewhere. Because of his—activities. He might not ever be able to return to this country or live a normal life."

*Connor knew that Sheldon was the Ghost!* Sophie's eyes widened. "I'm aware of his situation. Why are you saying this to me?"

"I know you want to meet him. But—you shouldn't count on it ever happening."

Sophie thought of their online chat. The Ghost had said he wanted to meet her "in real life." She had no doubt he could do that whenever he wanted to, in spite of being off the grid.

"I don't expect to meet him unless he finds me. If he can find me." She got into her truck, slammed the door, and rolled down the window to look into Connor's changeable eyes. "You think I'm still hunting him, and it's only fair to tell you that I am. But I don't know if I have an interest in turning him in, anymore."

"I'll tell him you said so."

"No need. I can tell him myself." Sophie turned on the truck, and drove away. In the rearview mirror Connor was staring after her, a diminishing shape, the sharp angles and still points of Anubis at his side.

THAT NIGHT, Sophie's phone pinged with an incoming message to the account she used to communicate with the Ghost. Already lying in bed on her blow-up mattress, she couldn't resist picking up her phone and opening the email.

She gasped, and covered her mouth with her hand.

The Ghost was naked in a series of black-and-white photos.

In the first one he hung, arms extended, legs crossed at the ankle, from a pull-up bar. In the next photo, he was halfway to the top, the muscles of his back standing out in stark relief, the wide V of his musculature ending in a pale, chiseled butt. In the third he'd reached the top, his chin over the bar. His legs extended down, the muscles of his shoulders and back tightly contracted in a pleasing topography. In the fourth, he'd lifted himself high above the bar on straight arms, and the line from the top of his head to the bottoms of his feet was breathtaking.

Sophie scanned the photos for clues—or so she told herself, as she brought the phone closer to her eyes, a smile lifting the corner of her mouth. *He was so beautiful.*

The Ghost must have put the camera on a timer. The background was pale gray in the photo, likely a white wall. The ceiling of the photo's setting, his private gym perhaps, was high enough to allow a wide range of motion—the steel rack of the bar had to be ten feet off the ground to allow the full extension of his body. Height was hard to judge with nothing to go by. Hair was dark and cut short, as Sheldon Hamilton's was from previous photos she'd seen of him.

But was it really the Ghost? *Who was this man?*

No way to know. She studied every detail she could find. The phone dinged with another incoming email.

*"Just so you don't feel alone in being seen naked."*

Sophie typed a reply with her thumbs. *"Yes, you do appear to take your fitness seriously. If that's you in the photos."*

It was hard not to say more—something about how incredible his body was, to begin with. But she had an agenda—and it was to lure him out of the shadows. Not that she knew what she planned to do with him once she'd caught him.

*"You damn me with faint praise, woman."*

*"So you thought I'd be impressed? Okay, I am. A little. But mostly, wondering where all this is going, why you're doing this."* Sophie bit her lip, sucking on that old bruise.

*"I enjoy this game we play. I enjoy a worthy adversary who's on the same team."*

*"I'm not on your team. I'm still trying to catch you. That's where this is going for me."* Sophie tried to calm her rapid breathing. *"I spent time with Remarkian today. Told him what I'd tell you...that I still want to capture you. But now I'm not sure what I want to do with you when that happens. I'm no longer an agent, and we already established that proving a case against you would be near impossible. So I don't know where to go from here."*

He must have been typing at the same time because her phone dinged with his reply. *"You're trying to do good in whatever role you're in. I'm doing the same. I don't want to be your enemy. I want to be more than a friend."*

Sophie stroked the glowing surface of the phone with her thumb. *More than a friend.* Clearly she wasn't the only one attracted. There was no reason for him to keep pursuing her otherwise. She was dangerous to him.

He must have read her reply because another email arrived. *"You don't have to know where to go from here. You'll meet me when the time is right."*

Sophie looked around the barren room, the heavy curtains blacking out the light, the only sound the soothing whuff of Ginger's breathing on the floor beside her. She didn't like that he thought he was in control.

*"You might find that difficult. I'm no longer at my former address,"* Sophie typed, and turned off the phone.

She was off the grid, and now she was glad she was. She wanted to be the one in control of where and when she finally met the Ghost.

# CHAPTER FIFTEEN

'MARY WATSON' held the floppy straw hat on with one hand so that the slight breeze at the Hilo airport would not tug it off of her head. She smiled at the other young women climbing into a large white passenger van headed for the Waipio Valley. The light rayon sundress she wore swirled around her legs as she settled beside another woman in the backseat.

"So excited to finally see the compound at Waipio," Sophie said. "Have you been there before?"

"No, this is my first time, too." The woman next to her was a pretty blonde. She tugged at her tight yoga pants and smoothed her tunic top. "Have you met Sandoval Jackson yet?"

"I have heard him speak. Mesmerizing," Sophie said. He did speak well on the YouTube videos she'd watched. "We're so lucky to be able to get on the list for this retreat."

The van got underway and in a very short time they were traveling along the verdant countryside of the east shore of the Big Island out of Hilo. They passed gigantic albizia trees draped in vines, great stands of hapu`u ferns, and tall waving patches of long pili grass framing glimpses of a distant blue ocean.

The driver of the van was a young mixed Hawaiian with long

hair in a ponytail and the orange clothing that Sophie recognized from her recon of the compound earlier. The hour-long drive took them through the broad grassy pasturelands of Waimea and beyond. The steep walls of spectacular Waipio Valley opened before them as the van rounded a bend.

This was the first time Sophie had entered the valley by car, and the one-lane precipitous access road carved in the cliff was intimidating from her wedged-in seat in the back of the van. Off to the right she could see the broad sweep of the bay at the mouth, the valley's river flowing into the ocean with the reddish-brown of runoff rainwater.

Finally reaching the valley floor they were met by small farms, lush with outsized banana and papaya trees, wandering loose horses, and sweeps of water-filled taro patches.

It seemed to take forever for the van to navigate the potholed, narrow dirt road with the obstacles of loose chickens, dogs, and mud puddles, but further back in the valley, where no one else was around, the road was better maintained. Sophie leaned her chin on her hand, watching the field she'd run through with a child holding her hand pass by.

Things certainly looked different in the light of day.

The doors of the compound were open to meet them when they arrived. Far from the fortified, forbidding aspect the compound had presented during her mission, today it looked welcoming and beautiful.

The children, dressed in orange dresses, T-shirts or shorts, ran up to greet them as the van pulled up. They greeted the retreat participants by draping fresh plumeria lei over their heads as they exited the vehicle. The oldest boy, who looked around thirteen, showed the eight women to their own spacious yurt. Inside, a series of four bunk beds formed corners in the round tent. In the center of the floor, a carpet patterned like a mandala gave the room a spacious, unified feel.

Sophie claimed a bottom bunk and her blonde companion, the top. She introduced herself. "I'm Mary Watson. And you are?"

"Gillie. Short for Gillian. Gillie Johnson."

"Have you been part of the Society of Light for long?"

"Just checking it out, actually. Looking to make some lifestyle changes." Gillie had the nervous energy and build of a whippet, and the skulls and rock band tattoos on her arms told a story of hard partying.

The boy returned. "What's your name?" Sophie asked.

"Zeus." He had large brown eyes, freckled skin, and a friendly smile. "I'm your guide. I'll take you to the yoga studio if you're ready."

They were, so Zeus led them to a large studio that was its own yurt. Spacious and inviting, shining floors reflected light from a pale cream roof. The familiar tools of yoga were piled in neat stacks against the walls. Folded blankets, foam blocks, webbing straps, and a large basket of silky, scented eye pillows all gave Sophie a reassuring sense of familiarity in spite of her mission.

The evening progressed in a straightforward manner with a yoga class, a group dinner in the dining room, and finally, a lecture from Sandoval Jackson in the yoga studio.

Jackson arrived draped in a wrapped orange loincloth worn with an embroidered tunic. From a distance, during their surveillance, it had been hard to see what he was like, and Sophie's research photos hadn't shown much more than an orange-draped figure. Up close, Jackson was lean and muscular, a young-looking sixty even with his flowing silver beard. He exuded a powerful calm that Sophie found herself responding to in spite of her feelings about the children, the Society, and what might lay in the garden.

Clearly the man had charisma.

Sophie chose a purple flax-filled pillow, and sat on it in a half-circle with the other participants around Jackson's place on a small raised dais. The residents of the compound filled in the area behind them, and the room settled into stillness as Jackson raised his hands.

"Close your eyes. Breathe." A long pause as everyone did so. "Notice the breath entering and exiting your body. Notice your body—how it feels in this moment, taking up space and time. You are eternal. Made of star particles, returning and recycling in different forms, but for now you have this moment. It will never come again. Be in this moment. Take it as yours. Fully inhabit it. And then let it go so the next can take its place."

It wasn't so much what Jackson said that was so hypnotic, as the low, resonant pitch of his deep timbred voice that held the surprising edge of a Scottish burr. Jackson had immigrated to the United States with his parents at fourteen from Scotland, but she'd thought his accent would be gone by now.

Perhaps that accent had its uses—because Sophie felt like she could listen to him talk all day.

And so, apparently, did the rest. Jackson said nothing really new, but it was rich. And as Sophie sat in the lotus position, fingers resting on her knees, she had to remind herself that this man was, quite possibly, a triple murderer.

# CHAPTER SIXTEEN

THE COMPOUND'S bathroom was a central complex that featured a catchment shower, a small gas water heater, and several composting toilets. It was rustic, but the appointments were top quality. Sinks were made of hand thrown clay, and beautifully woven tapestry adorned the walls. Sophie got ready for bed with the other women and waited for the right time to do her nighttime recon.

She waited as the lights went out, and the breathing of her new compatriots grew soft and long. Dressed in the black yoga pants and tank top she had chosen to minimize detection, Sophie tiptoed barefoot out of the yurt and along the winding path toward the large, half-acre vegetable garden. She had a story in place should she be stopped: she couldn't sleep. She needed to meditate, outside in nature.

Sophie walked slowly, with no illumination but the great black vault of sky, scattered with the pollen of stars brightened by the thin paring of a new moon. Coqui frogs, an invasive species from South America, chimed their shrill song from the surrounding jungle of the valley.

Her ears were tuned for any sounds of other humans, but there were none. Sophie reached the garden, defined by rows of lettuces, broccoli, staked teepees of beans and patches of chard and other leafy greens. It smelled rich and lush with new life, as she padded along a well-mulched row.

It was hard to imagine that there might be bodies under these lettuces.

She made her way down a well-maintained aisle of vegetables to a center area that was not immediately visible from the rest of the compound. Even in the dim light of the moon, she could make out the undulating curves of a labyrinth.

*Ah, the labyrinth.* A spiritual walking practice she hadn't been able to experience more than once or twice.

Her feet seemed to find the cool stones embedded in the dirt that marked the path almost by instinct, and she followed it. Every now and then she pulled a small, cigarette-sized stake out of the ankle sock of her tennis shoe, pushing it into the soil.

The plan for this trip was for her to attend the five-day retreat and check out the compound from within. Detect its security, its weaknesses, its patterns and procedures—and if able, gather any evidence she could find.

She was "off the grid" on this assignment, though Dunn was nearby, monitoring from the outpost they'd used before. Cell phones weren't allowed on the retreat, but she was scheduled to contact him twice daily with the extra-small satellite phone currently hiding in her bra.

Round and around, and back and forth the path led. Surely she should have reached the middle by now? And yet, she had not.

So far, she'd seen nothing alarming or out of place at the compound.

Her mind wandered back to the photos the Ghost had sent. Such unforgettable images. She wondered if he ever watched the video he had of her in her apartment.

*What was he playing at?*

Did Sheldon Hamilton really want some sort of relationship

with her? Was this his idea of courtship? And why was it so intriguing? She should really know better than to be so fascinated with this shady vigilante with his cat-and-mouse game.

Pain from the end of the relationship with Alika Wolcott, her former MMA coach, nagged her like the fading bruise on her mouth. Six months now, and no word from him, not even a text message—hers to him had gone unanswered, though she could see that he'd read them.

Clearly, whatever they'd had was over. It remained hard to accept. *She'd let herself have hopes.* But the fact that he'd chosen to return to Kaua`i permanently and cut her off still hurt.

"It wasn't love," Sophie muttered. *But it could have been.*

The center of the labyrinth was a smooth circle filled with pea gravel. She planted a few more of the stakes randomly around. She'd pick them up tomorrow, when the ninhydrin-infused paper pulp would have had time to react to any organic compounds thrown off by human decomposition. She sat down in the lotus position placing her hands on her knees. She closed her eyes, letting her senses take in the surroundings.

If she were Sandoval Jackson, this is where she'd bury the bodies: a central place, covered by gravel, where people with a mind to do so could pay their respects. Her nostrils flared. Could she smell them? Decomp had a powerful stench, and even once that phase had passed, unique organic compounds were emitted for months, even years, and could still be picked up by the spikes she'd planted, cadaver dogs, and the new LABRADOR body detection device Dunn had shown her from Security Solutions' tech lab.

"It uses scent assessment technology to find a buried body." Dunn had been enthused, showing her the handheld contraption, a series of gimbaled attachments that, while relatively small, would have been difficult to conceal in her backpack. He'd tried to get her to bring it, but it would have been impossible to explain if she were caught with it.

The shift and rustle of footsteps in the labyrinth warned her of someone approaching. She closed her eyes and settled into stillness.

"Is this seat taken?"

Sophie restrained herself from leaping to her feet at the sound of a deep male voice with a Scottish accent—but it wasn't Jackson. "Of course not. You are welcome." She lifted her head to see the man. He seemed large, backlit by the moon. He coiled himself and sat beside her. The moon cast a silvery illumination over craggy features and a bald head. "I couldn't sleep," she said.

"I assumed as much."

"I'm Mary Watson. What's your name? I didn't meet you at the orientation, or at dinner." They'd been introduced to the main staff of the retreat and community then.

He shrugged. "My name is Dougal Sloane. I'm Sandoval's head of security."

"Oh. Have I done something wrong?"

Sloane's teeth showed in a brief flash. "We discourage our guests from nighttime wandering. It might not be safe."

"How could it not be safe?" Sophie gestured to the moonlit scene, to the high, corrugated walls of the sheltering valley. "It's so beautiful here."

"If you want to meditate, go to the chapel." Sloane took hold of her arm. His spread fingers gripped her. She could feel, by the way he wrapped his thumb across her bicep, that he was taking a measure of her strength. "It's time to go back to bed." He gave her arm a little tug.

She rose to her feet meekly and followed him back along the winding route of the labyrinth, surprised that he led her that way and not across it—but they walked the whole thing. "I'm not sure I'm ready for bed."

"I'll escort you to the chapel, then." A motion-activated security light bloomed into a soft amber glow outside of a small square building set apart from the rest of the commune. "This is the chapel. You're free to spend as much time here as you like, but follow the footpath straight back to your sleeping quarters when you're done."

"All right. I'm sorry for any trouble."

The amber light gleamed on Sloane's head, and just momentarily, illuminated a tattoo of a pair of snakes forming a Celtic knot on his forearm as he slid a big hand up her arm as if he wanted to feel it again. He squeezed her muscle. "You're fit."

*This was no peaceful yogi.* This was a man of violence and action. She could feel it emanating off of him like a force field.

Sophie tilted her head, trying for flirtatious. "Thank you for showing me where I should be," she said, her voice soft.

"It was my pleasure." Sloane stroked his hand down her arm and gave it a final squeeze.

Sophie's skin crawled and she suppressed a shudder. She turned with a nod and a smile, and walked up the wooden steps into the chapel.

A candle guttered on a little altar at the far corner of the perfectly square room. A stack of seating pillows filled one wall, and Sophie helped herself to one, bringing it to sit in front of the plain wooden altar. She settled upon it, holding herself upright. Her back was beginning to ache from all of the sitting unsupported.

The phone tucked in her bra seemed to burn her skin. She checked again that there was no video surveillance in this room and that she was alone, and retrieved it.

She texted Dunn.

*"Security is tight and looks experienced."* She'd seen a couple of unobtrusive dark bubbles of cameras on the corners of the buildings. *"Not sure how much I'll be able to find."*

*"Recon only. Stay safe. I've got your back,"* Dunn answered promptly. Sophie let out a breath she didn't know she'd been holding.

# CHAPTER SEVENTEEN

THE NEXT MORNING dawned clear and glorious. Huge rafts of cumulus cloud, scudding over the ocean, seemed to be lit from within by the sunrise as it broke over the mouth of the bay. Sophie rose with her fellow retreat participants, arriving at the chapel for a period of meditation. Everyone sat in lotus position, facing the altar upon which a pillar candle burned.

Sophie tried to calm her racing thoughts but she'd begun to chafe internally, missing her technology. The oblivion of being "wired in" to her computers, absorbed and lost in streams of information, had become a huge part of her life. A free-floating anxiety rippled along her nerves, a sort of nagging itch like she imagined an addict must feel, longing for the needle. She'd wondered how she would do without her beloved computers—and now she knew. *Not well.*

This was also the subject of the meditation that Sandoval Jackson led them in. "For true peace, you must learn how to really live within your own skin, occupying your body, mind, and soul without external influences and stimulation except those found in nature. Accepting the here and now, without the outside influence of the world, will bring you a deeper experience of life."

Dunn could, at least, watch videos on his phone or something while he did push-ups or whatever it was he occupied himself with on a stakeout—while Sophie had to sit, cross-legged, eyes shut, with nothing to do but endure her thoughts. These inevitably spiraled into flashbacks of Assan's abuse, memories of her mother's indifference, and the familiar negative thoughts of the depression that stalked her like a jaguar.

Sophie made it through the meditation with difficulty and then she made it through the hour-long, strenuous yoga class that followed. Being able to move her body and focus on that was a relief. She made it through the simple morning meal, seated with the whole commune in the central cafeteria area, eating in silence. And she even made it through going out to work in the garden.

Simple chores out in the garden, picking slugs off the lettuces and pulling weeds, did have a meditative quality that seemed to still the restlessness—but she didn't want to retrieve the spikes she'd embedded in the dirt, because part of the feeling that crawled along her nerves was the sensation of being watched.

Sophie darted her eyes around, keeping Mary's hat brim low as she tried to observe who might be monitoring her. She'd already made a mental note of every location of a surveillance node that she could identify on the corners of the buildings.

Dougal Sloane was watching her.

Sophie spotted him leaning against one of the yurts, tattooed arms folded and one leg up with a bent knee as he observed the women working in the garden.

*What was he looking for?*

She felt his gaze on her like a touch. Could he be involved with choosing women for Sandoval Jackson's bed? Or was he simply considering her for his own? Either option did not appeal.

THE NOON MEAL was served under the fruit trees at one end of the compound, seated on lauhala mats. The children waited on them, respectful in their orange garb. Banana leaves, held on hands, were used as plates. The simple fare of rice, taro, and cooked garden vegetables was delicious and filling. She touched the hand of the eldest, the boy who'd met them the first night, as he handed her a bowl of poi—it couldn't hurt to fish for a little information. "Zeus. Your name is so unusual."

"I know it's unusual. Our father named us all for different gods and goddesses."

Sophie smiled. "So what are your brothers' and sisters' names?"

"Depends on which ones." he pushed a hank of curly hair out of his eyes. "There are ten of us. Well, eight now that Lono and Pele are gone."

"Where did they go?"

A shutter seemed to come down over the boy's clear brown eyes. "I can't talk about it." He withdrew, pulling away abruptly and heading back toward the kitchen.

"Zeus is still upset by what happened," Sophie's seat mate said. She was a pretty woman with lightly tanned skin and long, curly brown hair. The bulge of pregnancy pushed out her orange tunic. "Those children went to visit their mother, that's all. They'll be back soon." She turned placid brown eyes on Sophie. The certainty of her voice was chilling. "What's your name?"

"Mary. Mary Watson. You?"

"Jessie Sparks."

The back of Sophie's neck prickled with awareness—this was one of Jackson's two remaining consorts. "Are you enjoying the retreat so far?"

"I am." Sophie used the wooden spoon she'd been given with her banana leaf to mix a little poi with rice. She'd never had occasion to eat poi before, and it was filling, if a little bland. "It's great to get unplugged from technology—though it takes a little getting used to."

"You'll love it once you get used to it." Jessie's hand smoothed over her belly, stroking the curve of it. "I'm so glad to be raising my child here."

Sophie widened her eyes as if impressed. "Oh, then you must be with Jackson. One of his women?"

"I'm his wife." Jessie smiled. She really was lovely, and so young. "The children here are all his. It will be so wonderful for my baby to have so many brothers and sisters."

"It seems like a lot of children for one man? Did he have a wife before you?" Sophie probed.

"Oh, yes." Sparks laughed. "He has a different approach to marriage than most. We're only together in that way while having children, then the union is dissolved. The kids are the future—and the past, too. As you know, we believe in enhanced reincarnation. Sandoval thinks Zeus is the return of his brother, who died young. Sandoval says they are so much alike."

Sophie could think of a lot of reasons for that, beginning with wishful thinking and ending with shared genetics. "Fascinating. This is my first retreat, so while I've read Jackson's teachings, I am not familiar with how they play out in practice."

Sparks gave her an assessing glance. "Are you with someone?"

Sophie smiled. "No. I'm single."

"Well, maybe you want to apply to be with Sandoval at some point." Sparks dabbed her mouth delicately on a cotton napkin. "It's a great honor. Enhances your reincarnation return time."

Sophie couldn't find a response. She addressed her food, taking another bite. She'd never been quick on her feet verbally, unlike her friend Marcella, or even Lei. She could see either of her friends playing her current role so much more adeptly. She needed to pretend interest to find out more, though her stomach clenched with tension.

"I'm here because I'm such a fan of Jackson's," Sophie said softly. "His teachings—they hit me right here." She tapped her heart. "It would be an honor to be intimate with him."

Sparks nodded. "That's how it began for me. I came on a retreat. I caught Dougal's eye—you know, Sandoval's right hand man?" She pointed to Sloane's shiny pate across the room.

"He looks kind of intimidating." Sophie lifted her brows in Sloane's direction.

Sparks laughed. "Oh he is! He's Sandoval's pit bull. But he has his uses, and one of them is to make sure that everyone is getting along, and growing in their roles within the Society."

"How does he do that?" Sophie asked.

"He has the background to be able to read people and he always knows what Sandoval needs."

"I wouldn't want to get on his bad side."

Sparks flapped a hand. "Oh, his bark is worse than his bite. He's really a softie at heart."

Sophie eyed Sloane from across the room. He didn't look like a softie. "Well, you seem very happy here. With Jackson."

Sparks smiled. "I am. Very." And she patted her tummy, the picture of contentment. It gave Sophie a pang somewhere deep inside, in spite of the situation. She was far from even finding someone to date, let alone ever becoming a mother.

The afternoon was spent in a choice of various workshops: candle making, weaving, working with lauhala basketry, and even a hula class. A heavy rain kept them indoors, and Sophie did the lauhala and hula, figuring she might as well learn a few Hawaiian culture activities—and soon it was time for the evening routine again.

That evening the rain let up enough that Sophie was able to retrieve the ninhydrin stakes and stowed them in a paper bag, hiding them in the lining of her backpack. The frequent rain had degraded the paper pulp, though, and she worried that the results would be inconclusive—not to mention that the stakes would get moldy before they could be tested.

Two more days went by.

Each night, Sophie found her way to the chapel and texted Dunn her check-in for the day. He was getting restless. His brief answers had devolved into short diatribes about the mosquitoes, the heat, and the boredom. *"Haven't you ever been on a stakeout before?"* Sophie texted him.

*"Not if I can help it. Too much sitting around, and the phone reception is shit out here."* Dunn was nothing if not consistent. So much for her idea that he was sitting around watching videos.

On the fourth day, Sophie, working alone at the center of the labyrinth, wove some of the lauhala she had made into a basket. She looked up as Dougal Sloane approached her.

"Good afternoon, Mary."

"We meet again. Is this our special place?" Sophie wanted to charm him—but not too much. She was relieved he hadn't sought her out before now.

"Jessie Sparks told me you might be interested in an opportunity to get closer to Sandoval Jackson." *The man certainly got to the point.* "I came on behalf of our leader. What do you think of Sandoval Jackson after being here a while?" Sloane sat beside her, looping his tattooed arms around raised knees. She'd observed him during their yoga classes and he was ridiculously strong and flexible—but the bulk of his muscles had to come from some weight equipment—maybe in the one wooden building on the compound that she'd seen him go into daily.

"He is an amazing man. Everything he says has layers to it." Sophie kept her eyes modestly down as she tucked a stray bit of the fibrous leaf into the basket's curve.

"And he is taken with you as well. He told me so himself."

Sophie had not noticed any particular interest from Jackson. It was news to her that the cult leader was observing her. Her cheeks heated with nervous tension, which she hoped would translate into blushing interest. "I hope that's a good thing."

"You're a different type for him. He likes variety."

"Just what a girl wants to hear." Sophie ducked her head to hide her annoyance. She hated being called "exotic," let alone "different" and "variety." She had better things to do than be some old white man's fantasy—role or no role, it was racist. She slashed a fraying end of fiber with the sharp little paring knife the woman teaching the workshop had given her.

"I meant that as a compliment." For the first time, Sloane's confidence seemed to stumble.

"I've been wondering something. What happened to the children's mothers?" Sophie kept her voice soft with difficulty.

Sloane seemed to sit up straighter beside her. "They moved on."

"And left their children here?"

"I don't see how that's anything to do with this." Sloane narrowed his eyes. "This is just an initial encounter. It will still greatly enhance your possibilities of moving forward on the reincarnation wheel."

It chilled her how much these people believed Jackson's self-serving lies. "It seems odd to me that they had children with Jackson and then left."

"Their purpose with him had ended—and we aren't looking at you for that role."

So Sophie didn't rate being a baby maker for Jackson. *Of course not.* The women who became "wives" had money to put in the cult's coffers, and her cover identity Mary Watson was a mere data entry clerk. Sophie could push no further. "What do I need to do?"

"Meet with Jackson alone. Tonight. And see how it goes." Sloane picked up her hand, stroked her knuckles with his thumb. She felt his breath on her neck. "There's no pressure to do anything that you don't want to do."

*Liar.* Sophie removed her hand gently. "I appreciate that." She gathered her basketry materials together. "Tell me where and when."

SANDOVAL JACKSON'S large yurt in the corner of the compound was beautifully appointed. The interior was draped in woven tapestries, and silky Persian carpets created luxury underfoot. Window openings covered with screen admitted air that flowed through rooms within the yurt, defined by gauzy drapes.

Jackson met Sophie at the doorway and took her hands in both of his. She resisted the invisible pull of his charisma as he greeted her. "Come in, my dear." Jackson gestured toward a low table upon which rested a pot of tea and two cups. Seating was furnished by plump pillows. "Join me for a little refreshment?"

*What could be discovered by pretending to be interested in a sexual encounter with the cult leader?* But she had a job to do. *Marcella wouldn't be scared of this role.* Sophie squared her shoulders and put a smile on her face. She followed him across the front room. Through a gauzy white hanging, she could see a large bed draped in red coverings. She looked away quickly and sat across from Jackson on a small pillow. She accepted the cup of tea that he poured for her and her hands trembled. "I'm nervous."

Jackson smiled. His deep brown eyes held a soulful glow and it felt good to have his gaze on her. "You don't need to be. Dougal suggested that I get to know you better. We are both just travelers on this journey."

So this meeting had been Sloane's idea, as she'd suspected. What was that man's motive? Sophie sipped her tea. It tasted of jasmine and honey. "I'm curious about your relationships with women. It all seems rather unusual."

Jackson chuckled. "I guess to outsiders it is. But we in the

Society understand that these bodies are merely outward expressions of an inner truth. And your truth is particularly beautiful."

"I thank you for that." Giving him a measure of truth felt intuitively right. "I've been through a lot actually. My first marriage was not good."

"Then perhaps God has brought you here for healing. You have nothing to fear from me." Sophie looked up at Jackson. His expression had not changed: he regarded her calmly, kindly.

"Then what happened to your first three wives?" The question popped out of her mouth.

Jackson's face seemed to freeze. His lids lowered. He looked into the surface of his teacup. "They had new assignments."

"What does that mean?"

"It means that they moved on."

"Literally or metaphorically?"

Jackson met her gaze, unflinching. He stood with a graceful, fluid movement, remarkable for a man of his age. "I think our visit is over. We would not be a fit, I regret to say."

Sophie stood as well. She inclined her head. "Thank you for your patience. I meant no disrespect."

He did not reply.

Sophie exited and walked down the steps of the yurt. Dark had fallen early, with a massing of clouds over the steep walls of the valley. The promise of a storm had brought a damp thickness to the air that increased the apprehensive tightness in her chest.

*She'd tipped her hand.* This was why she was better behind her computers. Coming out here had been a mistake. Getting back and retrieving the phone, hidden under her mattress, was imperative. Sophie sped up, hurrying along the graveled pathway toward the group sleeping yurt.

"Going somewhere?" Dougal Sloane's silky brogue caught her from the shadows at the same time as his hand clamped around her arm just above the elbow. "Sandoval tells me you weren't his type. You ask too many questions."

Sophie hunched her shoulders and pretended a sob. "I'm so sorry. My ex was abusive, and I'm just not ready…"

Sloane kept a grip on her arm and swung in front of her to block her escape. "It's time we had a private talk." He towed her down a side path toward the two-story wooden building where he spent a lot of time. She'd never been inside, nor been told what it was used for. Could she still bluff or fake her way out of this?

*No.* Nothing good could come from letting this man get her inside that building.

Sophie yanked her arm down, breaking his grip, and spun away. But he was faster than expected. Lashing out with a fist, he hit her in the back of the head.

*Sophie flew forward and fell to her knees, reeling. Quick. Experienced dirty fighter. A lot bigger than me.*

She curled her fists, filling them with gravel as he leaped after her, grabbing her by her short-cropped, curly hair. Unfortunately, her hair was still long enough that he could get a grip and yank her back onto her feet. The pain was excruciating, bringing tears to her eyes, and she gave a cry. She flung a handful of the gravel into his face, and though he cursed, he kept towing her toward the door.

Sloane was clearly intent on getting her inside the building before she could attract any attention.

*Which meant she had to scream.* Sophie opened her mouth just as he yanked her forward against his side and clamped an arm over her throat in a yoke chokehold, cutting off her air. He tucked her under his thick arm like she was tiny, not a five foot nine athlete.

Sophie went limp, letting her body weight drop, hoping to loosen his hold—but that just tightened the chokehold on her neck. Her vision dimmed as he strode rapidly toward the door of the building, her feet dragging on the ground.

Sophie caught her feet back under her enough to push up suddenly, arching up to fling the handful of gravel into Sloane's face. He gave a furious grunt and his arm loosened. Sophie got her feet under her and kicked him backward in the knee. His leg buckled.

She spun loose from his grip, jumping backward into a ready stance. As he came after her with an inarticulate growl, she nailed him with an uppercut and then a left knee kick. He staggered back, and she moved in, taking advantage of his surprise at her aggressive attack to hit him with kick and punch combinations until he was up against the wooden wall, his arms up to protect his head—which left his kidneys and midsection for her to work over.

He rallied the moment she backed off to see if he was giving up, coming at her in a charge that caught her around the waist and drove her backward, lifting her off her feet. He heaved her up and threw her over his shoulder, knocking the wind out of her.

So far their struggle had been a quiet one, marked only by grunts and gasps and the rattle of gravel. She had to make noise, but couldn't draw a breath with his shoulder in her diaphragm as he spun and headed back toward the door again.

He smelled of sweat, rage, and musky garlic, and he outweighed her by close to a hundred pounds. She could tell by the grip he had on her ass that rape was on his mind, right after he beat the shit out of her.

Sophie arched up with upper back strength, flinging herself backward, using his shoulder as a lever—and the power of her move broke his hold so that she landed on her feet in front of him.

She dodged a huge roundhouse swing and drew enough breath to scream.

"Bitch!" Sloane snarled, and lashed out with his left foot, getting her in the side. Sophie groaned as air whooshed out of her and her ribs buckled. Rolling with the momentum of Sloane's move, Sophie pistoned off of her right foot and landed a punch to his jaw, rocking his head back—and she kept going, dodging under his reaching arm and leaping for freedom.

*If Mary Watson hadn't worn dresses, she might have gotten away.*

Sloane's fist captured the billow of her above-the-knee skirt. The garment tightened over her body, bringing her to a stumbling halt. He grabbed her hair again with the other hand and yanked her off her feet.

Sophie's scream was as loud as she could make it, but he punched her in the head and an abrupt explosion of colored light extinguished her voice.

# CHAPTER EIGHTEEN

Sophie woke in stages: a redness behind her eyelids. A sense of lying flat. And then a booting up of her hearing. Familiar voices were right above her.

"What do we tell them?" Jackson sounded worried.

"We tell them she was unstable and has had a nervous breakdown." Sloane's voice was tight with unspent anger.

Sophie's body sent pain signals from various points, but mostly from her ribs, which, if not broken, were seriously bruised. Her head throbbed. She kept her eyes shut, breathing evenly with difficulty.

"We tell them she's in the infirmary. If anyone even asks, which I doubt they will."

"Some of the retreat participants may." Jackson was moving away, by his feet echoing slightly on the creaky, hardwood floor.

"Send Zeus to tell the group she's sick and going home, and to pack up her things." Sloane said. "They won't ask him anything, and even if they did, he doesn't know anything."

"Good idea." A pause. "What are you going to do with her?" There was a quaver in Jackson's voice.

"It's best you don't know; don't you agree?" Sloane growled.

Sophie felt a draft of cool air over her exposed thighs as Jackson opened a door—*dear God, her skirt was rucked up around her waist.* The door shut behind Sandoval Jackson.

Sophie struggled against the instinct to curl up and hide herself, remaining sprawled and limp as if still unconscious. She had a pretty good idea, now, who had dealt with Jackson's wives, and how he could maintain such an air of innocence.

*Plausible deniability.* Jackson didn't know because he didn't want to know.

Now all she needed to find out was where the bodies were— but she might be getting a grave herself when that happened.

"I know you're awake." Sloane must have bent close, because his voice sounded right next to her ear.

Sophie lashed out—and he caught her fist, engulfing it. She heaved her body toward him, but he landed heavily on her injured side with his knee, wringing a cry out of her that was quickly cut off as he dropped his forearm across her throat and leaned on her neck.

"I didn't want to have to resort to this," he said conversationally. "But I think I'm going to need to restrain you for the things I have planned." Sophie tightened her abs and flung her leg up, catching him on the back, and though he grunted, he didn't move. Her vision was dimming. "You're the first woman to actually punch me. You've got a fist on you, I'll give you that, Mary Watson—but I can't say that I care for it overmuch. It's going to cost you."

Sophie thrashed, and got one hand from beneath her body. She grabbed his ear and brutally twisted. Sloane gave a howl as the cartilage tore. His weight lifted off her as agony took priority, and she rolled out from beneath him. Her breath was stolen by the pain of her ribs, but driven by the elemental need to survive, she sprang for the door and wrenched at the knob.

It was unlocked.

Sophie flew down the low wooden stoop and ran as hard as she could without breath, without direction, the headlong flight of extremity. She reached the first of the many outbuildings, and dove around the side of it into the deep shadows.

Her mind searched frantically for a way out as she sidled to the next building, listening for the sounds of pursuit. On one of her perambulations around the compound she'd noted that the razor wire she'd cut hadn't been fixed—but she had no way to climb the twelve-foot wooden wall. She hadn't seen the dogs that confronted them during their first raid, and that was a good thing—but if ever Sloane had a reason to set them on someone, it was now.

She heard a rush of footsteps behind her and the sound of Sloane's muffled voice speaking into a walkie-talkie. "Check under and around every building. She can't get out."

Sophie slid along the round exterior of a yurt, looking for an opening. If she could just hide for long enough, she could work her way closer to the gate or the gap in the wire, and find some way to escape. Worst-case scenario, she'd have to hide in the compound until Dunn came for her.

*And Dunn would come for her.*

Sophie knew that about him already, for a certainty.

A tiny bubble of hope expanded her ravaged chest. The safety measure of having him camped nearby, which had seemed such a waste of resources, might now save her life.

She could hear more footsteps running, but she still had a chance to get closer to the gate and the fence opening. She sprinted between the buildings, keeping to the darkness, ignoring the pain in her side, the bruising of her other injuries. She made it three buildings closer to the entrance of the compound before huge, bright arc lights came on, throwing the compound into brilliant light and burning her retinas.

Sophie flattened herself against the yurt she was hiding behind as the compound lit up like high noon. A small roof overhang provided her a shred of shadow, but it wasn't near enough. *She had to get out of sight.*

The yurt she was beside was raised off the ground on a wooden platform, with a latticework covering hiding the support posts. Sophie sidled along, tugging at the lattice until she found a loose corner. The edge lifted and she pulled, trying not to break the brittle wood.

The wood gave, with a loud *crack*. She lifted the broken section away and crawled through. On her hands and knees, she replaced the broken piece as best she could, fitting it into the gap she'd made. She was still holding it when she heard the rush of feet past her hiding place.

Sophie held the lattice still. She made sure it was in place and crawled backward, deep into the shadow under the building's center.

The soil was damp, and smelled moldy just from the humidity of the Big Island's steamy atmosphere. It was very dark in comparison to the glaring lights outside.

She heard the patter of the dogs' feet and saw them go by, leashed by a handler. Those Shepherds weren't scent dogs; she could tell by their raised heads—they were looking for her visually, so perhaps she was safe for a little while. She'd smeared her scent all over numerous buildings, and now was far from the edge of this one.

But how was she going to get out? How could Dunn reach and find her?

*She didn't have to have all the answers.* She just needed to catch her breath, rest a bit, and get a plan. Sophie lowered herself carefully onto her uninjured side, the most comfortable position she could find.

But now that she'd escaped, her body wanted to tell her all the things that were wrong.

The brutality of her ex's attacks had taught her to be the fighter she was, to handle pain and conflict and rise above it. She reminded herself of that, as hopelessness tried to rise up and swamp her mind.

She must have lost consciousness, or fallen asleep, because when she woke she heard the sound of sirens.

The grey pearl of new day had replaced the harsh artificial light. Stifling moans of pain, Sophie got up on her hands and knees and crawled to the entrance point she had made, trying to see out.

She couldn't see Sloane handing her over to police, if that's who was at the gate. She had too much to say for them to let her go. Sloane would stall, argue, deny, and maybe while they were doing that, she could get away.

The sirens had attracted the inhabitants of the yurt above her. She heard the creak of feet on wood, the muffled sound of conversation. Yes, this was a good distraction. Maybe she could make it to the hole in the razor wire of the fence.

Sophie pushed the broken lattice out and, after a quick check to see that the coast was clear, she burst out from under the yurt. She found a hidden vantage point where she could see that it wasn't police, but a yellow fire truck at the gates. The compound's refusal to open up had drawn a crowd of inhabitants as the firemen shouted and the cultists denied entry.

Sophie scuttled along the row of yurts set close together and worked her way toward the wall. It seemed impossibly high. She looked around wildly and spotted a small round table with a couple of chairs. She grabbed the table and dragged it over to the fence, jumping up onto it. Her ribs screamed a protest as she reached her arms up and jumped. Her fingertips scrabbled on the splintery wood and she slid down, almost falling backwards off the table but catching herself at the last moment.

She needed more power.

Sophie bent her legs, tightened her abs, and jumped as high as she could reach, her fingertips catching on the top of the fence. She brought her legs up with a groan, pushing herself higher to take some of the strain off as her arms flexed. Her shoes, sensible rubber-soled sandals with thin leather straps, gained a tiny purchase on the rough wood and pushed her just a little higher, enough so that her arms could haul her upright.

Poised at the top, she glanced back—and saw three of the children watching her. She lifted a finger to her lips, her gaze begging for their silence, and then she pitched herself over the wall.

She landed in a graceless heap on her shoulder, her whole body jarred violently by the fall. She lay there a moment, gathering breath and fortitude, listening for the sounds of pursuit. But there were none. There was only the sound of excited voices inside the compound and the flash of the fire truck's lights.

She didn't want to approach the truck. She wanted to check in with Dunn—who knew what Dunn had told them to get them to come to the compound's gate? But she felt certain Dunn was responsible for this distraction.

Sophie gathered herself and ran, holding her side, into the long, tall grass.

DUNN WAS NOT at the observation camp when she returned. The small, camouflage colored, waterproof shelter was still in place, as was the crude viewing area he had constructed.

Dunn was probably monitoring the situation from closer at hand. But was he working directly with the fire department? There was no way to know until he returned. Sophie found a jug of water and drank gratefully, then ate three protein bars in rapid succession, followed by a handful of ibuprofen from the medical kit.

The observation post was meant to look like a hunter's camp if discovered. Dunn had set the stage with a camp chair and a few empty beer cans, along with spent shotgun shells fallen on the ground. Dog-eared copies of *Guns & Ammo, Soldier of Fortune* and *Penthouse* gave a picture of his reading interests.

Her partner had taken his communication equipment with him, so there was nothing to do but wait. Sophie lay down in the shelter on a sleeping bag that smelled strongly of Dunn, and immediately fell asleep.

"I was hoping you would turn up here," Dunn said from above her.

Sophie woke abruptly and stared up at her partner. His expression was hidden in the shadow. Sophie pushed herself up on an elbow with a groan. Immediately Dunn dropped to his knees beside her, touching her shoulder, turning her face into the light. "Are you injured?"

She pushed his hand away. "I'm okay. It's just my ribs."

"You're the only woman who'd say that with the shiner and fat lip you've got. Let me get the medical kit." Dunn turned away, rustling around in a duffle bag. He insisted on dabbing her many small wounds with antibiotic ointment and a Q-tip, and finally, she stretched out so he could examine her ribs.

Dunn felt along the side she indicated, already purple and black with bruising. His fingers were deft and gentle, but she hissed in pain at his touch. He tugged her shirt down abruptly. "I don't think they're broken. Maybe cracked, but hopefully just some serious bruising." Dunn rocked back on his heels. "Got anywhere else I should check?"

"Took a couple of good ones on the head. Knocked me out."

"Let me get a look." He shone a flashlight over her head, feeling gently along her scalp. Sophie shut her eyes against the pain and the light. "Didn't break the skin except for a little wound back here, but you've got a couple of goose eggs going on. Someone beat the shit out of you."

"Dougal Sloane. An experienced fighter that likes inflicting pain." Sophie shuddered.

Dunn dug in his duffel and handed her a shiny metal flask. "Here. Medicinal purposes."

Sophie didn't argue. The whiskey felt hot and smoky and burned the bruise on her mouth, but the bomb of comfort it brought as it hit her belly felt relaxing. "Thank you for sending in the fire department. They provided enough of a distraction for me to get out of the camp."

"It was all I could come up with. I knew the cops weren't going to go down there on just an anonymous phone tip. I pretended to be a neighbor seeing suspicious smoke. Had to use the Bat-phone." He waggled the scrambler-equipped satellite device, a clunky black instrument with a rubber antenna. "I was getting ready to spring you myself after the cult turned the fire department away—but I thought I'd check if you'd come back here first."

"Dougal Sloane likely killed the women. He's Scottish. Some sort of ex-military. And he does Sandoval Jackson's dirty work." Sophie filled him in on her week in the cult and its denouement as Dunn began packing up the camp.

"So other than going to the police with your injuries and your experience with Sloane, you have no evidence for us to share with them?" he asked over his shoulder.

"I'm afraid not. The ninhydrin spikes were damaged by the rain and I suspect are inconclusive even if I could get my things back. But what I have now is a firm conviction that those women were murdered, and that their bodies are somewhere on the grounds. We need to move forward on this. Sloane won't hesitate to kill again."

# CHAPTER NINETEEN

BACK ON OAHU the next morning, freshly showered, her injuries treated, Sophie faced Kendall Bix, VP of Operations. "No, I did not gain any actionable evidence," Sophie said. "But I'm willing to share my personal experience at the hands of Sloane, and try to help Hilo Police Department get a search warrant."

"Certainly we should tell them about what you saw and experienced." Bix indicated her bruised face with a twirled finger. "But then we would have to tell them why you were there, what you were doing, and why it was under false pretenses. And anything they eventually discovered could be the fruit of a poisoned tree. If you follow me."

"I certainly do." Sophie's eyes felt gritty, her throat dry and sore, and pretty much every muscle in her body ached. The three of them sat, silent and glum, around the polished table. "I have some credibility. I was an FBI agent for five years."

"Then perhaps you can tell us exactly how Sloane identified you?" Bix drilled her with his gaze. "You're new with us. We hired you based on your record, and by your own admission you were never a field agent. Tell us exactly when and how Sloane was onto you."

"Sloane approached me to be Jackson's bed partner. I went along, to see how they recruited and treated women, to see what I could find out about the wives. Jackson decided we weren't a fit. I was relieved when he dismissed me, quite frankly. I'll do a lot for a case, but I'm not sleeping with someone to keep my cover. Maybe I played a little too hard to get, and that raised his suspicions. So be it." Sophie held Bix's gaze. "The man is hyper vigilant and paranoid, and Jackson gives him free rein and turns a blind eye. That's the dynamic."

Dunn spoke up at last. "It was a risky op. Why else was I hanging out for four days on that mosquito-infested ridge? That paradise down in the valley is really a little slice of hell. Give Sophie the day off, boss."

Bix smacked his hand down on the table. "We're still skunked until we have something we can go to Hilo PD with." He pinned Sophie with a glare. "I don't want all you went through to have been in vain."

"I have a friend, a detective at South Hilo PD. Let me talk to him. Give him a hypothetical about what Sophie found out and our case, and see what he says," Dunn said.

"All they need is to search that camp with cadaver dogs," Sophie said. "Those women, along with an accountant, are there. I just know it."

BACK AT HER APARTMENT, Sophie's burner phone was full of messages: three from her father, two from Marcella, and two forwarded texts from the Ghost.

She'd save those for last. A reward for getting through the others.

Sophie texted Marcella that she was back and safe from an off-island op, but not in shape for socializing. The return call to her father was much more difficult.

"Why aren't you in the apartment?" Her dad had a resonant voice, now wound tight with concern. "I've been trying to reach you all week. Are you safe?"

Sophie stifled an involuntary smile. *When had she ever been safe?* She looked down at the tattoo on the exterior of her thigh reminding her of *courage.* On the other thigh was *freedom.*

Sometimes one didn't come without the other. She'd chosen a career that pitted her against dangerous enemies. She'd never be entirely safe—but that was hardly the point.

"I'm fine, Dad. Like I told you in my message, I've left the FBI and I'm working for a private security firm. I had an operation on the Big Island for the company, so that is why I was out of touch. I went off the grid and left the apartment because I wanted to stay under everyone's radar with all that has been going on with the DAVID program."

She filled him in as best she could, and when he was finally reassured, she felt even more exhausted, ready to sleep for a week. But she had a couple of email notifications to read that she actually looked forward to.

*Did you like what I sent you?* That had come from the Ghost two days ago.

Then, another one yesterday.

*I guess you took offense. I'm sorry if the photos were over the line.*

Sophie opened her email again and looked at the photos he'd sent. God, he was beautiful—*what a set of back muscles and glutes.* They ought to be blown up and framed. That would give Marcella something to tease her about! Her involuntary smile hurt.

On impulse, Sophie stretched out on her bed and lifted her shirt. She took a photo of her abs that showed her navel surrounded by its mandala of elegant, tiny Thai writing. Some of the purple bruise from her ribs had crept down to mar her golden-brown skin, but it just looked like a shadow in the photo.

She emailed the photo to him, with a note: *I was AFK on a job.*

*Here's something private you will have missed in that video. You did not offend me with your photos. I approve of working out, as you know, and would not be averse to a few more.*

Was she being too forward? Had she showed this mysterious man, someone she was hiding from as much as the FBI, too many of her hopes, dreams, and desires? The message of her tattoo was right there to be translated if he so chose.

There was no way to tell, but it felt right.

She hit *Send* and turned out the light.

Ginger snuggled onto the air mattress, her nose resting on Sophie's back. Sophie let Ginger stay, as glad as the dog was to be reunited.

# CHAPTER TWENTY

SOPHIE SLEPT until Ginger's persistent licking woke her up. When she rolled painfully onto her good side to check the clock, she was shocked to see that eight hours had passed. Her phone, in vibration mode, buzzed around on the floor like an angry bumblebee. She picked it up, her voice gravelly. "Hello?"

"Sophie, it's Marcella. I got your text, but you agreed to let me come over when you were settled and I don't like not hearing from you for five days." A pause for breath. "What happened? You sound terrible."

"I told you. I was on a job on the Big Island. Things got a little rough." Sophie sat up with care and fended off Ginger's affection. "It's just as well that you called. I have to get up anyway. Ginger needs to go out. But you have to make sure you're not followed, coming to my place."

Marcella snorted. "I'm an agent. I know how to look for a tail. Who are you hiding from, anyway?"

"I don't know, really." Sophie straightened the tank top she slept in and levered herself up off of the air mattress. "I just know I didn't want to be in that apartment anymore, where anyone who wanted to could find me."

"That's not true. The Bureau keeps your address secret."

"Yes, but it's not secret from *them*." Sophie worked herself up to standing and padded into the bathroom, the phone at her ear. The sight of her battered face in the mirror was alarming. She turned on the sink and splashed a little water on her cheeks, wincing as it hit her split lip. "I'm not looking so very good today. My face looks like that time I got a pounding from the Punisher at Fight Club."

Marcella sucked in a breath. "That *was* a bad one. Okay, you don't have to go out if you don't want to. But let me come over."

"That's fine. I haven't eaten all day. I'll meet you at the front with Ginger. We have to take a walk around the block anyway. Let's get a bite at the noodle house and then you can come up and see this place." She looked around and shook her head. "Not that there's much to see." She told Marcella the address.

Sophie put on a Mary Watson floral tank dress and walked Ginger around the block a couple of times, breathing shallowly and moving slowly, though her ribs felt better.

Ginger nosed and sniffed and squatted, delighted that for once Sophie wasn't dragging her along at a run. Late summer in Honolulu was steamy, but evening brought cooler air in from the ocean, causing the shower tree near her building to drop bright petals onto the sidewalk, softening the warm concrete. Laundry flapped gently as bright flags, hanging from the railings of nearby apartments.

Marcella was parked in her black Honda sedan in front of Sophie's dilapidated apartment building upon her return. Her friend rolled down the window as Sophie approached.

"Can't say I care for the place." Marcella pushed large Jackie O sunglasses up onto her sleek, chocolate-brown head. "But I've seen worse."

"Mary Watson has simple tastes." Sophie said. "Can you drive us to the noodle place?" Marcella eyed Ginger, who panted and wagged in appeal.

"I'm not driving your dog anywhere in my nice clean car. Let me come up now, and you can leave her in the apartment."

"She's so happy I'm home. I can't bear to leave her again so soon." Ginger always acted grief-stricken at any separation. "But you wouldn't like Mary's car, either, so I'll leave her."

Marcella was unimpressed with the interior of Sophie's apartment. Hands on hips, she surveyed the bare space with a jaundiced eye. "This is not going to help your depression."

Sophie felt a waft of anger. Marcella was never short on opinions, and Sophie had heard enough of them. "My depression is not your concern."

Marcella's big brown eyes flashed with annoyance. "Right. I'm your best friend." She gestured to the barren space. "Why didn't you think of coming to stay with me and Marcus?" Marcella had moved in with the big Hawaiian detective not long ago, and they shared a cute little plantation home on the outskirts of Honolulu.

Sophie blinked. "You don't need me and Ginger getting in your space, reminding you what it's like to be single."

Marcella winced as if Sophie had slapped her. "What is with you today? Anything you need, you only have to ask. The fact that you're so paranoid that you went off the grid and assumed a new identity and rented this hole of an apartment for no good reason shows me how little we really know each other."

"This isn't about you, Marcella." Sophie's heart pounded with anxiety—she was offending her closest friend and ally. But she was angry, too, at being forced to explain a decision she didn't entirely understand herself. "This is about me needing to feel safe. Find my own way. Out from under Dad's money. Out from under the FBI. I'm figuring out who I am." The truth of this insight, so spontaneously reached, burst across her brain.

"And who you are is Mary Watson?" Marcella gestured to the light sundress skimming Sophie's body, the pretty sandals on her feet.

Sophie shrugged. "I don't know. Maybe. I'm kind of having

fun finding out. I like dressing up as Mary Watson. A lot of my life has been about reacting to what happened with my ex. Escaping him. Finding a way to defend myself—through my work, through Fight Club. Confronting him set me free in a way, but it's also taken a while for the effects to really be felt."

"I think you should talk to Dr. Wilson. She's a good shrink, and she might have something to say about how you're handling the stress of the DAVID situation. Who has threatened you so badly that you have to hide out?"

Marcella didn't know about the Ghost—her friend knew that he existed from Sophie's big last case, but never the extent of their communication or ongoing involvement.

And it wasn't that Sophie felt unsafe from the Ghost—it was more that she wanted to be in control of when and how she finally met him. She wanted to be in control of who knew her location, including visitors like Pillman and the other IA agent who'd shown up unannounced at her door.

"I have to do this right now. I don't expect you to understand. I'm not asking for your approval."

Marcella's well-marked brows rose and her mouth tightened. "Obviously."

She spun on a heel and stomped across the room, ending up at the sink with its small pile of unwashed dishes left over from before Sophie left for the Big Island five days ago. Bits of dried food had attracted a trail of ants into the sink. Marcella turned the water on and splashed noisily as she began washing the dishes.

She was just trying to get a handle on her hot Italian temper. Sophie refilled Ginger's water bowl and began blowing up her air mattress, which had lost air as she slept the night before. She groaned as the blowing strained her bruised ribs.

Marcella returned to the bedroom, sat down beside Sophie, took the plastic mattress from her, and finished blowing it up. She rearranged the sleeping bag on top of it, each fussy, decisive movement a sign of how much she cared. Gratitude warmed Sophie's bruised chest.

"Are you sure I can't talk you into coming and staying with us?" Marcella finally said.

"Thanks, Marcella. I'm fine. But can we get those noodles now?" Sophie asked plaintively. "I'm really hungry."

"Absolutely."

Ginger gave a sad bark as Sophie locked her in and they left.

Sophie's favorite saimin house, a spot she used to walk to in her previous neighborhood, was quiet on a weeknight in the early evening. The burly proprietor, a fan of Sophie's MMA fighting, wiped his hands on a towel and raised a brow at her appearance. "I hope you gave the other gal plenny lickins!"

"Not this time," Sophie said. They usually sat at the long, worn wooden bar, but this time the women took a table. Huge, steaming bowls of saimin arrived in short order. After sucking in several mouthfuls of noodles, Marcella lifted a brow. "So what does your dad think of your move?"

"He's worried." Sophie shrugged. "He's always worried."

"I would be too if you were my daughter. So tell me about your new partner."

Sophie lifted her bowl for a deep sip of the savory broth. The hot soup felt so good in her empty, sore belly. She set the bowl down and dabbed her bruised mouth gently with a paper napkin. "Dunn is a good operator. He's impulsive, too much of a risk-taker at times—but this is the first time I've worked so much out in the field, so what do I know? He hung in there, waiting for me on stakeout, even though the inactivity was killing him. When I didn't call to check in on time he created a good distraction that gave me a window to escape. Even though we haven't worked together long, I know he's got my back." Sophie told her friend about the case. "I really wish Waxman hadn't pulled the plug on the case when it came to the FBI. That was part of what pushed me over the edge into resignation."

"I think it was a bad call, too. Waxman's still on the warpath." Marcella chased a bit of egg with her spoon. "He's the one that provoked you into quitting, but I swear he's acting like you did it to spite him. Never seen him so grouchy."

"Not my problem." Guilt stabbed Sophie anyway. Waxman on the warpath was never a good thing. She had such mixed feelings about her former boss. She actually missed him, too.

"So. He's hot?" Marcella's eyes gleamed with a teasing light.

"Who? Dunn? I already told you he was."

"When do I get to meet this mystery man?"

"I could call him right now. He'd probably come."

"Are you serious? He'd drop whatever he's doing and come, just 'cause you called?"

Sophie considered, then nodded. "Pretty sure. He might have a little crush on me. It'll pass."

"Ha! I bet his little crush just gets worse, poor sap." Marcella gestured to Sophie's phone. "I want to meet him. Put your theory to the test."

Jake Dunn, entering the noodle house, drew every eye. It wasn't just his size, though that was imposing. It wasn't just his appearance, though he was handsome. It was something more—a crackling energy, a charisma. Sophie was amused by the way Marcella's eyes widened, by the way her unflappable friend got tongue-tied as Sophie introduced them. Dunn charmed Marcella with bantering small talk as he sat down beside Sophie, who diligently addressed her noodles.

"So. Tell us about yourself, Jake Dunn. What brought a guy like you to a place like this?" Marcella gestured to the noodle house, encompassing Hawaii. Her natural insouciance and flirtatiousness had rebooted after the initial overwhelm.

"Ex-Special Forces. I was looking for something to do after my tours were up and Hawaii seemed like a great place to live." Dunn's white smile was as brilliant as Marcella's. Too bad her friend was already taken; Marcella would have been a good match for him. "I like Hawaii. The surf, the mountains. The women." He gestured between the two of them as if making a point, and Marcella laughed. "Private contracting is a good gig. Been here three years now, and we even get some pretty hairy action, right, Sophie?"

Sophie kept her eyes on her bowl and nodded. "Right."

"I'm making you do stakeout next time. How are you feeling, by the way? You look like hell." Dunn touched her cheek gently with the back of his fingers.

Sophie moved away, uncomfortable with the gesture. "I'm fine. I'll be back at work tomorrow. Slept all day, today, though." She lifted her bowl to sip the last of the broth.

Marcella cleared her throat. "You got a family?"

"Divorced parents. Two sisters. Single, but looking. You?" Dunn's brows rose. His saimin order arrived, and he picked up the spoon.

"Taken, I regret to say, now that we've met," Marcella said.

Dunn laughed. "He's a lucky guy. So what does it take to get your friend here to give a guy a chance?"

Marcella shook her head. "Years of selfless adoration finally earned the last guy she went out with one date."

"Hey!" Sophie set down her bowl abruptly. "It was a complicated situation. I'm not ready to joke about it." The wound of Alika's departure throbbed like a bruise when poked.

"I'm sorry." Marcella's full mouth turned down. "You know me, always trying to lighten the mood."

Sophie was having none of it. She turned to Dunn. "You want to know a little more about why I don't date? Right out of school when I was too young to know better, I married a sexual sadist who abused me in ways you can't imagine. Is that enough for you?"

Dunn's eyes widened as he raised his hands. "Hey, whoa. I'm sorry."

"Don't be. It's in the past. But even if I'd date a partner, which

I'm too intelligent to do, you don't want to be with me. I'm all messed up." Sophie tried the American phrase and it felt right. Old, familiar darkness seemed to rise around her, a paralyzing fog. She stood, fumbled in Mary Watson's straw bag for a couple of twenties, and threw them on the table. "Sorry I'm not more fun."

Marcella grabbed her purse to leave as well. "See you around, Jake."

Dunn put his hand on Sophie's arm. His full attention on her felt weighty and his touch seemed to burn. She twitched her arm away and he opened his hands in appeal. His gunmetal eyes shone with sincerity. "Sophie, I'm really damn sorry I put my foot in your private business. Please sit down. I finally got my saimin, and we were just getting to know each other outside of work a little bit. You told me a ways back to mind my manners, and I will. I respect you. We're partners, and I want that to work."

Sophie vibrated with the need to flee as she looked down at him. She absorbed the regret in his gaze. His playful mouth was a serious line.

He seemed to mean it.

"Okay. As long as I never have to talk about that again. Or deal with your off-color jokes and attempts to ask me out. It is not happening, so forget it." Sophie sat back down.

Dunn whooshed out a breath in exaggerated relief, wiping imaginary sweat off his forehead. "My passes are usually better received." He was irrepressible, just as Connor had said. Sophie felt a smile tug her mouth. Dunn addressed Marcella. "She always this touchy?"

"You got away without her punching you," Marcella said. "I usually get slugged when I piss her off."

So Sophie knuckle-punched Dunn in the shoulder, hard, and he howled in mock anguish. The rest of the evening passed with too much Kirin beer and enough laughter that her ribs were doubly sore the next morning.

# CHAPTER TWENTY-ONE

SOPHIE RETURNED to her office after a lengthy morning meeting with Dunn and Bix. Frustration tightened her muscles and made her breath short. Dunn followed, but she shut him out of her office with a firm bang of the door.

She pushed the small conference table to the side and unloaded her gym bag, taking out a weighted jump rope. She took a few moments to remove a large rubber exercise ball from the bag, inflating it with a small handheld pump. Set up, she got on the jump rope, and soon the rhythmic thwack of the rope smacking the carpeted floor began to soothe her jangled nerves.

Even with her bruises and sore ribs, only movement would help.

"There's a gym one floor down," Dunn said, through the door.

"But then I would have to see other people," Sophie snarled. "Like you."

She felt rather than heard Dunn's footfalls as he beat a retreat.

Their Skype conference with Hilo PD had not gone well. Sophie had shared her notes and showed her physical damage to an impassive Lieutenant Ohale. The station chief and two detectives had reviewed all that she and Dunn had submitted, but finally Ohale shook his buzzcut head.

"The cult has strong legal representation and we need a clear reason to search the premises." Ohale's big brown hands shuffled the notes Sophie had faxed over. "Without some physical evidence connecting the cult, the cult leader, even this enforcer Dougal Sloane to the missing women, I don't have grounds for a search warrant. No missing persons reports have been filed in Hawaii on the women."

Sophie had known that, from her experience as an agent. Still, hearing it out loud, when her body ached from a near-fatal beating, was another thing.

Her role in the FBI had been a layer of protection like a bullet-proof vest. Secure in that role, within the bounds of the law, her work had clear consequences even when cases didn't end the way she wanted them to.

Now she was just another civilian, and getting beat up was part of her new job.

The frustration made Sophie jump harder, her breath rasping against her bruised ribs. Her clothing was soon soaked with sweat. The fervent exercise was the only thing keeping the depression at bay.

Maybe she should try therapy. Perhaps even medication. It wasn't just her circumstances she was fighting; it was her family history. Her mother's crippling depression had overshadowed everything in Pim Wat Smithson's life. Sophie could sometimes sense that same fog bank waiting, waiting, waiting for her guard to be down so it could roll over her permanently.

Sophie switched to the exercise ball, lying on her back to do ab crunches, but they hurt too much. She rolled out a yoga mat for some gentle stretches.

*There had to be something she could do.* Ohale had said, "Find me something actionable. Find me some legitimate reason to get into that compound and search it, and I'll bring cadaver dogs."

DAVID was the only way. Perhaps DAVID could find a financial trail leading from the women to Jackson's cult, a way to lever open the cult so that its real, rotten core could be revealed. The FBI had used tax evasion to bring down mob bosses for years when no witnesses or evidence could be obtained of the murders that they had committed. This cult might be the same.

Sophie finished her workout, drank some water, and got behind her desk, firing up the laptop with DAVID on it.

She inputted Dougal Sloane and the names of the women, family members, and the new wife she had met. She sent an algorithm to monitor the cult's online activity, and searched for their tax records. Setting up a new confidence ratio, she queried DAVID about the probability that reported income was truthful given the cult's known asset portfolio.

DAVID did not take long to produce a low probability of twenty-four percent.

This meant that tax evasion was a definite possibility if she could track the flow of money. Maybe more digging with the families of the missing women would turn up information leading to where their assets had gone.

Several phone calls later, it was time for another interaction with Dunn. She had to steel herself for it—his personality was so intense. He was exhausting for an introvert like her. A few yoga stretches later, Sophie was ready to deal with him. She collected her laptop and went to his office.

Dunn was behind his computer, but his eyes brightened at the sight of her as he looked up. "Feeling better?"

"As a matter of fact, I am." Sophie smiled and set her laptop down on the table. "I have some thoughts I want to share."

Dunn joined her, lacing his big hands together and resting his elbows on the table. Even in a passive pose, he always looked ready to bound up and tackle something or someone. "I was thinking we could do a raid. Get all those kids out of there. Hand them over to child welfare."

Sophie shook her head. "It won't work. The children are not being abused. Yes, they work, but on closer observation, it's not inappropriate lengths of time except for maybe all the hours in the taro patch. They're healthy, fed, clothed, and educated, even if it isn't the way we would like to see it done. Child Welfare won't have a case, and the children will be traumatized by being forcibly removed."

Dunn cocked a brow. "I'm surprised to hear you say that. You seemed so—motivated regarding those children."

"I got to see their lifestyle up close and personal. It's unconventional, but the children are happy from what I can tell. Jackson is their father. If we get Jackson for the murders, the children's world will change as a result, and we really have no control over what that will look like. Some of them might end up in foster care, and I'm not sure that's an improvement over their current situation."

"Okay, but I think we should hold that as a back pocket strategy. So what's this update you have for me?"

Sophie filled him in on her inquiries using DAVID and her idea to follow the money trail and get the families to file missing persons reports. "We have to focus on finding a reason for a search warrant. Once Hilo PD has that in place, they can take in cadaver dogs based on the hearsay testimony of our client. When they do, I feel confident they will find the women's remains."

"So what do you need me to do?"

Sophie slanted Dunn a glance. That was one of the things she liked about him: he was never afraid to get in and do whatever needed to be done, including a stakeout that had probably driven him close to crazy.

"You're going to hate this. I want you to pull together copies of all of the cult's tax returns and call the women's parents for copies of their wills, and while you've got them on the phone, encourage them to file missing persons reports with Hilo PD. DAVID has already confirmed that the income streams into the cult do not match their reported income. If we can find where the gap is, we can alert law enforcement to move in on them for tax evasion. I also think that the women's families would not want their daughters' estates going into Jackson's pockets. Maybe we can prompt them to challenge the women's financial arrangements, and drag the cult into court."

"Yeah. Without death certificates, the women's money will keep rolling into the Society's coffers. I'm sure they won't want that to continue." Dunn gave a brisk nod. "I'm on it."

By the end of the next day, Dunn and Sophie had shepherded the families of the missing women through filing missing persons reports with the Hilo PD. They also obtained copies of the women's wills and copies of the Society of Light's tax returns going back years.

Sophie programmed DAVID to dig deeper into tracking the sources of income in the Society's accounts. She set the algorithm to drilling all night, and locked up her office.

Dunn clapped her on the shoulder in the hall outside her office, and Sophie winced. He lifted his hand away as if burned. "Sorry, sorry. I keep forgetting you were just in a major fight."

Sophie gestured to her face. "I would think you would remember, having had to look at this all day."

"I don't know. It must be a kind of a normal look for you, with your MMA fighting." His bantering tone reminding her of all the days that she'd dressed so carefully in Hong Kong, hiding the damage that Assan had done—but he'd always been careful to leave her face unmarked, and perhaps that was why she didn't mind the bruises that she got in the MMA ring. They were honestly won. But Dunn was right—her face was bruised more often than not.

That had begun to bother her. Mary Watson, with her flowy dresses, didn't look right with a black eye and a split lip.

Sophie gave a brief wave goodbye and turned into the company locker room, where she changed into Watson's modest floral exercise clothes: a tank top and pink shorts—and walked downstairs to the battered truck, wondering, not for the first time, what and whom she was hiding from.

Assan was behind bars, his case tied up in extradition orders; the IA agents had already visited and could summon her any time they wanted. And the Ghost? She wanted to meet him face to face, anyway.

And still she felt compelled to don this other identity, and hide in a dingy apartment to sleep on a blow-up mattress with her dog.

*Maybe it really was time for therapy.* She could always call Dr. Wilson, the consultant whom she'd worked with several times on FBI cases. The petite blonde psychologist had been helpful more than once. But she'd liked Dr. Kinoshita, the Security Solutions psychologist, too...

Long evening shadows fell, wafting in the gold-edge galleons of cumulus cloud that were such a part of the Waikiki skyline at dusk. After picking up Ginger from doggie daycare, Sophie drove down to Ala Moana Beach Park.

She bought hot dogs at a street vendor, and after eating, she and Ginger walked briskly through the park. Sophie listened to the chatter of hundreds of mynah birds settling into one of the banyans to sleep as she passed by a knot of homeless people setting up tents for the night. Her workout earlier in the day had taken the edge off of her need to exercise, but Sophie was still troubled on some deep level.

Not to be able to see Dougal Sloane taken down at the compound was a huge setback. The fact that he could assault her the way he had and get away with it felt fundamentally wrong. She could push to press charges, but she'd then have to reveal the identity she'd used, and why.

In the new case they were constructing, would Sloane even come up as a suspect? It was doubtful he had anything to do with the finances of the cult, so this new angle might capture Jackson, but Sloane would still be free.

The limitations of being a civilian investigator were being brought to the fore.

Darkness fell as Sophie jogged slowly along the Ala Wai Canal's cement walkway. Waikiki was everything the tourists came for: with the daytime crowd gone, the full moon sparkled on the peaceful canal, and a cool evening breeze made a subtle rustle through the palms.

Ginger tugged at her leash, pulling Sophie forward with a happy, excited bark. There was someone near the canal's edge—someone with a dog, someone Ginger knew. Sophie allowed the Lab to tow her toward the silhouetted figures.

"Sophie?" Connor Remarkian's voice was sharp with surprise, and Anubis, in a rare display of disobedience, dragged the man toward the straining Ginger. The dogs met, sniffing, Ginger making little ecstatic noises of happiness as she greeted her friend from their hikes. "What are you doing out here?"

"I might ask you the same, Connor," Sophie replied, her spirits lifting at encountering the man and his dog. She stepped in for the polite hug that was an appropriate greeting in Hawaii. She had never gotten used to all the physical touching that was a part of the culture here, but she'd learned to deal with it. Connor smelled unexpectedly good, of sandalwood aftershave and warm, clean male.

He seemed to think the same about her, his hands cupping the rounded muscles of her shoulders as he leaned in to kiss her cheek. "What a delightful surprise this is. And here I was, feeling a little lonely and sorry for myself."

Sophie laughed. "You, lonely? How is that even possible? You must have women chasing you every day."

He shrugged, a movement in the darkness. "You'd be surprised. So do you come here often?"

"That sounds like one of those things men say in a bar," Sophie said. "But yes. I do. A couple of times a week, at least."

"So do I. We should coordinate."

"That's a possibility." But Sophie didn't always want to share her alone times jogging the nighttime beach or canal area. They fell into step, walking along the canal's edge. Sophie liked the feel of his easy-moving bulk beside her.

"We talked about doing the Stairway to Heaven this weekend," Connor said.

Another rigorous hike with him and Anubis would be fun. But when she bent to release Ginger's leash, her bruised ribs still hurt.

Sophie shook her head. "I got a few injuries on my last job. I should probably take it easy."

"What? Sophie Ang taking it easy?" She could almost hear Connor smiling in the dark, though only the moon gilded the top of his blond head and his broad shoulders, gleaming in a tank shirt. He released Anubis, too, and the Doberman and Lab commenced playing, leaping, and chasing each other like puppies in a little park area.

"I'm trying to listen to and respect my body more." Sophie was surprised by the truth of her words even as she spoke them. Driving herself, punishing herself, beating others down and letting them beat her up—those days were over.

The realization felt like a small detonation.

What would that mean for her MMA fighting? She didn't know, only that she didn't want to show up for work covered with bruises anymore, didn't want to see a battered face in the mirror every day.

"Did I—overstep myself?" Connor's voice was hesitant.

"No. I'm just…figuring out some things." Sophie lifted her head, straightened her spine. Enough with the foolish crush she'd been entertaining toward the Ghost. It would never go anywhere.

Sheldon Hamilton was overseas somewhere, unlikely to return, and Connor was flesh and bone, right here, and he made her feel good. That was something, at least, and more than most. "Would you— like to go out with me? On a date?"

Connor halted and they faced each other. Sophie wished it were brighter so she could see the expression in his eyes, but they were hidden by shadows. His voice was rough. "I'd like nothing better. I was working up the courage to ask you, but I was afraid I wouldn't even have our hikes to look forward to if you said no."

Sophie laughed. It sounded nervous, thin, her breath hitching. "I'm not very good at this dating thing. And I should warn you, I seem to be cursed. Bad things happen around me."

"You trying to talk me out of it? Not going to happen." Connor lifted his hands slowly as if approaching some wild, shy creature. He set them on her shoulders, his fingers squeezing, stroking. "You have the most marvelous deltoids."

This time Sophie's laugh was free and genuine. "Now that is one I doubt you say to all the girls."

"Only to you, Sophie." Connor's voice was husky. He leaned forward slowly, giving her plenty of time to pull away, but Sophie didn't want to. She stepped in to meet him, her hands coming up to rest lightly on his shoulders. His face descended to hers, backlit by the moon, and his lips touched hers gently. Sophie shut her eyes, the better to take in whatever there was to know from this experience.

She was surprised by an unfamiliar tug of desire at the base of her spine as the kiss deepened, surprised by an impulse to lean deeper into Connor, to slide her hands up over his shoulders, to cup the back of his head. She drew him down closer into her, pressing her body to his. Connor had made a sound, something between a groan and a whisper, as his arms slid down and tightened around her, bringing her flush against his hard torso.

Sophie remembered the last time she had been kissed by Alika, a moment so magical that she hadn't allowed herself to recall it until this right now.

Connor wasn't Alika, but he was a little bit wonderful, too.

She opened her mouth to his, and they tasted each other. Their hands traveled lightly over each other's bodies, exploring. Sophie's skin felt sensitized, every touch igniting heat, but still not sure. She stopped moving, standing passively and allowing his hands to caress the deep curve of her waist, slide along the muscles of her back, the contours of her arms.

She needed to know what she was feeling, if this was right, or too soon, or the wrong man. He took advantage of her pliancy to bend her so that her head rested against him, angling her jaw so that he could kiss her deeper. One hand held her close, as the other slid up her side, and back down, feathering over her butt.

Connor noticed her stillness and paused, lifting his head to gaze down at her. Sophie opened her eyes. She couldn't see his face, and wished she could.

"Are you all right?" He was gentle and alert to her. She liked that he was paying attention.

"Just taking it all in. This may be—moving a little fast for me." Her voice sounded breathless.

"We have all the time in the world." Connor let go of her, his hands sliding down to take hers. "No rush. I'm not going anywhere."

The acceptance in his words, his willingness to let her set the pace—all of that gave Sophie the confidence to rise up on her toes, clasp his face in her hands, and pull him down for one more kiss.

"Let's have dinner on Saturday," she said. His teeth gleamed briefly in the dark as he smiled.

"It's a date. Thanks for asking me."

# CHAPTER TWENTY-TWO

DUNN BARGED into her office the next morning, practically hopping with amped-up energy. "My surveillance camera picked up some unusual activity."

Sophie frowned, looking up from checking DAVID's cache files. "What are you talking about?"

"I'm talking about the lo-res, time lapse surveillance camera I set up pointed at the compound." Dunn threw himself into one of the chairs at her little conference table without invitation. "Also, our informant Corbett made contact to let me know that the cult is packing up and leaving the Waipio Valley location. They're going to South America."

"Sounds like they're doing damage control. Why didn't you tell me you were setting up a cam?" Sophie asked sharply.

Dunn shrugged. "It never came up. Check this out." He opened the slim laptop he had brought in and turned it to face her. "This footage was sent remotely, and as you recall the signal isn't too good out there. The resolution isn't great, but you can see that they're digging up the garden. With a backhoe. At night."

Sophie hurried around her desk to lean over his shoulder. The images were grainy, shot through a night vision scope, but even so

Sophie could see the small backhoe, planted square in the middle of what would have been the mandala labyrinth in the garden, and it was digging, creating a mound of soil. "They're moving the bodies."

"It looks that way. Any luck with your online hunt for a reason for a search warrant?"

"I've isolated a couple of possible sources of unreported funds. But—I'm afraid it is not enough yet."

Dunn pointed a finger at the screen. "This was last night. I should have been monitoring the cam all night, but I left the laptop at work. My bad. Who knows what they've done by now." He punched a few more buttons, and a new window popped up. Morning light was dawning over the Waipio Valley, throwing the high, velvety-green, corrugated sides of the valley into sharp relief.

Sophie frowned. "We have to talk to Hilo PD."

"What will they be able to do?" Dunn threw his hands up in frustration. "You know that isn't actionable. But maybe—" he leaned forward, his thick forearms bunching. "Maybe, if we're able to sample that soil using the new sniffer technology device, we can get them to come check that hole."

Sophie lifted an eyebrow, feeling a smile tug her lips. "You just want to go back in and use that device."

"So what if I do? Thing cost thousands, and we haven't had a case to use it on since we bought it. This is the perfect test situation."

The cadaver detection device, a handheld contraption utilizing the ninhydrin-based decomposition gas detection technology, was being touted as a replacement for cadaver dogs. Sophie had her doubts, but clearly Dunn was eager to try the thing out.

"So what if we do find something?" Sophie leaned back and tapped her lips with a forefinger as her eyes wandered the acoustic tile ceiling. "So we find something that indicates the presence of a human body. Then what? How do we stop the cult from disposing of it, and get Hilo PD there in time to confiscate the remains?"

Her gaze fell, to find Dunn looking her over, a pinched expression on his face. Clearly he didn't care for the Mary Watson outfit she'd dressed in today: long Bermuda shorts, sensible sandals that fastened with Velcro, and a button-down floral shirt with the sleeves rolled to her elbows. It seemed like the kind of outfit that was appropriate for a casual office setting like theirs.

"What's with the new threads? You look like you're going to a church luncheon—with my grandmother."

Sophie shrugged, her cheeks heating. She was experimenting with clothing styles for the first time in her life, and his comment hurt a bit. "I was getting sick of always looking like an FBI agent, or like I was going to the gym. Can we get back to the topic at hand?"

"You have to take me shopping with you next time you go. I can help you with wardrobe choices." Dunn looked serious, though she grinned at the thought of him trailing her through clothing aisles, holding her bags and advising her on purses. "I know how you should dress."

"Oh really?" She scoffed. "Probably something tight and slinky. You men are all the same."

"No, really. You are what I'd call a 'classic.' You should dress like Audrey Hepburn. Little black dress, cream silk blouse, tailored pants. Pearl earrings." The tops of Dunn's ears had gone red.

Sophie met his gaze. "You've thought about this," she said in astonishment.

The color spread from Dunn's ears to his cheeks. "My mother was a model. Worked closely with some designers in New York. I got dragged to a lot of shows as a kid."

"Fascinating. Turns out I agree with you about the pearls, at least. I have a nice pair of earrings at home." Sophie took a sip of her mug of morning tea. "All right. Where were we?"

"Planning a raid on the compound with the sniffer device." Dunn stood. "Let's run this by Bix and see what he says."

Sophie laughed. "I think you're starting to appreciate the benefits of the chain of command."

Dunn glanced back at her from the doorway and winked. "I am, as a matter fact. I'm beginning to like the feeling of having my butt covered."

It took them all day to prepare: prepping their strategy with Bix, packing and sorting gear, communicating with and setting up the situation with Hilo PD, who agreed to be standing by to move in on their positive ID of human remains biologicals.

Stepping up into the helicopter in the long, slanting rays of sunset, Sophie ticked over the plan as she fastened her four-point harness. Her wardrobe dilemmas were resolved by being decked out in dark, gray-green camouflage wear; underneath she wore the newest, latest version of a bulletproof vest made of lightweight, high-technology fabric that was supposed to be able to stop any bullet. Knowing Sloane and the sniper on duty at the compound, Sophie wished this didn't have to be her first time wearing it, or that she'd at least had time to watch the demo videos of how it worked.

Before they put on their flight helmets, Dunn leaned over. He smelled like lemon and breath mints. "I'm kind of shocked Hilo PD is standing by at the edge of the valley. I thought Ohale would give us more of a hassle."

"I think he wants Jackson as much as we do," Sophie said. "And he knows this is their last chance for someone else to get inside." They donned the helmets and conversation ceased as Security Solutions' small, lightweight stealth helicopter rose from the pad on top of their building. Sophie tried to enjoy the sight of the city beneath them, spread like a sparkling carpet of jewels, but the small size of the aircraft, the buffered, silent engine technology, and the sleek shape, built for speed, not stability, all contributed to a rough, bouncy flight all the way across the black ocean to the Big Island.

Sophie's stomach was churning with airsickness by the time

they swooped into the furthest corner of Waipio Valley. Per usual, they would have to work their way closer on foot.

It was beginning to feel almost like a familiar routine to drop out of the hovering helicopter into long grass, give a thumbs up to their pilot, drop the visor of her night vision helmet, engage comms, and follow Dunn's rapid progress through the jungle. Dunn had a GPS heading on the compound and made a beeline for it—regardless of trees, fences, the river, or taro patches in the way.

They reached the compound in an hour.

The moon was still high, and detection was easily possible as they flattened themselves into deep shadow against the high wooden wall. Dunn carried the cadaver detection device in his backpack, and Sophie carried evidence bags and a trowel to store soil samples in.

The gap they'd made in the razor wire of the fence had been fixed.

"Doesn't matter." Dunn's eyes were invisible behind the faceplate of his visor but he seemed to sense her dismay. "We have to get in closer to the digging area anyway. The compound's security is going to be on alert with any organics exposed."

*Organics.* What a way to describe whatever was left of three beautiful women.

But they needed to reduce their mission to a series of neutral components. Sophie gave a brisk nod.

"This looks good." Dunn's whisper went from the microphone, so close to his lips, straight into Sophie's ear. They worked their way around the compound to the shadowed area directly opposite their target. Per their plan, Sophie loosened her weapon and turned her back to Dunn as he strapped on climbing spikes and took out his wire cutting tools.

The night was silent but for the chorus of coqui frogs, their high-pitched calls creating a backdrop of white noise that screened the soft clinking of Dunn's equipment as he prepared. In no time her partner was at the top of the fence.

Sophie kept an eye on his movements even as she scanned the quiet area surrounding them. But suddenly Dunn went rigid as sparks flew up from the bolt cutters he'd set to the wire. He flew backward, falling to hit the fence with a heavy thump. He dangled from his climbing gear, head down, arms and legs limp.

*"Venomous yak worms!"* Sophie exclaimed. *They'd electrified the wire!*

She jumped up high enough to grasp hold of Dunn, clearly unconscious. Whipping out her combat knife, she cut the rope tying him to the top of the fence and caught his heavy body, breaking its fall and lowering him to the ground at her feet.

Sophie scanned for danger, but heard nothing. Saw nothing.

*They had to have surveillance cams or some sort of monitoring system for the electrified fence. They had to know that the current had been breached.*

Sophie checked Dunn's vitals. His heart was beating—rapidly, irregularly. He was still breathing, but unconscious. His color was pale even in the dark. There was nothing she could do for him right now but leave him to rest. Hopefully he'd come around soon.

The thought of going away empty-handed was intolerable. Dunn had breached the electrical circuit. Maybe this mission wasn't over yet, because it didn't seem as if they'd been detected.

*It could be a trap.* But if so, why hadn't Sloane and his helpers come after them already, with Dunn passed out on the ground? It was worth taking a chance, because it was going to be the last chance they had to gather evidence about the missing women.

Sophie stripped off Dunn's climbing harness, strapped on his spikes, and removed the backpack with the sniffer device in it from his body. She stowed a few more evidence bags from her bag into his, donned the pack, and hit the fence. At the top, she scanned the compound. All was quiet.

Sophie's skin crawled with tension as she made the first cut into the razor wire. With her NV visor, she could see the electrified wire that Dunn had cut on his initial attempt. She cleared away a two-foot section of wire and tossed it back down on the other side of Dunn, who had begun to move his arms and legs, making tiny moaning sounds.

She whispered into her comm unit. "I'm going in, Dunn. When you feel up to it, keep an eye out for me." And over the fence she went.

# CHAPTER TWENTY-THREE

SOPHIE HIT THE GROUND, her knees bent to absorb the drop. She sank into the soft, dislodged soil of the garden's disruption and moved forward quickly to a heavy-duty dump truck next to the hole, already piled high with dirt from the digging site.

Watching the daytime surveillance, they'd seen the dump truck already make a trip to the entrance of the bay to empty the garden soil into the ocean. This was the reason they had had to move so quickly.

Sophie swung the backpack off of her back, extracting the sniffer device. A long steel rod ended in the ninhydrin technology unit, a round attachment. A stabilizer clamp around her forearm and a handle to hold gave the device the look and feel of a metal detector. Sophie swung the device along the edges of the deep excavation hole, watching the LED display attached to the rod for a green light that would indicate human remains.

It was hard to keep an eye on both the LED display and the surrounding area with the helmet on. It also inhibited her hearing, which at this point she concluded would be her best indication of someone approaching. She removed the helmet, setting it on the ground, and moved away from the hole to scan the mound of dirt in the back of the dump truck. Her eyes flitted over the destroyed garden, the amber-lit yurts in the distance, the dark shadow of the fence nearby. All of it felt so familiar from her time at the retreat, but menacing now.

The LED display lit suddenly, a strong green seeming to leap off of the small black square to pulse in her vision. Sophie fumbled to take out an evidence bag, and scooped a handful of dirt from where the signal had showed. She hadn't packed the trowel—that was still in her backpack on the other side of the fence—so she used her hands to scoop the dirt into the bag. Her fingers encountered something hard—probably a stone. She fumbled it out of the soil.

She held a bone, darkened with dirt but still pale enough to discern. Probably a phalange. Smooth, round and about the size of a half-smoked cigarette, it lay like a talisman in her palm.

"I was hoping you'd come back." Dougal Sloane's voice was casual. Sophie spun, dropped the bone into her pocket and reached for her weapon with her spare hand—but froze as moonlight shone on the chrome-plated Beretta in Sloane's hand. "I knew it would be you, Mary Watson." The way he said her name confirmed he knew it wasn't real.

It was a bad idea to test her new, untried vest with a 9mm at close range, and her lifeline to help was four feet away in the helmet she'd foolishly taken off. "They say men with big guns are overcompensating," she said, equally conversational.

Sloane snorted an almost-laugh and took another step toward her. His eyes were dark caves, the bald top of his head gleamed, his teeth flashed white. "Psychoanalyzing me, eh? Don't think you want to do that, m'dear. You won't like what you find."

Sophie fumbled the sniffer detection unit's forearm grip off, letting the unit drop to the ground. Her mind scrabbled to think of a way out as Sloane took another step closer. "Not sure how you got out of here the first time, but I won't make the mistake of leaving you alive again. This is an ideal opportunity to bury you with the rest."

*So that's how it was going to be.*

A deep calm settled over Sophie.

Time seemed to slow. The details surrounding her impressed themselves on each of her senses: the rich, loamy scent of the dirt around them. Moonlight on the chrome barrel of the Beretta was oddly beautiful, as was its ominous black bore. Even Sloane's Scottish accent felt rich, grace notes over the aural tapestry that was the song of the coqui frogs in the background. The humid night air felt like satin on her skin.

*Maybe this is where all your struggles are meant to end, the depression whispered. He is going to kill you.*

*Hello, darkness, my old friend. I won't give in to you now, or ever. I have to at least try to live.*

Sophie gathered her strength from her core, an invisible inward coiling, and leaped at Sloane, the longest standing broad jump of her life. Her hands caught his wrist, deflecting the weapon upward.

The massive boom of the gun going off felt like a bomb in her hands. She felt a blast of heat on her face—then she felt nothing.

# CHAPTER TWENTY-FOUR

VOICES SOUNDED NEARBY BUT MUFFLED, as if heard through a thick cotton blanket. "You're going to be all right. Stay with me, Sophie. Stay with me!"

*Dunn.* He was always so bossy, so demanding. Always wanting more than she had to give.

There was a long stretch of nothing. Perhaps. Or maybe it was only a moment or two.

She was drifting, somewhere gray, like walking in the morning fog through the marsh of a rice paddy, as she'd done as a child in Thailand. The ground was spongy below her, the sky too close and the color of lead. Memories played intermittently, like glitchy videos.

Her mother Pim Wat's beautiful face close to hers, kissing her cheek, stroking her hair. Sophie had been sick, and it was one of the few times her mother had been well enough to take care of her. "You are going to be beautiful." Her mother's voice was so loving, her small hand sliding around the outside of Sophie's face, stroking the bones. "Even with this hair from your father."

Her mother's hair was long, straight, black, and shimmery as a fall of silk. Sophie's was dense, curly, with the structure she'd inherited from her father's African-American roots. She'd dealt with it by cropping it short, too impatient to figure out how to manage the wayward locks.

She heard a rumble in the gray mist—her father's voice. She'd always loved his voice, so deep and melodic, a good part of his success as an ambassador. He could talk anyone into anything with that voice. Now it was nothing but a rumble in the distance, a rumble that felt like home.

*But where was home?* Certainly not the bare little apartment Mary Watson had rented. She really just wanted to sleep. If she could just lie down and rest, maybe all of this would make sense.

Someone was talking over her head.

*Marcella.* Her friend sounded upset, with that edge she could get in her tone when something was bothering her. "I'm going to tell you this and assume you can hear me. They say you can hear things. Maybe you'll even remember them, and you better listen when I tell you..." Marcella's voice caught. "Don't do this. Wake up, Sophie. You're my best friend. I need you."

Sophie hated the sadness in Marcella's voice. She looked around in the gray, but couldn't see a way out. She tried to run forward but her legs felt too heavy.

"Thanks for sitting with her," Dunn's voice said.

"You don't have to thank me. She was my friend a long time before she was your partner." Marcella sounded harsh, angry.

"I'm sorry I let this happen to her."

"You should be."

Dunn and Marcella did not sound like they were getting along, and it really wasn't fair to Dunn. He was unconscious when she went over the wall. He would have stopped her if he could have; he would have taken the bullet for her. Somehow she knew this.

Remembering that about Dunn felt like it meant something.

The struggle to get through each day, to keep the depression from crippling her, that familiar sense of futility, hopelessness, and loneliness—it was gone. If this was the afterlife, it was boring, but it was peaceful.

Perhaps time passed. She heard snatches of conversation, but not anything that she connected with enough to notice until Waxman.

Waxman was close to her. She could imagine herself, lying on the hospital bed or wherever it was. Her former mentor and boss was speaking directly into her ear on the left side. Maybe the light gleamed on his prematurely silver hair like it used to.

"Sophie. I want you to return to the Bureau. We need your skills. We always did. We can reinstate you with no loss in seniority, I promise. We were wrong to try to take DAVID from you… I should have looked the other way about your use of the program, but I worried about controlling it, about the legal issues…and I'll be honest. I wanted it for the Bureau. But now I just want…you to come back."

Sophie honestly wished she could lift a hand and touch Waxman's face. Reassure him. He sounded so broken. But even when she yelled, nothing happened in the gray.

Another stretch of time. Or not. Maybe she was getting closer to getting out, but she wasn't sure she wanted to.

"Sophie. Sophie. I know you can hear me." This voice was speaking from her right side this time. A sensation accompanied it, something tingly, dimly felt and far off, like circulation returning to a frozen limb. "This is Sheldon. I've gone through a lot of trouble to come see you."

*Sheldon. Sheldon Hamilton. The Ghost.* She felt a small, warm feeling at the thought of that brilliant, enigmatic, beautiful man sitting beside her, speaking into her ear, stroking her hand, her arm. That's what he was doing, even though she couldn't feel anything but the far-off knowledge of a sensation.

"We're all alone in this room, Sophie. I thought I would have so much longer to figure out how to make all of this work."

What was he talking about? His shady dealings in Hong Kong,

his desertion of Security Solutions, the real reason for his disappearance—his vigilante activities? She had to get out of here! *The Ghost was sitting right beside her and she could catch him at last.* Was that why she wanted to catch him, or was it the crazy attraction she had for him? "I thought I'd have time to build trust, to let you know how I felt about you and figure out how we could meet. From the first time I saw you, I felt something new. You were a worthy opponent. A worthy—counterpart."

Sophie tried to call out. She tried to move, and in the gray she was able to, but she knew that in the stubborn, unresponsive body she was trapped in, none of that was visible. It was painful to hear his voice, Dunn's voice, Marcella's voice, her father's voice—even Waxman's voice—and not be able to respond.

"We could have a future. That's what I want with you. I know you don't agree with my methods, but I know you agree with their utility, their necessity. I hoped that somehow we could find our way through all that to be partners. Friends. *Lovers.*" Sheldon's voice shook on the last word. "Please come back."

Oh, she wanted to. How hard she tried.

Fighting the gray was like the worst episode of depression she had ever had, the heavy inertia of it pinning down every limb. She was trapped here, stuck here, and peaceful as it was, it no longer felt like a place she wanted to stay.

She had things to do, and there were people who needed her... people who loved her.

# CHAPTER TWENTY-FIVE

SOPHIE'S BED was cranked up so she could see the view out of a top floor window of Queen's Hospital. Poufs of cumulus cloud sailed by over a cerulean ocean dotted with sailboats, white lines of breaking waves at popular Waikiki surf spots a punctuation. High-rises glittered like fool's gold in the sun, and Sophie could even see the waving palms along busy Kapiolani Boulevard, fronting the beaches.

She'd woken during the night, grateful for the dimness of her room, illuminated only by the LED lights on the monitoring equipment. Her movement seemed to have set off some sort of alarm, because a nurse appeared at once. She pulled up Sophie's eyelids and shone a blinding light into them, waking her father, whose voice came anxiously from a reclining chair in the corner. "Sophie? Sophie, are you there?"

"Yes." It was all Sophie could do to make her throat work enough to get the word out. She was in terrible pain, her head and face throbbing, her throat dry, and for a moment, she wished she could stay in the comfortable gray forever.

But only for a moment. She was glad to have escaped.

Now, hours later, hydrated and medicated for pain, her father

Francis Smithson beside her, Sophie watched the sunrise. Because the sun came up on the other side of the island, she could see the line of its light hit the water out in the ocean and gradually recede to strike the tops of the buildings, the palm trees, the surf, the beach.

Her father held her hand. She couldn't remember that happening since she was a child. He had large hands, long-fingered like her own, the backs the color of buttery leather, soft and pinkish on the palms. Her thumb stroked a callous around the web of his thumb.

"That's my signing hand." She could hear the smile in his voice. "I sign a lot of papers."

Sophie would have nodded but moving her head hurt too much. She had been injured in some terrible way that she was afraid to know exactly. The bandages on the right side of her face and head felt stiff and bulky, and adhesive pulled at her skin. She'd asked for them to be loosened and had been told they were on so tight because they were pressure bandages.

At some point she had been intubated and so her throat still felt dry and abraded. Her father squeezed her hand. "I'm so glad you're awake. You're going to be okay, Sophie."

Sophie turned toward him very carefully, keeping her head propped on the pillow. Even with pain medication it throbbed, as if her brain was too big for her skull, which was probably what had happened. The round must have creased her skull, creating enough swelling to keep her unconscious for a while. "How long was I sleeping?"

"You were in a coma for three days. It was touch and go there for a while." He squeezed her hand again as she gazed into his large brown eyes. She shared those eyes, but lighter brown and set at a tilt, the evidence of her mother's Thai heritage. Francis Smithson was the product of her white grandmother and black grandfather. This pairing had given him an angular face, full lips, and level brows. His hair was buzzed short and looked just like Sophie's, but for the swatches of gray at his temples.

There was a guardedness in the way her father looked at her, in the way the nurses treated her—there was something very wrong about her face, and it was time to ask about it. "Why are there so many bandages on my face?"

Her father let go of her hand and rubbed the short nap of his hair, looking out the window. "When that man fired on you, the bullet went through your mouth, destroyed your cheekbone, and creased your temple."

Sophie tried to comprehend this.

She remembered leaping for the weapon. Moonlight, gleaming on the chrome barrel of the gun. Her hands grabbing Sloane's wrist, thrusting upward. She thought she'd been able to deflect the barrel from her face—but apparently not.

"Through my mouth?" No wonder it hurt so much to talk, to move the muscles of her jaw. "My teeth?"

"Your mouth was open. The round missed your teeth by a fraction. You were so lucky." He took her hand again. His trembled.

She didn't feel lucky. Now that she knew the extent of her injury, the strange pulpy sensation in her cheek made sense. The round had gone through her cheekbone on its way to creasing her skull. Her face must be destroyed on one side.

"As soon as the swelling goes down, we're having the best plastic surgeon in the United States flown in. You'll be good as new in no time," Her father declared, in the official speechmaking voice he used for United Nations addresses.

"I think I need some more medication."

"Now that you're awake they took you off the morphine drip. We have to make do with these." Her father fumbled some pills from a small paper cup into his hand and poured her some water. She swallowed the medication with difficulty. "They want you off the hard stuff and to be able to monitor your own pain levels."

Sophie wanted to ask about the case, but her father was not the one to speak to about that. The pain pills worked quickly, making her pleasantly floaty and drowsy. "I'd like to speak with Jake Dunn when I wake up from my nap."

"He will be relieved. That man has made a pest of himself. I had to send him away."

Sophie could well imagine Dunn's restless pacing and bossy manner, and she would have smiled if it hadn't hurt so much.

"YOU ALMOST GAVE ME A HEART ATTACK." Dunn glared at Sophie, gray eyes accusing.

"Like how I felt when you got electrocuted?" Sophie raised her brows, and winced. The muscles of her face were still traumatized by the gunshot wound. She was actually looking forward to being under general anesthesia for the repairs to her face. She didn't let herself think about what her face currently looked like, or even what it was going to look like after the surgery.

"Yeah, about that. Can't believe I made a rookie mistake like that. My excuses: it was dark and I was in a hurry. Just goes to show you it never pays to be in a hurry." Dunn winked to make his comment into an innuendo as he lowered his bulk into the hard plastic chair beside her bed. "I spent a lot of time on this chair in the last few days. And these don't get any more comfortable."

"I didn't ask you to hang around," Sophie said defensively. "My father is here. Marcella is here. Just give me a situation report."

"You wound me, madam. You're my partner. And it should've been me shot in the head, quite frankly." Dunn's brows drew together as his face grew serious, his gray eyes intent. "You should never have gone in without backup."

"That doesn't make me feel better." Sophie took a sip of water to ease her scratchy throat. "Just tell me what happened. I thought I got his gun hand up in time, but I guess not."

"What's not good is that I didn't get a good enough look to positively identify the shooter. I got to the top of the fence, just in time to see you jump at him as he shot you in the head. I fired at him, and he threw you into the pit and ran off."

"He threw me into the pit?" Sophie's stomach lurched at the thought of that deep, twenty-foot round gash in the earth, already the grave of three women.

Dunn's voice was flat, his jaw tight. "I got over that fence as fast as I could. I thought you were dead, but I climbed down into the pit to check. My helmet's electronics had been fried by cutting the wire, but I was able to call Hilo PD on the radio by using your helmet. They were on their way by the time the noise from our exchange of fire brought the floodlights up and the cult people came running out to investigate." Dunn blew out a breath. "We ended up flying out on the Security Solutions' helicopter, because it was faster than an ambulance or any of the first responders that Hilo PD could get to come to that remote location. I flew with you..." Dunn looked down, opening and shutting his big hands. "I carried you."

Clearly that had been traumatic for brash Jake Dunn. She tried to picture him climbing out of the pit with her in his arms, the helicopter landing inside the compound, the police breaching the exterior gate, him climbing aboard and taking off, flying all the way to Queen's Hospital with her in his arms. "I bet I ruined your clothes," she said with an attempt at a smile. "I hear head wounds bleed a lot."

"You have no idea." He shut his eyes. "I wasn't sure you were going to make it."

Guilt made Sophie move restlessly. "So what happened with Dougal Sloane? And the case?"

"Hilo PD came in at my call, like I said. They tried to find Sloane, but he's gone to ground. They scooped up Sandoval Jackson and took him in for questioning. They sent in the cadaver dogs. They found evidence of bodies in spite of a lot of the dirt being dumped in Hilo Bay. A judge is reviewing the case to make a judgment on whether or not the evidence was illegally gained and will be excluded from any court proceedings."

Sophie's dry throat tightened further. "I thought they'd be able to get a search warrant."

"The Society of Light has excellent representation. Jackson lawyered up right away when they took him in, and they've challenged any basis for you and me to be inside the compound. That could make the forensic evidence gained from the dirt pile inadmissible, the bone you found, everything—depending on what the judge decides. Jackson has been charged with the murders, but he claims to have no knowledge of the women's whereabouts—that this whole thing was Sloane, acting independently."

"Sloane's a convenient scapegoat for Jackson." Sophie shut her eyes, overwhelmed by pain and tiredness all of a sudden. "Jackson knew what Sloane was doing." She remembered overhearing their conversation over her inert body back at the compound. "He knew, but he didn't want to know."

Francis Smithson's resonant voice woke Sophie with a start. "Time for my daughter's surgery prep, Mr. Dunn. You'll have to check in tomorrow and see how she did."

Sophie opened her eyes. Warmth departed when Jake Dunn let go of her hand and stood up in a blur of motion. She hadn't known he was holding it, or even that she'd fallen asleep so abruptly.

"Be well." Dunn leaned over to kiss her forehead. "You'll be fine, and good as new in no time. I'll check in tomorrow." His over-hearty tone told her that he was afraid for her, and she couldn't muster a response as he left.

# CHAPTER TWENTY-SIX

SOPHIE CAME AROUND SLOWLY, blinded by a light in her eyes as a hand held open one eyelid.

"Response is good."

Sophie recognized the voice of her plastic surgeon, Dr. Littleton. Littleton had come to work on her from Washington, D.C., and she'd met him yesterday during surgery prep. A friend of her father's, he worked on combat vets, politicians, and people with enough money to build their own hospitals.

Littleton let go of her eyelid. "Sophie, can you hear me? Blink if you can."

Sophie blinked. Speaking or moving was impossible—her head was immobilized in some sort of frame.

"Good. Now, I want you to just rest, while I talk to you and your father about the operation. You can listen in if you feel up to it, and ask any questions you might have."

Sophie blinked again. Her head felt unwieldy as a bowling ball, and her face was too tightly strapped to move her jaw. She couldn't imagine trying to speak.

"To begin, I rebuilt your cheekbone with a prosthetic device.

We will have to see if the material takes, but so far, I've never had a reject on my hands."

*Never had a reject on my hands.* It sounded like something said about a defective factory part.

"Secondly, I repaired the skin over the wound area. That was the reason the surgery took so long." Sophie opened her eyes to make an effort to show that she was paying attention. She really did want to know what had been done to her face. "Sophie, I was at it for eight hours. Your injury is much like that of many of our troops returning from Iraq and Afghanistan, so I've had a good deal of practice working on this kind of damage to the face." He paused, looking down at notes on a clipboard. "The exit wound area was rather extensive. I had to do a graft."

"How—how will she look?" Francis Smithson's voice was tight with anxiety. He seemed more worried about her appearance than Sophie felt herself. Maybe he didn't know how little that mattered to her. How could they have had such a miscommunication?

"We will need to do several surgeries to minimize the scar. The bullet entered your mouth, broke the cheekbone, and continued up the side of your head, creasing your skull. You are very lucky that your skull wasn't damaged further, or we wouldn't be having this conversation right now. You'd be planning a funeral, Frank." Littleton's voice was definite, leaving no room for argument. It appeared he needed to convince her father that Sophie had bigger things to worry about than the plastic surgery to her face. "When the round exited, it tore off a large flap of skin at the cheekbone area, leaving an open wound. After I put in the prosthetic cheekbone, I took a patch of skin off of Sophie's hip and sewed it over the wound. It's a little…" Littleton cleared his throat. "It's a little rough, but we'll get it to where you can live with it."

Sophie opened her eyes again with an effort. She hadn't realized they'd closed. "I'm sure you did all you could."

"Indeed I did, young lady." Littleton patted Sophie's hand

through the bedclothes. "I hope you'll be as beautiful as ever in time—with a few scars to add character."

"I'm just happy to be alive." Sophie closed her eyes and sank back into sleep.

A WEEK LATER, Sophie finished a very quiet, gentle yoga practice in the corner of her father's penthouse suite. He wouldn't hear of her going anywhere but "home" to recover, and she'd been at their familiar, luxurious apartment for three days after discharge from the hospital.

It was finally time to remove the surgery bandages, though she hadn't told her father that. She wanted only the company of one friend to support her during a moment she'd been dreading. The thought of seeing the mutilated side of her face and head was giving her more anxiety than she had anticipated.

Ginger, in her cozy dog bed, lifted her head and rose at the sound of the doorbell. Sophie stood up and unwound from a stretch that opened up the vertebrae of her lower back. It still hurt to move, and she was often dizzy when standing up. The doctors had assured her that these side effects from the head injury would eventually fade.

Sophie opened the door. "Hey."

Marcella embraced Sophie without hesitation as she stepped inside. Her friend's arms felt strong, warm, and life-giving. Sophie had fended off multiple attempted visits from Dunn, Connor Remarkian, and even Ben Waxman. She'd had a long phone conversation with Lei Texeira on Maui, and a post-shoot debrief meeting with Dr. Kinoshita, but other than them, she just wasn't ready to see anyone besides her father and Marcella until she had assessed the extent of her injury.

"There's just something about getting shot in the face," Sophie said, gazing into Marcella's warm brown eyes. "Just something really demoralizing about it."

"I can't even imagine." Marcella cupped Sophie's good cheek. "But you know that you're beautiful regardless. Are you sure you want to do this now?"

"Dr. Littleton said I can remove the bandages today, and that's what I want to do. Let's just get it over with." Sophie could hear the steel in her own voice.

The two women walked into the bathroom, where the mirror Sophie had been avoiding was lit with a strong neon glare.

Marcella seated her on the toilet, and began to tug and lift at the bandages covering the right side of her face as Sophie watched Marcella's face closely. Marcella gave nothing away. Her brown eyes were intent, her full mouth relaxed, holding the same expression she'd had when beginning to lift the bandages off. "Not bad," Marcella said, looking over the area in question. "Seems like the skin graft took, thank the good Lord."

Sophie stood up and walked to the sink. She turned her face to be able to see the surgery area. Her cheek on the injured side was twice as big. Her eye was sunk in a pouch of black and blue swelling. The skin graft was clearly visible, beginning in the middle of her cheekbone and extending up the side of her face into her hairline and around into her scalp. She'd already known the size of graft area, because she had a matching wound on her hip. "Where your bikini will hide it," Littleton had said, with his gift for optimism.

A row of black stitches surrounded the graft, giving the area the look of a crude patchwork quilt. When Sophie looked closer, she could see how tiny the stitches were. They were almost too small to have been done by human hands.

Littleton was one of the best in his field, her father had said. There was no reconstructive surgery on the face that he hadn't had extensive experience practicing. When the stitches were out, the wound's distorted, horrible outline would be much less obvious—but the fact remained that the area was dented and dimpled, too.

"I look like a pirate," Sophie said. "I look like..." She couldn't find words.

"You look like a beautiful, brave woman who's been shot in the face and surgically repaired by the best," Marcella said. She burst into tears, covering her face with her hands.

"That doesn't reassure me." Sophie hugged her friend as Marcella pulled toilet paper off of the roll, dabbing her eyes and blowing her nose noisily. "I'm a freak."

"You are not. I'm just so glad you're alive. We all have to remember that, going forward. And that's why I'm crying," Marcella said. "Because I'm happy you're still here, and you're going to be good as new in no time."

"People keep saying that to me." Sophie turned back to her disturbing image in the mirror. She traced the outline of the skin graft's stitching with a fingertip. "I won't have hair here. I guess I'll have to grow my hair out and find a way to cover up the bald spot."

"You can't get discouraged by this. Dr. Littleton said this was only the beginning of the repairs."

Sophie shrugged. She couldn't take her eyes off of the wasteland of her face. "Good thing I don't have a boyfriend."

"This won't make a bit of difference to anyone who really cares about you," Marcella snapped.

"You know who has been missing from this whole thing? Alika. It's really over with him. If he cared about me at all, he would have visited me. He would have called."

Marcella set a hand on her shoulder. "I did call him to tell him the news. He said he'd be praying for you."

Tears prickled Sophie's eyes for the first time.

Some part of her had still been hoping that with this crisis in her life, Alika would come, like she'd come for him when he was in need. *But he hadn't.* At least Connor Remarkian had tried to see her. And Dunn would have moved right into the apartment if her father had let him. And even the Ghost… She had some memory of his voice, a sense that he had come to her when she was in that gray place, but no real memory of it.

*The Ghost.* She thought of their exchange of photos. What would he want with her now? Would their online game of attraction survive her mutilation? Maybe, since it seemed to be about a lot more than the physical. She couldn't help a persistent feeling that somehow, the Ghost had something to do with waking her from the coma.

But right now the last thing she needed to worry about was some man's opinion of her face.

# CHAPTER TWENTY-SEVEN

Dunn was next to see Sophie's scars besides her father a day later. Shock showed in the widening of his gunmetal eyes and the flare of his nostrils before he schooled his expression into an impassive mask. "Looking good, Sophie."

She rolled her eyes "That's the best you can do, Jake?"

"I don't know what to say, damn it." Dunn ducked his head, pushed a hand through hair still damp from a shower. Wearing a teal-colored polo shirt and chinos, he looked like someone her father would play golf with on the weekend. "I'm sure it's going to get better."

"I'm not that concerned about it, actually." She opened the door further to let him in. "What did you come for?"

"I came to see you. And to tell you there have been some new developments in the case. Hello, Ambassador." Francis Smithson, seated at the couch with the Wall Street Journal open, shook out his paper and stood.

"Nice to see you outside the hospital, Jake." Her father had been the best possible company—warm and supportive, but leaving her alone whenever she wanted to retreat into her computer world or stare out the windows. Sophie wasn't ready to go out in public and be seen, still hoping the lurid color and swelling of her face would go down. "I'll give you two some privacy."

The apartment was set up in such a way that each of their bedrooms had an office/work area, and her father disappeared into his large, formal bedroom, closing the door. Dunn sat on the couch across from her. His gaze flicked to her face, then back down to a file he had brought in.

Was this always going to be the way people looked at her in the future? Glances, side looks, not wanting to make eye contact or seem to stare, but also not wanting to look at her face, either?

After another week, she was getting a little more used to it. The stitches would be coming out in another day or so, and they would begin a round of laser treatments to reduce the raised, red ridging around the edges of the scar. She kept her hopes small, though—it was better to get used to being what she was now than to hope for more.

Dunn cleared his throat and opened the file on the coffee table. "Big breaking news. Sloane was spotted here on Oahu."

Sophie's eyes widened. "Where?"

"Airport. Preliminary identification points to Dougal Sloane." Dunn pulled a grainy surveillance photo out of the folder. "Check this out."

Sophie picked up the printout of a dark silhouetted face. "I can't make out anything about this photo."

"See this?" Dunn's thick finger pointed to the ridge of light at the top of the head. "That's a light reflecting off of a scalp. Height and build are also consistent with Sloane."

"So how close is Hilo PD to picking him up?"

"That's why I'm here." Dunn gazed at her squarely at last—it was as if he'd had to work up to it, and the thought hollowed her belly. "I think we need you and your DAVID program to find him. Hilo PD has put an all-island warrant out on him, and his photo is circulating, but no one has seen him since he arrived, likely traveling under an alias. He seems to have a hideout here. Probably a

Society of Light connection of some kind. Wish we were in on that investigation."

Sophie settled deep into the love seat, curling her legs up onto the couch. "I can't officially use DAVID while its possession is in contention with the FBI. And even if I found any information, how could I give it to the police? It would open the door for an appeal from Sloane later, if he were prosecuted. As it is, we can't even make a case for those murdered women without the evidence being compromised."

"You were using DAVID before. And, on an encouraging note, the judge ruled the evidence admissible in the case against Jackson. The ruling was based on your work as a private contractor working for a client, with no directive from law enforcement. I brought your laptop back." Dunn opened the case at his feet and lifted out Sophie's familiar laptop. "You have more security on this laptop than I've run into in years."

"You tried to get into my computer?"

Dunn shrugged, the dimple in his cheek flashing, his teeth white. "Of course."

She took the laptop from him. "I don't use wireless with this. I had security issues working from home last year, part of why I left the FBI. I don't feel comfortable using this apartment as a base of operations for DAVID, especially with my father here. He is a diplomat, and has his own security concerns."

Dunn nodded agreement. "Would never expect you to compromise your safety," he said. It seemed like it was getting easier for him to look at her, and now he was staring.

She frowned. "Like what you see?"

"Sophie, you will always be a beautiful woman. Even if this is as good as they could do, you'd still be beautiful. The scars add character. They make you look even more interesting." Dunn's voice was pitched low and sincere. "Kind of badass, actually."

Sophie stood, agitated. She rubbed her hands up and down her yoga pants and walked over to the tall glass windows framing the beautiful skyline view of downtown Honolulu. "I kind of liked being Mary Watson. I got to disappear as her whenever I wanted to. I'm not sure I know who Sophie Ang is anymore, and now I don't even recognize her face."

Dunn stood up and walked over to where she stood. He squeezed her shoulder gently. "I've always thought work was the best antidote to almost anything, and I think you need to get back to work, sooner rather than later. You'll get more closure by finding Sloane than any therapy."

Sophie looked up at him and smiled for the first time. "I never thought I would say this, but you're not half bad as a therapist yourself." He was standing too close, and his hand slid down her back. She broke away and walked back to the couch. "So what's happening with the cult and the children?"

Dunn shrugged as he walked around to sit across from her, collecting his file. "Well, Jackson's out of jail on huge bail, but his absence gave the children's grandparents a chance to sue for custody, which is promising for them—they are currently with their grandparents, and as we know with custody cases, possession is nine-tenths of the law. Our client has cut us loose and closed our contract. She paid for us to find out what happened to those women, and we did. Now it's up to the police to make their case." He cleared his throat. "Speaking of Hilo PD. They really grilled me about who I saw when I took the shot to try to save you, and I had to admit I couldn't positively identify Sloane."

"So I'm the only eyewitness to what he did to me at the pit." Sophie's throat felt dry. "And to what he did to me when I was Mary Watson." Being Dougal Sloane's only living witness did not seem like a good thing.

"At the moment. According to Ohale, who called me yesterday, none of the cult members are admitting to seeing him the night you were shot—though they do admit he's gone."

"Don't they think that's a little suspicious? Who else would have shot me?" Sophie snapped.

"Of course. But info I have is through the cult's attorney—you know how it is."

"Unfortunately, I do. Well, thanks for bringing my laptop, but until I find a secure location to work, I won't be able to use it."

"You should consider what I said. About closure." Dunn leaned forward, dangling his big hands between his knees. "You're welcome back at the office whenever you're ready."

"I'm not ready." Formless panic at the thought of leaving the apartment rose up to grab Sophie by the throat. She'd been plagued by nightmares and had trouble sleeping, and even taking Ginger out was difficult. "I may not be, for a while. Until after all my repair surgeries."

"Bix told me to tell you to take all the time off you need. Our injury insurance will cover your leave, your health care. Security Solutions is keeping you on the payroll, but I wish it were more. Don't let this injury put you on your ass in here, hiding from the world."

"I'll take that under advisement," she said stiffly.

"Listen. I can tell by those circles under your eyes that you're having trouble sleeping. If it's any consolation, I am too. I went on many combat missions for the military, but retrieving your body from that pit and flying you back to Oahu—it did something to me, too." Dunn's gray gaze was intense. "I'm talking to Dr. Kinoshita about it...and the rest of my past. Please consider seeing her too."

She wanted to scream. His trauma was only a shadow of hers, and Sloane was here on Oahu. "I think that's enough of a visit for today, Jake." Sophie stood, giving him no room for argument.

Dunn walked slowly to the door and turned back at the opening that she held ajar. "I'm not giving up on you. I meant what I said about that. Come back to work."

"I'll think about it." She shut the door and leaned on it, closing her eyes just to breathe.

# CHAPTER TWENTY-EIGHT

S<small>OPHIE</small> <small>SETTLED</small> a small straw cloche-style hat onto her head and smoothed the black fitted sheath dress she'd ordered online, along with a pair of kitten-heeled pumps. Makeup, except for lipstick, was a waste of time, but a cherry-sized green Tahitian pearl at her throat gave a nice focal point for people to look at other than her face.

She was dressed a whole lot like Audrey Hepburn today.

*Dunn was right.* This look felt like it might be her style, and she couldn't look less like an FBI agent.

"You ready in there?" Her lawyer tapped lightly on the bathroom door. Smithers had called her two days ago to tell her that the FBI wanted a meeting, and that she was getting on the next plane to come over and attend with Sophie. "Not going isn't an option. This could be them escalating the situation—or, better yet, dismissing it," Smithers had said.

"Coming." Sophie gave herself a spritz of gardenia body spray, and opened the door. "Ready as I'll never be."

"You're getting pretty adept at those Americanisms." Bettina Smithers wore a sleek red suit, gold winking at her ears and throat, contrasting nicely with her mocha skin. The lawyer looked every inch a competent professional—from somewhere other than Hawaii. "If you didn't have that little bit of an accent, I'd think you were a local."

"I'll take that as a compliment," Sophie said. "It takes years to be a real *kama'aina* in Hawaii." She walked past Smithers, practicing some calming breaths and drying her sweaty hands by slipping them into the slash pockets on either side of her hips. She retrieved her purse and slid on her sunglasses. "Let's go."

"Not so fast." Francis Smithson got up from the desk in the corner and came to put his hands on her shoulders, kissing her cheek, careful to avoid her lipstick. "You look gorgeous."

"You're my daddy. Of course you'd say that." Sophie blinked through tears she'd been fighting all day. The stitches had come out yesterday and she'd been fighting the depression, a blinding headache, and anxiety about going out of the apartment.

"I second that. You're gorgeous. The scars add character, an element of mystery and danger," Smithers said now, smiling. "They say, 'no one better mess with me.'"

Sophie smiled. "And no one better. I have the best lawyer in LA by my side."

"You sure you ladies don't want me to come too? For moral support?" Her father seemed rather taken by Smithers, and clearly wouldn't have minded a little more time with the stylish litigator.

"Not appropriate for this meeting, Frank, but perhaps you could meet us for a celebratory, or a consolation drink after, as the case may be?" Smithers raised elegant brows. Her father accepted with alacrity.

Sophie decided she would be coming straight home, and would leave the two of them to that drink alone, whatever the outcome of today's meeting.

RISING in the familiar elevator to the tenth floor of the FBI offices in the Prince Kuhio Building in downtown Honolulu felt like déjà vu—but like a life that had happened years ago. The New Agent Trainee at the check-in desk buzzed them into the locked hallway.

"I was keeping an eye out for you." Marcella emerged from her office and gave Sophie a quick hug. "You're in Conference Room A."

"Oh good. Friendly interrogation room." Sophie's smile felt like a tic.

Marcella raised her brows, smoothed her chocolate hair back. "Waxman pushed for this meeting. We'll talk later." She ducked back into her office, and Sophie saw why—Special Agent in Charge Ben Waxman, her former supervisor and mentor, approached. Slim and dapper, the SAC was followed by his right hand man, Agent Gundersohn, a hulking Swede with a passion for detail.

"Ms. Ang." It was strange not to have Waxman call her Special Agent. His steel-blue gaze flicked over Sophie, who kept her hat and sunglasses on. "It's good to see you up and about. You were down for the count the last time I saw you, and we were all concerned. You're looking terrific." Waxman's greeting sounded forced. Gundersohn said nothing, per usual.

*He'd visited her in the hospital? She had no recollection of it.*

"This is my attorney, Bettina Smithers," Sophie said.

"Well, we have someone from Legal coming too, but it's strictly a formality." Waxman turned on a heel and led them past several offices and meeting rooms to Conference Room A.

"Strictly a formality?" Smithers preceded Sophie into the cozily decorated room with its homelike seating arrangement around a coffee table. "Except for the part about you suing Ms. Ang for ownership of her program, and sending two Internal Affairs agents to her door."

"That investigation has ended, I'm happy to say." Waxman sat on one of the armchairs and Gundersohn held down one end of the couch. That left the loveseat facing them for the two women.

Sophie hadn't spent a lot of time in this room, but she'd watched plenty of footage recorded in here. Everything they did or said was being recorded and observed. The furniture, slightly off-kilter and too far away from the coffee table, was bolted down, contributing to a subtle sense of unease. She'd briefed Smithers on the psychology of the room's setup, but even knowing the purpose of the room's deceptive appearance, she had to resist an urge to resettle the loveseat at a better angle or scoot forward. She made herself sit back quietly and fold her hands in her lap.

Smithers extracted a small black device. "I'm recording these proceedings."

"And we are as well," Gundersohn rumbled. "As I'm sure Ms. Ang told you."

The door opened. An older man with a neatly trimmed white goatee and charcoal-gray suit entered. "Aloha, all. I'm Peter Jameson, Esquire, from the FBI's legal department."

As soon as he was seated beside Gundersohn, Smithers squared off.

"I hope there's a good reason for dragging us in for this meeting. Ms. Ang is still recovering from extensive injuries, as you can see."

Sophie took the sunglasses off, and Waxman's regard fastened on her face. "I'm fine. Ms. Smithers is just concerned for me."

"And we apologize for the inconvenience," Jameson said smoothly. "I think you'll be pleased with the purpose for this meeting, which is to dismiss claims and legal action against Ms. Ang and the computer program known as DAVID."

"This is indeed good news." Smithers eked out a smile and accepted a clipboard with a stack of papers on it from Jameson. She began to read through the papers, pen in hand.

Sophie made eye contact with Waxman at last. "What brought this on, sir?"

Waxman shook his head, smiled. "Call me Ben, please. After all this time."

"Ben. What brought this on?"

He lifted his hands. "We had no claim on the program. I convinced the higher-ups of that at last. Besides, without you to run it, the DAVID program is useless even if we could eventually work out all the legal issues involved with the program's ability to gain access to other law enforcement databases to do its searches."

"Why did you put me through all that, and why stop now? You'd likely win." Sophie's voice sounded bitter, even to her own ears.

Smithers snorted loudly. "I wouldn't count on that."

"Your lawyer's right. And we were wrong to push it this far." Waxman leaned forward, straightened his tie. "We miss you around here. If we could reinstate your benefits and seniority with the Bureau, perhaps even a raise, would you come back?"

Sophie took a moment to consider it—her familiar IT cave, routines, the job challenges that were primarily behind a computer. "No. I'm sorry, Ben. I loved working here, but it's not a fit for me anymore." She hadn't realized the truth of this so deeply until this moment.

Waxman's gaze was kind, and sad. "I wish you would reconsider."

"I'd consider coming in to contract with you and the team for special assignments," Sophie said. "But no. I'm enjoying the challenges of being out of the lab…for the most part." She gestured ruefully to her face and tried a smile, but that hurt too much.

"These agreements look to be in order." Smithers's voice was brisk. "Except for the part about never using DAVID again, at any time, for any reason. We will not be signing this contract. Ms. Ang has a right to continue to utilize her proprietary software."

"DAVID poses a threat to the security of every national database, and part of our mission as the FBI is to address those kinds of threats," Jameson said.

"We will not be signing this contract. We can revisit the terms if you remove that clause." Smithers stood up. "Ms. Ang, we're done here. We will not be responding to anything less than a court order banning DAVID's use."

"Then I will be filing a motion to that effect in Federal as well as state court." Jameson's hands flickered around the coffee table, gathering the rejected contract pages Smithers had let fall. "DAVID is a threat to national security."

"Such hyperbole. Now I know the kind of inflammatory language you will use in your motion, the hysteria you will try to incite—and how prejudicial that is to my client." Smithers stood and crossed her arms.

"Well. Ms. Ang is a foreign national." Jameson also rose. He twitched at his lapels, his hair.

"Ms. Ang is not a foreign national, as you know perfectly well. She has dual citizenship in Thailand and the U.S. She is the daughter of a United States Ambassador, for goodness' sake. You will not get far with this slander." Smithers paused to reload. "Ms. Ang has an obligation to obtain the necessary consents for DAVID to access law enforcement databases, and she will pursue those consents through the proper channels. But you don't have the right to deny her that process." She picked up her purse. "Let's go, Sophie."

Sophie met Waxman's gaze. "I almost trusted you there, Ben, for a moment."

"I didn't know about that clause. And this is not personal. This was never personal, this thing with DAVID." Sophie had never seen Waxman's face so stark. "We should talk about this. Privately."

"How could this not be personal? DAVID is an extension of my abilities. First you tried to steal it, then to kill it." Sophie tugged the brim of the cloche lower, to hide her eyes. She felt an actual pain in her chest as she followed Smithers out.

She'd loved Waxman, just a little bit, and she hadn't known it until it was over.

# CHAPTER TWENTY-NINE

MARY WATSON PULLED up in front of her rundown apartment building three weeks later. She held open the door for Ginger to hop down from the cab, and gave the floppy brim of her hat a tug, pulling it down firmly to hide her face.

Ascending the exterior metal stairs, Sophie felt oddly disconnected from her surroundings. She'd had a post-shooting debrief and several more meetings with Dr. Kinoshita, Security Solutions' psychologist. The petite Japanese psychologist's words had helped her sort out what was going on. The panic she'd struggled with about leaving the apartment and the persistent sensation of unreality were all part of post-traumatic stress.

"But it seems to me that you were going through something of an identity crisis *before* you were shot," Dr. Kinoshita said, keen brown eyes gazing at Sophie's mutilated face unflinchingly. She leaned forward to touch Sophie's hand. "I've read your file. You escaped an abusive husband into the FBI, where you learned to fight and defend yourself, eventually bringing him down...but you never learned who *you* really were. You were married so young, to a sadistic man—how could you discover what the rest of us have a chance to, when your goal was survival? What has happened to your face is a metaphor, in a way, for the changes that you're going through. You're in the middle of becoming someone new, and what you will ultimately look like, be like—who you'll be with as a romantic partner, what you'll do for a living…all of it is in flux."

Two rounds of laser scar removal had helped minimize the edges of the skin graft area, but one side of her face was still raised, oddly contoured, and a different color than the rest of her facial skin. The prosthetic cheekbone had settled "as well as could be expected," according to Dr. Littleton, but now her eyes were off-kilter: one appeared higher than the other, and tight skin pulled it wider. Sophie's hair was still too short to cover the bald area of the skin graft as it went up into her temple, so she continued to wear hats.

Her face would never be the same.

Dougal Sloane was still at large, and she'd found she couldn't relax in her father's apartment, even with the building's security detail and the other measures she'd installed after the previous breach.

Too many people knew where she lived. The only thing she could think of that would make her feel safe was to be someone else, somewhere else, off the grid.

Her father, of course, had not agreed with this plan. "You're having some sort of breakdown," he said. "And it's understand-able. Just keep going to that therapist you're talking to. It seems to be helping." But in the end, he'd had to return to work in Washing-ton. The minute he was gone, Sophie packed her backpack, a few more things from the penthouse, and here she was again. *Mary Watson.*

Sophie reached Mary Watson's door and fumbled out her keys, unlocking it. There was no good reason for the feeling of relief she had to be in this place versus her father's luxurious penthouse. This building had no doorman, no security but the motion detector and extra locks she'd installed—and still it felt more like home than the penthouse.

Ginger gave a happy bark and bounced into the apartment as Sophie bent to pick up pamphlets and flyers left on the mat by Jehovah's Witnesses, a car detailer, and a pizza joint.

She stepped inside and locked the door behind her, engaging the extra security measures that she'd installed—and then she paused, sniffing the air, and turned.

The apartment smelled fresh, not musty. Marcella had asked for a key to the place, and she must have stopped by.

Sophie took a few steps in, to peer around the dividing wall beside the door. One of the windows over the sink was open, allowing a breeze. A tablecloth printed with palm trees covered a small round table with a couple of chairs in the kitchen alcove, and a vase of red and yellow ginger both brightened the place and sweetened the air. A small futon couch with a coffee table had been positioned in front of the glass sliders, and when she peeked into the bedroom, she gasped at the sight of a pretty bedroom set in rattan, with a mirror on the wall.

Tears filled her eyes and she covered her mouth with a hand. Marcella must have done this, and her father had probably paid for it. *She was loved.*

Sophie lowered the backpack of clothing she had brought from her father's apartment, and set the laptop that was still her lifeline to the online world she knew so well on the table, where a note was folded and tucked under the vase of flowers.

---

*Your dad, Marcus, and I wanted you to be a little more at home in your place. Hope you like what we did! We love you, beautiful. ~ Marcella, Marcus, and Frank*

---

She opened the sliders, letting the evening breeze blow in. Ginger lay down on a brand-new dog bed her friends had put near the door. She called Marcella and her dad and left tearful messages thanking them for the surprise. "You don't know what it meant to me to open the door and find the apartment looking like this." She set the phone down, but it almost immediately buzzed again.

"Marcella?" She answered it without checking the caller ID.

"I wondered if today was finally the day you were going to pick up." Connor Remarkian's cheerful Aussie accent brought a flush to her cheeks.

She'd been dodging his phone calls ever since the hospital and hadn't seen him in all that time. It was hard to forget that the last time she'd seen him, they'd kissed. What would he think of her now? And how much did she care?

She still wasn't sure.

"I needed some time to recover from the injuries I got on the Big Island." Sophie hated how wooden her voice sounded. She was so bad at this relationship thing.

"Totally understandable. Bix has kept me informed of your progress. But I had hoped we were at least friends, and you would let me...help you somehow. Be a support."

"I've been going through a lot. I'm sure you heard I was shot in the face, and I don't look...like me anymore." Her voice broke on the last word and she covered her eyes against the prickle of tears. She hadn't cried throughout the whole ordeal. Why was she crying now?

"I have to see you." His voice sounded rough. "When can I see you?"

Sophie dashed the tears off her cheeks, feeling the sag of her eye, the dented, dimpled surface of her skin with her fingertips. The truth hit her as she rubbed the wetness away—she didn't want things to go any further with Connor, because she couldn't stop thinking about the Ghost.

And he hadn't written her in all this time.

Fuzzy memories of the Ghost talking to her in the hospital still made her skin prickle. Had Sheldon Hamilton visited her there, or had that just been wishful thinking? No one could tell her if he had or not, but the feeling that he'd had something to do with her waking up was too persistent to ignore.

This was a conversation that needed to be had in person with Connor—he deserved that much. She glanced around the apartment. She might have furniture now, but the fridge was still empty.

"I need to go out for something to eat. Why don't I meet you for a night beach walk at Ala Moana Beach Park after?"

"Can we eat together, too? Could that count as the date you asked me on that we never had?"

Sophie pinched the bridge of her nose, embarrassed. "I guess." She named her favorite noodle house, and they set a time.

Sophie brought in the rest of her things, fed the dog, and put away her clothes. Wearing a pair of slim black jeans and a tank top with pearl earrings and Mary Watson's straw hat, Sophie drove to the noodle house.

Connor was already seated at a corner table. Sophie was surprised at the lift in her spirits to see him. He rose to greet her, sea-blue eyes intense as they traveled over her face, body, and clothing, registering the changes as she approached. He hugged her, knocking her hat back and making her laugh.

"You look great. It's so good to see you."

"Likewise." Sophie liked the feel of his arms around her, but detached herself. They sat.

"What's your favorite dish here?"

"Saimin."

"Good thing. It's a saimin place." They laughed.

Sophie was relieved that he didn't comment on her face. It must be improving.

After eating, they walked down toward the beach park along the sidewalk. "I feel naked without Ginger," Sophie said. "But the restaurant changed their rules. They used to let me tie her up on the sidewalk outside."

"Anubis is moping at home, too. He always likes an occasion to see her, as do I." Connor took Sophie's hand, squeezed.

Sophie felt the words she needed to say about the Ghost on the tip of her tongue, but couldn't bring herself to speak them yet. *This was so nice.* He felt good beside her—his acceptance a balm, his presence easy.

They reached the park, and headed for the water's edge, where they slipped off their shoes. Little wavelets splashed their feet, and the night wind thrummed in the palm trees. The moon on the water lit their way.

"I expected you to look much worse, with the way you've been hiding from me. Hideous. A Halloween witch with a single eye, at the very least." Connor swung her hand, clearly trying to broach the subject in a lighthearted way. "And for the record, it wouldn't have mattered to me if you did look like a witch."

Sophie couldn't even smile. "I don't know how much better I'm going to look than this."

"You're beautiful. But then, I suspect that it doesn't matter how many times people tell you that, you won't believe them. I wonder if you believed it even before your injury." He stopped her, turning to place one hand on her shoulder, one on her mutilated cheek. "This was never about your looks for me... Well, okay, it might have started that way—but it hasn't been about that for a while now."

Sophie took a step back. Her heart hammered with anxiety. She hated to hurt him, she wasn't sure she wanted to—but she owed it to him to be honest. "I have feelings for someone else."

"I don't think Alika Wolcott is coming back to Honolulu." Connor's eyes were hidden and dark with the moonlight on them from above, but his voice low and definite.

"So you know about him, then. And you're right, that's over between us. It's not him I was talking about."

"Who, then?"

Sophie hadn't expected his urgent persistence. "I'm not ready to talk about it. Just like I'm not ready...to talk about what we might be to each other."

"Fine. We'll go as slow as you need to." Connor was making an effort to rein in the frustration she could still hear in his voice. "But it's hard knowing that some mystery man is making a move on you while I'm being a gentleman."

"I'm trying to be fair by telling you." Sophie bit her lip. She pulled her hat off and slapped it against her leg, releasing tension. "Okay, then, since you won't let it go. It's Sheldon. We've been in touch online, and I need to know...what's between us. He visited me in the hospital, I'm sure of it, and I think he has feelings for me too."

Connor tipped his head back to speak to the heavens, throwing his hands up. "Of all the people!"

"I'm sorry. I know he's your friend."

They fell in step together again. Sophie was surprised at the relief she felt at having told Connor the truth. "You know that he's the Ghost. But what you probably don't know is that...we've kept in touch since last year's case. I know it's crazy to feel this way... and believe me, I wish I didn't."

"I warned you when we went hiking that he wasn't ever going to be available. For a relationship, or anything else." Connor's voice was tight with tension, the words bitten off.

"But he came to me in the hospital. He said he'd see me when the time was right." She heard the pleading in her voice. "You know him better than anyone. Tell him I need to see him. I need to know if he..."

"Why would I help you with that?" Connor picked up a stone, skipped it across the ruffled surface of the black ocean. They were close enough for the warm tropical waves to splash over their feet. "The guy is competition."

"I thought he was your friend."

"Hell if I'm going to help him take you from me." Having declared himself, Connor seemed as relieved as Sophie was to have acknowledged the proverbial elephant. He took her hand again and swung it a little in the dark as they walked.

Sophie felt the constriction in her chest lifting and something else replace it, something light and bubbly. She'd told him, been as honest as she could be, and they were still talking. "So I guess I'll just have to keep looking for the Ghost on my own."

"Better yet, you can give that shit up." She could see the crinkles of humor beside Connor's eyes as he tried to lighten his tone. "Let the Ghost play his little online mind games with criminals. I'm here, and I'm real." His hand felt big and warm, pleasant. "And I want to be with you."

She wondered how it would be to have Sheldon's hand holding hers—and almost couldn't breathe at the thought.

The spit of a silencer at close range was almost lost in the sighing of the waves, but Sophie couldn't miss the sear of pain on the outside of her left bicep. She gasped. "Gun!"

She ducked low and spun to face the threat, but Connor shoved her behind him.

Somehow she wasn't surprised to see moonlight shine on Dougal Sloane's bald pate as the big Scot walked toward them, gun hand extended, the familiar chrome Beretta lengthened by a cigar-like black protrusion—a silencer. Connor had gone very still, and for some reason she was reminded of the way Anubis could stand like a statue, all coiled menace.

"You're hard to kill, Mary Watson." Sloane kept advancing. The next shot couldn't miss. Sophie edged out from behind Connor. Her mind settled into that focused place where she went when she needed to. *Just another couple of feet, and she could reach him.*

But Sloane stopped just outside of range and lifted the pistol, waggling it back and forth between them.

"Which one of you would like it first? This is nothing personal." *Why did they always say that? It was such bullshit.* "Just cleaning up loose ends, Mary. With you out of the way, there's no case against me."

Connor shoved Sophie down and aside, and leapt for Sloane's gun hand.

Sophie gave a cry, falling to the sand as the weapon fired. Connor's body hit Sloane. The two men went down, landing in the shallow water at the water's edge and rolling in the surf as they grappled with each other.

Sophie scrambled to her feet, belly tightening with nausea as adrenaline flooded to her system.

*Connor had to have been shot.*

There was no way Sloane had missed at that range.

Sure enough, it was Sloane who stood up in the shallow water. He turned to push his foot down on Connor, submerging his motionless body.

Sophie launched herself with all her strength, hitting the big bald man in the back of the neck with her protruding elbow, knocking him face down into the water. But he was still holding the pistol, and he brought it up out of the water, *firing, firing, firing,* the spit of the rounds a deadly rain—fortunately he couldn't get an angle to hit her.

Sophie used her body weight to keep Sloane submerged, her knee between his shoulder blades. She grabbed the arm holding the pistol, and using all her upper body strength, twisted it behind his back until she heard, and felt, the pop of his shoulder dislocating. His body jerked beneath her as he released a gust of bubbles, and the pistol fell from his fingers and sank to the bottom.

Sloane thrashed, trying to get a purchase to stand and toss her off. Small waves, the uneven sandy bottom, and his strength all contributed to Sophie having trouble staying on his back and holding him under.

Sloane managed to get his feet underneath him, and surged upwards with a gasp that threw her backwards. She landed in the shallow water, scrabbling backwards crabwise on her hands and feet towards the shore as he spun to face her.

One arm dangled useless, but Sloane's good hand reached

toward her as he coughed and bellowed in rage, staggering out of the shallows toward her.

Sophie lashed out and caught his knee from the side, a tricky move she had learned in her MMA fights. In matches it had to be done carefully or it would break the knee joint—but this time, she wanted to break it.

Sloane went down with a cry, his leg collapsing, bringing him to his knees in the water. Sophie burst up to hit him from the front, capturing his head in a chokehold and drawing him up against her hip. Holding her wrist with the opposite hand, Sophie winched down the pressure on his windpipe as he tore at her arm, punched at her legs. Dougal Sloane wasn't going down easy.

Her eyes strayed to Connor, floating face up in the water. He was going to drown, if he wasn't dead already.

She choked Sloane into unconsciousness, and the minute he went limp, she dropped him with a splash.

She ran to Connor's body, grabbed him under the arms, and hauled him up onto the beach. She could see an oozing black hole where the round from the Beretta had penetrated his upper chest near the shoulder.

Sophie laid Connor on his back. His mouth flopped open and water flowed out of it as she turned him onto his side and thumped on his back. An ear against his back told her his heart was still beating.

She heard splashing, and looked up to see Dougal Sloane standing, big as a mountain, staggering in the water. She turned Connor over so more of the water could drain out. It was the best she could do at the moment.

Sophie hurtled back into the water with all the momentum she could muster and caught Sloane around the waist. Hitting him with her shoulder in the groin, she startled an exhalation of air out of him as she knocked him backwards into the water, arms churning. She landed on his chest with her knees and shoved his head under, all the way to the bottom.

She held him down by the neck.

Waves splashed into her face as Sloane thrashed, but she kept her knees on his chest, sucking gulps of air between waves as she held him down with all her strength.

His whole body seized, spasming. He heaved convulsively beneath her as he inhaled ocean water. Whatever people said about drowning, it wasn't a peaceful death.

But Dougal Sloane didn't deserve a peaceful death.

Sophie stayed on him until the last tremors and shudders were gone, until she was absolutely certain he wasn't getting back up.

She splashed back to Connor's body on the beach. There was foam at his lips and he still wasn't breathing. Sophie took a pulse. His heart was beating sluggishly, but regularly.

She had to get the water out of him. She had to get him breathing again.

Sophie hauled Connor up onto his stomach, so that his solar plexus landed across her bent knees. She made sure his head, inclined downward, was turned to the side and that his mouth was open. She lifted one of her knees, increasing the downward angle, and pounded on his back with all her strength.

Water gushed out of Connor's mouth. Every time she hit him, more came out. In between blows to his back, she screamed for help.

# CHAPTER THIRTY

Sophie sat down on the beige suede couch in Dr. Kinoshita's office at Security Solutions. She crossed her legs, hands locked around one knee. After telling her tale multiple times to the police and spending the night in an interrogation room, Sophie was in no mood to repeat it again—but Bix had sent her a text ordering the interview with the psychologist.

Her eyes felt gritty from lack of sleep, her body bruised and sore, and her throat still hurt from screaming for help two days ago.

Dr. Kinoshita came out from around her desk and seated herself opposite Sophie in a wingback armchair. The psychologist's dark brown eyes searched her face. "You look exhausted, Sophie. How are you holding up?"

"I wouldn't be here if Bix hadn't ordered it."

"I totally understand. Can I get you some tea?"

"I'd love some, thanks."

Kinoshita remembered that she wasn't a coffee drinker. Not too many people did, and it showed the psychologist's thoughtful attention to detail. Kinoshita turned on an electric kettle over on a sideboard, fussing with a tea bag and mug. "I am personally so grateful to you for saving Todd." Kinoshita slanted a glance at Sophie over her shoulder. "Mr. Remarkian is essential to Security Solutions, especially with Sheldon Hamilton's departure."

Sophie had to consciously remember that Todd was Connor's first name. Apparently Kinoshita wasn't close enough to the CEO to know that. "It was really frightening trying to bring him back from drowning. The doctors are still not sure if he sustained some permanent neurological damage from oxygen deprivation—but at least he's going to make it." Sophie hadn't even been able to visit Connor in the hospital with the police on her like fleas on a dog. Dunn had kept her informed of Connor's changing medical situation via text messages. "I heard he had surgery for the bullet wound, and is due to be discharged tomorrow."

Kinoshita brought Sophie the mug of tea and a coaster for the blond, Danish-style wood coffee table. "Now that we're all settled, why don't you take me through what happened step-by-step."

Sophie took a moment to muster her thoughts, smoothing Mary Watson's linen pants down to her knees, flexing her fingers. "It started with my leaving my father's apartment." Sophie took Dr. Kinoshita through the series of events, keeping it as simple and factual as she could. There were many points in the story when her voice trembled, or she needed to get up and pace—particularly when describing the Faustian dilemma of killing Sloane, or saving Connor.

"I gambled. And I'm not sure I won."

"The fact that you could subdue Sloane at all is practically a miracle," Kinoshita said.

Sophie smiled. "You and I clearly have a different standard. I'm a trained FBI agent and an MMA fighter. I'd gone against him before and almost lost, so I knew what I was up against, but Remarkian gave me a chance by attacking him first."

"Yes. It appears that he pushed you out of the way and made a grab for the man's weapon." Kinoshita poured more tea into Sophie's mug. "Are you two dating?"

Sophie moved uncomfortably, kicking her foot in its pretty but sensible sandal. "I guess you could call it that. It's more like— spending time together."

Kinoshita sipped her tea. "Well, he certainly tried to help you."

"I know." Sophie twisted her hands together, unsure how much to tell the psychologist, but in need of someone to discuss her situation with. "I had just finished telling Remarkian that I had feelings for someone else. Someone—not available." Sophie plucked at a loose thread on Mary Watson's linen pants.

"And how did he take that?"

"He seemed to accept it." Perhaps that wasn't true, though. She remembered the tight line of Connor's jaw, the way he had skipped that stone so forcefully into the ocean. "You were right a while ago when you told me you thought I was having an identity crisis. It's true. I needed to leave my father's penthouse after being stuck there with anxiety and depression problems right after the shooting. Now I only feel safe in that off-the-grid apartment, and I'm clearly still figuring out my wardrobe choices." She gestured to the pants. "I've realized I don't want to get beaten up anymore. I'm really quite sick of it. And what that will mean for my MMA fighting, I don't know yet. I still need an intense physical outlet to manage my depression, but getting pounded in the ring just doesn't appeal anymore."

"What about coaching?" Kinoshita said. "You could take the skills you've worked so hard for, and help others learn—and maybe not have to take so many hits yourself."

"That's a good idea. I haven't been back to Fight Club since I went underground as Mary Watson." Sophie sipped her tea. "I miss it."

"Something to think about, at least. Let's meet again next week. And sooner, if you have any further stress symptoms, like nightmares, persistent anxiety, or flashbacks."

Dunn was waiting for Sophie outside Kinoshita's office door when she finished with the session, dressed for action in his usual black cargo pants and tee. "I have a possible new case for us. You might like this one. It's over on Maui."

Sophie smiled, and felt the tug of the skin graft tighten across her cheek. "You're nothing if not persistent. Not going to let me have even a few days more off for this latest incident, are you?"

"The best way to move on is to get back on the horse," Dunn said. Sophie couldn't even be irritated with him because he was probably right. She followed Dunn to his office.

"I'm not coming back for at least a few more days. But you can try to get me interested."

"How does looting of artifacts at an important archaeological dig site sound?"

"Wonderfully nonviolent after what we've been through on this last case. Tell me more."

"I don't know a lot more, except to tell you that they're putting us up in a hotel, and there's an expense account." Dunn wiggled his brows. "Possibly including a bar tab."

Sophie loved Maui, from its beautiful beaches to its mountaintop cloud forests. The Valley Isle always felt like a vacation to visit even when she was working. She'd be able to see her friend Lei and her family, too.

"Sounds like something I'd be interested in. When I get back." She gave Dunn a playful shove at his exaggerated expression of relief. "Get everything set up and keep me informed."

Her phone buzzed with a text from Connor on her way downstairs.

*They discharged me. I'm at home, at the Pendragon Arches apartment. I think you know the address. Can you come by? Want to see you.*

Connor must be feeling better. She smiled and her fingers flew as she typed a response. *Definitely. On my way.*

# CHAPTER THIRTY-ONE

SOPHIE REMEMBERED the Pendragon Arches building well from her last big case. The monolithic, Art Deco style apartment building in the ritzy Nuuanu area of Honolulu was one of the premier addresses for the well-heeled living downtown. Security Solutions maintained a couple of corporate apartments there, but she was surprised to find that Connor still lived in the rather sterile unit they'd originally interviewed him in.

She entered the building, checking in with the reception desk in the foyer. The majestic lobby was decorated in subdued jewel tones, with smoked glass doors and windows, rich burgundy patterned carpet, and crystal chandeliers: quite formal for Honolulu, and an indication of the security concern and wealth of the residents of the building.

The desk called up to Connor's apartment and then directed Sophie to the elevators. The case that had gotten her involved with Security Solutions had ended up with a body in one of the company's apartments and a confrontation with the man who'd done everything he could to ruin her life.

Sophie squelched the traumatic memory and focused on the

task at hand as she rose nine floors in the beautifully appointed elevator car.

Connor had not changed the two brass urns that marked the doorway of the apartment. She knocked, and almost immediately a young Filipina woman in a white nurse's uniform answered the door. A nametag identified her as Monique. "Please come in."

"Hi Monique. I'm Sophie. Glad to see that Mr. Remarkian is getting some professional care." Sophie entered the living area at the nurse's welcoming gesture, stepping into the familiar room with its leather couches, large flat screen TV, and another brass urn holding bamboo canes and long imitation tikis, a designer's idea of tropical decorating.

"Yes. He's finally resting comfortably. The move over from the hospital put a good deal of strain on him."

Sophie frowned. Where were Connor's parents? The closest people in his life should be there to take care of him in this crisis. What would she have done without her father helping her recover from her injuries? It made her throat tight to think of Connor so alone. "Who engaged your services?"

"I've been retained by Security Solutions and I'm here full-time until he recovers."

Sophie paused the woman with a hand before they left the living room, her heart thumping. "How bad is he?"

Monique smiled. "He's going to be fine. Doctor told me there's no evidence of any brain trauma, and while painful, he's having a normal recovery for a gunshot wound of this type. He'll be up and around in a week or so." She patted Sophie's arm. "Eventually there will be nothing to show for it but a sexy scar and a good story."

This woman thought she was Connor's girlfriend. Sophie cleared her throat. "Happy to hear my friend is going to make a full recovery," she said stiffly. "Where's his dog, Anubis?"

"The dog was here at the apartment when Mr. Remarkian was

injured. His housekeeper took Anubis to the pet sitting service he uses when out of town."

"Oh, good." Sophie wished she'd thought of this earlier. Poor Anubis must be so stressed without his master. "Can I get that information? Maybe I can take him out for a walk."

Monique wrote the name and number down and handed it to Sophie. "I'm sure Mr. Remarkian would be relieved to have a friend look in on his dog. Follow me."

Connor was propped up on pillows in a masculine-looking bedroom done in shades of jade and plum. His head was turned away on the pillow, his eyes shut. His color was sallow in spite of his tan, the stark white dressing wrapping his upper shoulder and chest, a sharp contrast. Monique held a finger to her lips and pointed to a round, comfortable armchair placed beside the bed. Sophie sat down, drawing her legs up into it, curling up to wait as Monique gently closed the door on them.

She heard the soft rustle of Monique doing something in the kitchen. She rested her head on the back of the chair and relaxed.

Sophie wasn't aware of falling asleep, but she woke to the sound of Connor's voice.

"What a sight for sore eyes." Connor's voice sounded like a rusty hinge. Sophie stretched her legs and sat up with a smile. His changeable eyes were pouched in dark circles, and his tan lay like paint over his pale skin.

"Monique seems nice. But where is your family? I know from having my dad around that recovering from a gunshot is a good time to be surrounded by family."

"I'm an only child. Both my parents are gone, and I don't get along with the relatives who are left."

"I'm sorry." Sophie uncoiled from the chair. "Do you need anything? Water, pain meds?"

He scooted to one side of the bed, grimacing, and patted the pristine sheets beside him. "Just sit with me. You make me feel better just being here."

Sophie carefully lowered herself into the spot next to him. She wanted to make Connor feel better, she wanted to comfort him—but Sheldon Hamilton was a *ghost* never far from her thoughts.

She had made a pun, but it wasn't funny.

She couldn't lead Connor on. She made sure several inches separated them and put a pillow behind her back. "Monique told me you're going to be okay. What do you remember about the attack?"

"I remember making a jump for the gun. Nothing else." His tone was grim. Connor reached for her hand. His was warm and dry. She lifted it and turned it over, traced the calluses on it—he had thicker skin on his fingertips, and in the web of his palm beside his thumb.

"I thought you were mostly on computers, like I am. But these calluses tell a different story."

He pulled his hand away, tucked it under the bedclothes beside him. "Rock climbing and martial arts are my hobbies, besides hiking. I like using a *bo* staff. There's a lot about me that you don't know." He seemed to be withdrawing from her.

Sophie was uncomfortable with the proximity anyway, and got up off the bed. "Well, I just wanted to see that you were all right. I'll come back another time."

Connor stared up at her. "We were having a conversation about something important when we were rudely interrupted by Sloane's attack. I'd like to revisit that."

Sophie didn't want to revisit that conversation about where their relationship wasn't going. "Now does not seem like the time. Get some rest." She stepped away, but Connor leaned forward, catching her hand, and groaned at the pain of the abrupt movement. He gave a firm tug, and she stumbled toward him, kneeling on the bed in the place she had just vacated.

"Look at me, Sophie."

Sophie didn't want to hurt him. Eventually she raised her eyes to his. There was more gray than blue in them now.

"Every day that goes by, Sheldon looms larger between us."

"That's ridiculous." Never mind that Sophie was obsessively checking her email, looking for more of those beautiful photographs.

"Please go lock the door."

"Why?" But she got up to lock it, feeling a curl of apprehension.

"There's something you need to know about Sheldon." Sophie didn't like the set, white determination on Connor's face.

*Maybe Hamilton was married. Maybe he was an international porn king.* Maybe he was something even worse than the murdering vigilante she already knew he was.

She shook her head. "Don't tell me anything. Let him tell me."

Connor struggled upright, wincing. "Help me up."

"I'm sure that's against doctor's orders."

"Screw the doctor's orders." Connor swung his legs to the side and pushed himself upright. "I have to show you something."

"Why can't it wait?" But Sophie helped him anyway, because he gave her no choice. She looped an arm under his and lifted him to his feet. The effort made him white with pain.

"The bedroom door is locked. Where are we going?"

Connor pointed to the closet.

Sophie shook her head. "You need something, I will get it for you."

"Get me walking."

She staggered, his weight solid and heavy as they navigated to the closet door. He fumbled in his pocket for something. She spotted a key fob in his hand, much like the one she used to use when she turned on the computer rigs in her apartment. "Open the door."

Sophie slid the door open to reveal a big, deep closet with a large wood organizer, thick with folded shirts, neatly hung ties, and polished dress shoes. Connor hit the fob, and the organizer moved aside and folded back against the wall with a gentle creak. A doorway was revealed, just an outline against the back wall.

A breathless dizziness tightened Sophie's gut. "What is this?" The setup reminded her way too much of the hidden 'safe room' where Assan Ang had performed his most intimate tortures on her.

Connor didn't answer. He hit the fob again, and the door on the far wall retracted smoothly, revealing a bedroom identical to the one she was standing in.

Signs of a man's occupation were evident inside: a shirt was draped over a leather bench at the base of a king-sized bed dressed in a garnet-colored spread. A modern abstract in bold, hot shades on the opposite wall gave a feeling of the molten lava of the Big Island. A clutter of personal items filled a calabash on the dresser: watch, a handheld grip exerciser, a dog's toy ball. Unlike the designer room they stood in, this one was very personal.

Sophie helped Connor forward, biting her tongue on all of her questions. She sat him on the edge of the bed because she couldn't hold him up anymore.

She glanced back through the opening into Connor's bedroom, then at his face. His eyes were closed, and one hand pressed against the wound on his chest.

"Tell me what this is about," she whispered.

"It's easier to show you. But we have to go to another room. I just need a minute to get my breath."

Sophie scanned the bedroom, looking for clues. Nothing of interest on the koa entertainment unit. A large dog bed next to the bed they sat on made her frown. *Could that be for Anubis?*

He draped an arm over her shoulders. "I'm ready. It's just in the next room." He pointed.

Sophie hefted Connor's weight. He hissed in pain and she gave his hand a comforting squeeze. They limped to the door and Sophie inhaled sharply as she opened it.

The home office was set up much like how she arranged her computer rigs: three large monitors with the computers hidden under a desk. A rack of exercise equipment filled one wall and a second work area, complete with three more computer monitors, was set up in the L of the desk.

Violins in different sizes hung from a wooden rack on one of the walls.

The air was cooler than normal, optimal for computers, and soft, dim natural light came in through heavily tinted windows. Sophie lowered Connor into one of the office chairs.

"Sheldon's a programmer. Is this his office? Has he been here all this time, right here in Honolulu?" A potent sense of fury and betrayal raised Sophie's voice.

"Yes. And this is his office." Connor pinched the bridge of his nose, clearly in pain.

She looked over at the exercise equipment and recognized the chin-up bar.

Sheldon Hamilton must have set up a camera on a timer and posed naked for her on that very rack, creating images of his body she would never forget.

"I thought he was overseas. And all the time he was right here, playing a game with me." Sophie's gut churned. "I should have known."

Connor used his foot to pull out the second office chair. "Sit."

Sophie sat, grinding her teeth. "Where is he?" Her hands fisted and twitched with the need to hit something. Maybe her days in the MMA ring weren't over yet.

"Right here. He's right here."

Sophie's breath blew out in a gust. "What are you talking about?"

"I'm Sheldon Hamilton." Connor shut his eyes, pinched the bridge of his nose. The Aussie accent was gone. "Always have been."

But Hamilton had dark hair, dark eyes. Glasses. A goatee… Nausea rose to choke her.

"Why?" It was the only word she could force past the obstruction in her throat, and she knew it sounded tiny, just a minuscule puff of air that couldn't begin to express the pain and disillusionment swamping her.

"The short answer?" Connor pushed a hand through his blond hair, tufty and unstyled from his stay in the hospital. "Plausible deniability."

"Is there anything you've told me that is true?" Sophie stood up, balling her fists.

"My real name is Connor. Not Todd. Not Sheldon. Only you know that it's my real name."

"Oh, what a gift. A generic first name. I feel special and important to you." Sarcasm wasn't her style, but Sophie wanted to hit him—and she couldn't because he was already folded over in pain from a bullet he took trying to save her. She wanted to run, but that wouldn't help the bombshell of this revelation be any different.

So she stood up and paced, up and down the length of the room, calming herself with movement as she always had.

"You had to hide the identity of the vigilante, the Ghost."

"Exactly." Connor blew out a breath. "I couldn't risk being caught, by either law enforcement or by those I had manipulated into…doing things. Not all of them are dead, you know."

The kidnapping gone wrong that had uncovered the Ghost on her last case leaped into her mind: carrying Anna Adams, six-year-old kidnap victim, past the sprawled bodies of criminals who'd shot each other after receiving a mysterious text from an unknown sender.

"You've been mixed up with organized crime. You've manipulated a lot of people into killing each other and turning each other in."

"Yes, I have. The mob has its uses, and they have expiration dates when those uses are done."

"But why? Why the Ghost? I asked you this before…" Sophie found herself rubbing the numb-but-tingly skin graft on her face.

"Because there are too many who will get away with what they do. I feel compelled to tip the balance of the scales. Because someone must, and I can. You're not so above it all that you didn't ask me for the kind of favor only I could do."

"An honest answer at last." Sophie made herself stop rubbing the scar and spun to walk back again, fighting an urge to use the chin-up bar—but he would see that as acceptance, some obscure reference to the photos—*the photos of him!* And she was far from accepting this. "I told you that I couldn't agree with what you were doing. There are too many dangers in circumventing the system."

"And we agreed to disagree, but I knew you saw me as a handy ace in the hole for cases that didn't go the way you wanted. And I was okay with that." Connor looked up at her at last. "Want to know how I did it?"

"I don't need to see your hair dye, your fake glasses, your glue-on goatee," Sophie snarled. "But I do need to know why you played with my emotions as Sheldon Hamilton. And why you're revealing yourself to me now." Tears stung as she stared into his eyes, breathing too fast.

"I discovered you as Hamilton. I fell in love with you as Hamilton: through watching you on video. Through our duel of wits. Through getting to know the woman you are." Connor held her gaze. "I love you. I'm not afraid to say those words. I've never known another woman like you, nor will I ever meet anyone to equal you."

Sophie sat back down in the chair, a puppet with cut strings.

"I encouraged you to become attached to Hamilton because he was all I had to connect to you, and I didn't know how to bridge the gap between his identity and Todd's. I tried to build a friend-ship with you through Todd, but from the first, I knew it was already too late—I could tell you felt no attraction to Todd, and I couldn't help hoping it was because your emotions were engaged elsewhere. And then you told me you had feelings for Hamilton the other night, even though I'd been able to kiss you as Todd..." He paused, and through her own labored breathing, Sophie heard his anguish. "I almost died the other day. I can't go on living a lie with you. I see no way out but to trust you as myself. Trust you to keep my identity as the Ghost secret—or turn me in, as you see fit. Whatever you choose, I won't fight it."

"I have to get out of here." The room's walls seemed to be closing in on her. Sophie tried to stand but her knees buckled. *Relax. Breathe. He's not going to hurt you. The bastard just said he loves you.*

"I'm so sorry," Connor said. "I would like to start over."

His words got her on her feet. Sophie turned to spear him with a glance. "With who? Hamilton? Remarkian? Who *are* you? You know my history. How could you imagine I'd ever be able to trust you after this?"

"Connor! I'm Connor, and that's the truth, and all that really matters!" Connor's face was white with effort and pain as he thumped his chest, his wound. "See me, I'm right here. Have the courage to know me! You're a hypocrite, *Mary Watson!*"

Sophie winced as the arrow struck. They stared at each other for a long moment. There was no sound in the quiet room but both of their ragged breathing.

"Goodbye, whoever you are," Sophie said.

She turned and left—but she didn't run out, because that would have given him too much power. She squelched the little voice that told her how hard it was going to be for him to make it back to bed alone with his wound. She didn't walk out of the secret apartment, either, because she hadn't yet decided what to do about the Ghost, and Monique would wonder how she'd disappeared.

No, she went back through the secret door, and out through his bedroom, shutting the door behind her and telling Monique something had come up and that she had to go. "Mr. Remarkian is resting. Don't go in until he calls for you."

And once she was safe and alone in her car in the underground garage, Sophie covered her face with her hands and cried.

# CHAPTER THIRTY-TWO

THREE DAYS LATER, the Security Solutions helicopter entered the Waipio Valley through the wide, deep opening of its bay. As always, the sight of the place stole Sophie's breath: the patchwork of small farms, the winding green snake of the river, the thick vivid layers of green vegetation, the steep, velvety slopes of the valley, and the tumbling plume of the huge waterfall at the back.

"This is a stupid idea," Dunn said into Sophie's comm. "There's nothing new here. I don't know why we're doing this."

Sophie didn't reply, because she could see the stress in Dunn's tight muscles, in the big hand he clenched and unclenched on his thigh. This field trip was Dr. Kinoshita's idea, since both of them were having trouble sleeping and flashbacks relating to the case. "You need to have closure, a different experience out there. I will come with you. We'll process," the psychologist had insisted.

Sophie had cursed long and fluently in Thai as Dunn got up and walked out of the conference room when Kinoshita had delivered her bomb—but now, here they both were, with the psychologist up front with the pilot.

The cult compound came into view, the gate around it still closed.

Hilo PD had informed them that the site was empty, the crime scene tape removed now that they had recovered the remains from the garden area. The cult, expelled by police, had taken the opportunity to relocate to their location in Costa Rica—with the exception of Sandoval Jackson, prevented from leaving the country by removal of his passport and a million-dollar bail pending his court date.

Sophie felt her pulse pick up as she identified the place where she and Dunn had gone over the wall, marked by a gap in the wire.

The dump truck was gone, as was the pit, now filled in with sifted soil. The accountant who'd committed suicide and the first woman to disappear, Mandy Newburt, had been buried deep, under the labyrinth's central mandala. Sophie could almost feel the toe bone she'd found in the dark that night in her hand—forensics had matched it to the missing Amy Fillmore.

Amy Fillmore and Jennifer Roberts had been dismembered and integrated into the compost heap. The rich black compost, made of yard waste and manure, had been run through a shredder after it was well broken down. The bodies had then been spread over the huge garden. *No wonder those lettuces were so lush.*

Sophie wasn't sure if she was airsick or just nauseated by the thought of the salads she'd eaten at the retreat.

The chopper settled into the center of the compound. The pilot got out, checking something on the landing gear and giving them a moment of privacy. Kinoshita turned back to face them as they removed their helmets. "How are you two doing?"

Dunn looked pale. His eyes were the gray of a winter storm. "Never wanted to see this place again, quite frankly." He glanced at Sophie. "Last time I was here, my partner was bleeding like a stuck pig, her face all shot to hell, and I was carrying her to this chopper wondering if she was going to live."

"I'm fine now, thanks to you." Sophie touched his arm. "I'm absolutely sure I'd be dead right now if you hadn't got up from being electrocuted to rescue me."

"And maybe I'd be the one with the pirate look now. Damn, you stole that sexy scar from me." Dunn was trying to make light of it, but Sophie could see the strain in his face, his body. "And then, because I didn't kill him, Sloane came after you again, and Remarkian almost died."

"It's not your fault." Sophie said. "Can you two give me a moment of privacy? I want to go check out the gravesite. Alone."

Dunn shook his head no, but Kinoshita nodded in agreement, so Sophie hit the handle of the helicopter and pushed the door open.

The humid air smelled of diesel fumes from the chopper, but also of the lush green growing scent that was such a part of the valley. The yurts were deserted, their doors closed, as Sophie walked around a couple of them toward the former garden. Nothing stirred in the compound but a forgotten towel, flapping on a clothesline behind one of the buildings, and a loose chicken that ran squawking at the sight of her.

The silence was strange when she remembered so much sound during the retreat: the background cluck of the chickens, the chatter of the children, the music of guitar and flute.

Sophie hadn't expected to be sad that this place was over and done.

The huge hole she remembered standing on the lip of had been filled—smooth, raked-looking soil made a blank expanse. Sophie knelt at the edge of the disturbed area, lifted a handful of soil, sifted it through her fingers. *Of course.* The police had gone through all of it looking for bits of the bodies. What a messy unpleasant job that must have been...

"I can't believe you had the nerve to come back."

Sophie stood, the handful of soil clutched in her fist.

Jessie Sparks faced her from twenty yards away. The woman before her looked like a scarecrow ghost of the pretty woman she'd been, the bulge of her pregnancy distending a smock-like orange dress. Her shiny, curling brown hair now hung in matted clumps, her plump cheeks were caved in, and her legs looked too skinny to support her swollen body.

Sparks held a gun, pointed at Sophie—a chrome Beretta.

*The cult must have bought them in bulk on sale.* The irrelevant thought appeared and seemed to hover, as if in a comment bubble, over Sophie's head.

*I'm getting awfully tired of looking down the barrel of this particular model.*

Sparks had been concealed in one of the yurts whose door still hung open. They should have checked all the buildings to make sure that the compound was clear.

*So much for the therapeutic visit.*

*Dunn is going to be so pissed.*

Each thought blipped through her mind separately.

*So this is the kind of stupid thing that you think about right before you die.*

"I'm sorry." Sophie slowly raised her hands. "For whatever it is you think I've done."

The helicopter's view of her position was blocked by one of the yurts. She flicked her gaze around, looking for Dunn. She had her weapon, but it was snapped into her shoulder holster and might as well be on another planet.

"You killed him." Sparks's hands shook. She raised the pistol and tracked from Sophie's head, to her chest, to her abdomen and back again as if unable to decide what to shoot first. "You killed the love of my life. My baby's father."

"What do you mean? Jackson's alive." Sophie's lips felt numb. The madness in the young woman's eyes was somehow more terrifying than Dougal Sloane's murderous intent.

Someone had come to the door of the yurt. A man stood behind Sparks.

"Jessie." The resonant voice with its Scottish burr was smooth as cream liqueur. "Jessie, what are you doing?"

"This woman killed Dougal." Sparks's hands trembled but her

eyes were steel. Sophie could feel the young woman's emotional instability oscillating around them like a force field.

"Did I hear you say—Dougal was the love of your life?" Jackson was descending the stairs behind Sparks. "But you're with me."

"No, no, I'm not. Never was. This is Dougal's baby." Sparks let go of the gun with one hand so the other could caress her rounded abdomen. "I slept with you so I wouldn't get kicked out of the Society."

Jackson approached her, his voice flowing like oil over troubled waters, his gaze serene, as Sparks divided a glare between him and Sophie. "We can work all of this out. You shouldn't stress yourself. It's not good for the child. Perhaps it's Dougal coming to join you again, when you give birth."

Sparks reared back in revulsion. "That's totally perverted! You are a fake, Sandoval, and I'm done swallowing your lies!"

She turned and shot Jackson, the report of the weapon shockingly loud.

Sophie dove for the ground as the cult leader's hands came up to clutch his neck, blood spurting between his fingers. Sparks spun back and shot the place where Sophie had just been standing.

She fired again and again, screaming with rage, as Sophie rolled frantically—until the sound of another gunshot, much louder, silenced the onslaught.

*Jake Dunn, saving her again.*

Sparks's wailing cry showed she was still alive. Sophie, face turned sideways in the soft loam of the gravesite, closed her eyes and murmured a prayer of gratitude.

She turned her head at the thunder of Dunn's footsteps passing and saw him kick the pistol away from Sparks's foot as the woman screamed in outraged horror and pain. Even from where Sophie lay, she could see that Sparks was missing two fingers.

"You okay?"

"Good shot, Jake." Sophie let Dunn pull her to her feet. "Good thing Sparks has terrible aim."

"Tell that to Sandoval Jackson." Dunn gestured with his head to where Dr. Kinoshita and the pilot were vainly trying to administer first aid to the cult leader as he bled out messily. "We really screwed up not checking that the compound was clear."

"I know. *Son of a two-headed yak.* This could all have been prevented." Sophie walked over to Sparks.

The pregnant woman had collapsed to the ground, her bleeding hand wrapped in her skirt and pressed between her thighs. She'd stopped screaming, but her gaze up at Sophie was just as hate-filled as before.

Sophie stared down at her. "I pity your child. It will be taken from you as soon as it's born, while you serve a sentence for murder."

"Screw you," Sparks hissed. "You don't know true love."

No, Sophie didn't—and if this was where it ended, she didn't want to.

# CHAPTER THIRTY-THREE

SOPHIE TUGGED at her ex-FBI gray suit jacket as she left the Honolulu PD video conference room, where she'd just finished giving an official statement to Hilo PD regarding the death of Dougal Sloane and the events at the compound. The case was on its way to being officially ruled self-defense by the Honolulu investigators on their case, and her step was a little lighter leaving than it had been going in.

Dunn had insisted on coming in with her for "moral support" even though the detectives interviewing her had made him wait outside. He fell in step with her as Sophie strode down the hall and out the front door of the Honolulu Police Department building. He'd been relentless in his attempts to get her back to work at Security Solutions. "Since you're out and about, I was hoping you could come into the office for a few. I have someone who wants to see you."

Sophie stopped on the cement steps outside and turned to him, her heart kicking into overdrive. *Would Connor show up at the Security Solutions building?* It would be perfectly normal for him to do that, considering he was the boss.

Light wind played with the few curls long enough to cover

some of the scar on her head, but the damn skin graft hurt every time she went into the sun. Sophie fumbled in her oversized purse, smacked on her hat and pushed on her sunglasses. "Who is it?"

"Our former client. Sharon Blumfield. Who were you expecting? You look like you've seen a ghost."

Sophie gave a snort of hysterical laughter. She'd hardly slept or eaten in the last couple of days with the depression so bad, the wrestling match in her mind so severe. She'd only been able to get herself together enough to come down to the station because the alternative was a bench warrant for her arrest.

Dunn clapped her on the back.

"Get it together, woman. This is a good thing. Come with me. I promise you'll like it."

"Okay. Since you promise I'll like it. I've had too many things I really didn't like lately."

She followed Dunn down the steps and got into her vehicle. Dunn was refreshingly transparent and heavy-handed. Whatever else he was, there was no subterfuge in him—and subterfuge was something she'd had enough of.

SHARON BLUMFIELD MET them in the reception area on the ground floor of the Security Solutions building, and she wasn't alone.

Her children, the boy, Lono and girl, Pele, who Sophie and Jake had rescued, put down comic books and stood to greet her—and two more children behind them also rose. Zeus, the thirteen-year-old boy she'd met at the retreat, and his sister Hera were brushed and scrubbed, wearing bright new clothing. Sophie came to a halt in front of the four kids and took off her sunglasses. "Hello. I'm Sophie Ang."

"And I'm Jake Dunn. Forget shaking hands. You can high-five." Jake got Zeus to try it, along with a complicated fist-bump combination that made them all laugh. Ice broken, Sophie helped Sharon tug chairs into a rough circle.

"You were Mary Watson at the Society. We wondered where you'd gone," Zeus said, when they were all seated. "Dougal told me you didn't like the yoga class and ran for the hills."

"That's true, in a manner of speaking."

"What happened to your face?" Pele asked.

"I got shot. This is a skin graft. They took skin from my hip and put it on my face." Sophie smiled, hoping it wasn't too scary of an effect, but their expressions weren't encouraging. She turned back to their former client. "Ms. Blumfield, thanks so much for bringing the kids in to talk with us."

"The least I could do. Zeus and Hera are going to live with us —their other relatives can't care for them right now, and the therapist we're all seeing suggested we all get some closure by seeing our rescuers in person—and the kids really wanted to see you again."

Dunn told the story of rescuing Lono and Pele to Zeus and Hera with many an embellishment—enough to make Sophie roll her eyes.

"How do you feel about…Sandoval Jackson's death?" Sophie asked.

"Our father, you mean?" Zeus was perfectly composed. "He's going to come back soon. Probably in the body of someone close by, so he can be near us."

Sophie met Blumfield's gaze over the top of the boy's head. The woman gave a slight headshake.

"That's good then," Sophie said lamely. "So. Have you any questions for us?"

"We want to see your equipment lab! All the stuff you have, like Batman!" Pele exclaimed.

Sharon laughed. "The kids have been glutting themselves on TV since we all got outside. Old Batman reruns seemed harmless, and now the kids think Jake is Batman and Sophie is Catwoman."

"Not really. I just think you're kind of like superheroes," Pele said, ducking her head in embarrassment.

"It so happens I've got a few things I can show you in our lab," Dunn said. "Follow me." He took off like the Pied Piper, the kids in pursuit.

"I heard Sloane was the one who shot you," Blumfield said.

Sophie turned her face away from Blumfield's gaze. "Yes."

"The man was a pig. I hated him."

"He's dead now. And not coming back." The memory of Sloane's drowning body under her knee made her shudder.

Blumfield set a hand on Sophie's arm. "Your face will get better. And your heart will too. We just really wanted to thank you. All of the children are doing remarkably well in their new homes, with their grandparents and other relatives. I was delighted to take Zeus and Hera—my kids were so used to the group living situation that they cried for days, missing their brothers and sisters. We're going to bring them all together often."

"It was very good to see you, to know there's been a happy outcome for your family. Thank you." Sophie said goodbye, and left. Dunn would track her down soon enough, probably sooner than she was ready for, as usual.

She needed to go to the beach and unwind—and revisit the scene of the crime.

She wasn't going to let the hideous memory of what had happened there with Sloane ruin one of her favorite places in Honolulu.

Sophie picked up Ginger from the pet sitter, and drove down to Ala Moana Beach Park.

She used the restroom to change into some running clothes and pulled a billed hat down, slathering her face with sunscreen—not something she'd had to do in the past with her tawny complexion, but the plastic surgeon had warned her that the new skin was delicate and sensitive to the sun.

Afternoon was cooling things down as Sophie leashed Ginger and moved out, picking up a slow jog in the deep warm sand.

She passed the location of the attack. The crime scene tape they'd used to rope it off with was gone.

There was nothing to mark the life-and-death struggle that had taken place there between Sophie and two men. Cool, calm turquoise water lapped against fine-grained sand, dimpled with thousands of happy tourist footprints.

Sophie hit the break wall at the end of the beach and jogged back. She reversed and did it again. When she'd done the length of the beach four times and Ginger was panting and begging to go into the ocean, she peeled off the exercise clothes she'd worn over her bikini and went in, laughing as the Lab chased her. They swam and splashed, and finally Sophie grabbed Ginger's tail and let the dog tow her into shallow water.

*Where would she be without Ginger?* The dog brought so much laughter and surprise into her life, helping beat back the depression's talons.

She spread out her beach towel and lay down on her stomach, the hat back on, protecting her face. Ginger flopped beside her, tongue hanging out.

Sophie just rested there for a long, sweet time.

The late afternoon sun dried the water on her back. The sound of beachgoers laughing and playing in the gentle water and the breeze in the nearby monkeypod trees—all of it soothed her.

She had a place of her own, interesting work, and friends. She was recovering well from her injuries, and she was discovering new things about herself: what she liked and what she didn't, and she was making a life out from behind her computers.

That didn't mean she didn't still love the tech world. She'd recently set up Ying, Amara, and JinJai, her computers, in the apartment—and the niggle of a new program idea had her playing with code for the first time in months.

But the security concerns about using DAVID remained along

with the unanswered consent questions. It was easier, for the moment, just to let DAVID rest awhile.

*She didn't have to know exactly where she was going, or what came next.*

But she was lonely.

She missed Connor.

*Todd.*

*Sheldon.*

Whoever he was, she missed that brilliant, complicated, fascinating man who obviously played violin as well as all the other things he was able to do—if those callouses on his fingers were anything to go by.

She wanted to hear him play violin.

After days of wrestling with her conscience, she'd come to a decision.

Sophie sat up on her elbows and dug into the pocket of her discarded nylon shorts, bringing out her phone. She clicked to the encoded site she used to communicate with the Ghost, and typed in a message.

*Been thinking a lot about our conversation. You were right. I'm a hypocrite.*

The little green cursor in the old-school DOS-style format pulsed at her, then green letters unspooled and her heart rate picked up.

*Took you long enough to admit it. Two whole days was way too long not to hear from you.*

*A girl has her pride. I felt betrayed. But I've thought it through and I understand why you couldn't tell me.*

*Are you going to keep my secret?*

Sophie bit her lip. *Yes. For now. Subject to review.*

*I'll take it, and thanks. I wish Todd had met you first. Everything would have been simpler.*

*Would Todd have liked me as much as Sheldon did?*

*Definitely. He'd have turned on his Aussie charm and swept you off your feet.*

*I'm glad you're both—because I never liked that accent much.*

A long pause. Ginger wriggled closer and snuffled against Sophie's side, tickling her, and Sophie scratched under her chin.

*I'm afraid you'll have to put up with the accent in public, because Todd is planning to ask you out. But it's Connor you'll really get to know, Mary Watson.*

Sophie's fingers flew as she texted. *That's 'Sophie Watson,' to you. Bring Anubis down to the beach when you're feeling better, and we'll see where we go from there.*

*It's a start. I'll be up and around soon.*

*Thanks for taking a bullet for me, by the way.*

*And thanks for saving my life. Things can only get better from here.*

Sophie smiled. "You're right, Connor. Things can only get better from here." She turned the phone off and lay back down to enjoy the last of the warm Waikiki afternoon sun, Ginger at her side.

**Turn the page for a sneak peek of, *Wired Hard*, Paradise Crime Thrillers book 3.**

# SNEAK PEEK

Two nights later, Sophie was sitting in a semi-trance watching the monitors when one of the sensor lights went off, accompanied by a loud banging on the metal gate of the site's fenced enclosure. "Sophie!"

Sophie was already on her feet. She started in surprise at the sight of her partner at Security Solutions, Jake Dunn, in the monitor. His all-black, combat-ready clothing projected an intimidating message, as did his height and build—but his ready grin was pure masculine charm.

Jake was a badass, but also a big softie who loved Ninja Turtle cartoons on Saturday, too much relish on his hotdog, and to give her fashion advice.

Sophie jogged out of the trailer and unlocked the gate to let her partner in, feeling a distinct lift in her spirits. "Jake! What are you doing here?"

Jake swung her up in his arms for a too-long hug. He never really stopped flirting in spite of her many reminders, and after months of working together, she had to admit she wasn't totally averse to it.

Jake kissed her cheek with a resounding smack. "Had to come

over to make a pitch for another contract, and couldn't resist breaking up my favorite partner's exciting evening."

"And thank God you did. I was about to disgrace myself by falling asleep again." Sophie pushed against Jake's chest to get him to let go of her. "What job is this?"

"I might as well tell you inside. We can get more comfortable." He bounced his brows, incorrigible.

"Come into my palace." Sophie led him to the dilapidated trailer. "When you told me this was a job at a royal Hawaiian archaeological site, I had something a bit grander in mind."

Jake followed her up the rickety step. Inside, he looked around, hands on hips, overhead light gleaming on short dark hair, highlighting his shoulders in the tight black shirt. "This was not what I was told on the phone. They told me expense account. Air conditioning. A nice condo. We should never take jobs sight unseen— hence my trip over to check out this new one."

"Well, I suppose technically that's all true." Sophie hit the button on the ancient wall AC, and the unit rumbled into life. Condensation dripped into a can set beneath it. "I turned it off because somehow the noise makes me sleepier, and doesn't really do anything temperature-wise."

Jake pulled a folding metal chair over to the desk and sat on it, extending long legs in black combat boots up to the desk's surface and crossing them at the ankle. "Yeah. I was sold a bill of goods on this job. I should have taken it, not you."

"Well, except that I wanted it. I wanted to come see my friend Lei, get a change of scenery. I love Maui. And as for the job, except for the part where I'm a glorified night watchman, the situation at the nonprofit is interesting. It appears the thieves are looking for something specific as they dig these holes." Sophie unlocked one of the desk drawers, and took out a thick report. "This is the interpretation of the ground penetrating radar survey done by the archaeology firm contracted by the Hui to Restore Kakela. This shows possible burial sites and concentrations of artifacts on the actual island, which is what this trailer is standing on. Most of the field you see out there is a former lagoon filled with dirt from the construction of the road leading out of Lahaina. It is unlikely to have had anything in it that didn't decompose in the water. But the part that is the island..." Sophie unrolled the blue surveyor's map of the site and spread it on the desk for Jake to see. "This island might even hold the burial site of one of Kamehameha's queens."

Jake steepled his thick fingers. "How real is that? Because if it is, that's something that would really put Kakela on the map."

"I don't know how real it is. But, I'm getting to understand a little better what the archaeologists' priorities are." Sophie paged to the section in the report that seemed to indicate possible burials and relics on the island. "The GPR can't distinguish small details, but these shapes indicate a possible buried canoe, which Brett Taggart, the archaeologist I'm working with, seems to think could be the queen's burial site."

"So why hasn't anyone excavated that? It seems like the first thing they would do."

"Dr. Taggart's archaeology firm was hired to survey the site and locate all the edges of the island area. The Army Corps of Engineers is slated to come remove all the fill dirt in the former lagoon area in a few months. Once that is done, restoration of the actual island area will begin. The burial site will likely remain undisturbed. Hawaiian cultural value is to leave the burials the way they were and not excavate them."

"But that could leave the site open to vandals or thieves." Jake frowned. "Which is why Security Solutions is involved at all. Wouldn't finding the queen's burial site increase those problems?"

"Not if no one knew it was found." Sophie traced the oblong shape of the possible canoe in the report's illustration. "This report is highly confidential. Only the inner circle of leadership at the Hui has access to it. And you're right. That's one of the risks with a specific burial. If they build any sort of marker or monument, it could attract the kind of negative attention they've struggled with in Egypt."

"There's no silver, gold, or precious gems here in Hawaii."

"No, but look at this example." Sophie flicked open pictures on her phone. Pomai Magnuson had shared a photo of a chief's necklace made entirely from polished dogs' teeth. The lei had a hypnotizing, barbaric beauty. "This is a relic that was found on the site of a hotel built here on Maui. The body was reburied with this artifact, and blessed by a kahu, priest, on the grounds. It's hidden beneath a rock formation so no one knows where it is. But don't you think this is the kind of thing that a Hawaiiana collector would do just about anything to get his hands on?"

Jake leaned in close to look at the photo on her phone. He pinched his fingers to open it wider, examining the detail of the polished ivory canines. "I see what you mean."

"And here's a drawing of one of the human bone hooks found at this site." Sophie scrolled to the illustration. The bone hook was an arc of the polished, tea-colored bone with holes drilled in the top and bottom. "Taggart told me these are not photographed, in order to show respect."

"Where is the barb to keep the fish on?"

"The Hawaiians were master fishermen. They didn't want a precious bone, infused with the mana of their ancestors, to be broken. Two separate barbs were lashed onto the hook's body with animal hide at the bottom, and they could break off if necessary, from here." Sophie leaned over to point, and heard the soft sound of a deeply indrawn breath—Jake inhaling.

*Was he...smelling her?*

Sophie pulled back, her neck instantly hot, but Jake continued to look down at the phone as if nothing had happened. She cleared her throat. "So, anyway, I wish there was a picture of a completely restored bone hook that I could show you, but this is an idea of what we're dealing with. The bone is this color because of staining from the surrounding soil."

"I think I have more of an idea about these, and I can see the appeal." Jake looked up at her. "You do any fishing?"

"A little bit when I was a child growing up in Thailand, but nothing since."

"I'll take you sometime. Great way to spend time in nature and bring something home to eat too."

"Sounds fun." *But would he try to turn it into a date?* She'd told him she was seeing someone, but he didn't seem to take the hint—or even the outright slapdown. "Tell me about this job you're here to pitch."

"Shank Miller, a rock star with a beach house in Wailea, has become a part of a kayak tour." Jake leaned back and away, lacing his hands behind his head. "The tour is technically staying outside of the no-harassment zone, but the tourists and paparazzi are camping out on the beach, trying to get a shot of him or his girl-friend sunning naked." Jake reached into his pocket and pulled out a plastic-wrapped rod of beef jerky. "Want some?"

"No, thanks." Sophie sat back down in her chair to watch the monitors as he unwrapped the snack.

"Anyway, Miller wants a full security system and he's had a couple of incursions, so he wants to hire permanent bodyguards to keep the riffraff out of his area. As you know, no one can own Hawaii beaches, so rabid fans are able to get closer to celebrities here than just about anywhere."

"Sounds like you'll be the one with the expense account and the nice condo."

"So far, so good on that score. Open bar and kitchen with a chef in the main house. Miller's putting me up in a 'cottage.'" Jake made air quotes. "It's bigger than our office area on Oahu."

"I take it you're pretty motivated to get the gig."

"Well, I made my best effort today, but there are several firms that sent over reps and estimates, so…" Jake shrugged. "But if Security Solutions gets the job, I'll need a partner."

*Staying in a cottage with Jake 24/7 wasn't such a good idea…*

"But I'm already busy, so if these two Maui situations overlap, I won't be available."

"Miller's got his mainland security team holding down the fort, and you're only on this Hui contract for two weeks, right? So it could work out. In fact, I'm going to propose to Remarkian that we open a satellite office over here on Maui, since we fly over so much and we both like it here." Jake grinned, but his gunmetal-gray eyes were flinty. "Not that I think Remarkian will let you leave Oahu."

"We're dating. Remarkian doesn't own me," Sophie said. "Time for a perimeter check." She stood up, picking up the heavy metal flashlight and Taser. She needed to get a breath away from Jake.

She walked outside of the trailer and deliberately out through the gate, outside of the fenced enclosure and range of the sensor lights. The cool night air, sweet with the smell of plumeria and dust, tickled her nose and calmed her nerves.

Jake just needed to be reminded of boundaries—and that she was halfway in love with someone else.

*Connor.*

Connor, who could play the violin like a virtuoso, and computers just as well. Connor, who liked to rock climb and scuba dive and run-hike challenging trails with her and their dogs. Connor, who had told her that he loved her, and had taken a bullet to prove it.

*Connor, who had a mysterious and deadly alter ego.*

**Continue reading *Wired Hard*: tobyneal.net/WHwb**

# ACKNOWLEDGMENTS

Aloha dear readers!

Thanks so much for coming along for another adventure with Sophie! I am already plotting and writing *Wired Hard*, Book 3 in the Paradise Crime Series, and it involves a nefarious plot on Maui to steal artifacts from a sacred buried royal Hawaiian island...But I get ahead of myself.

I so enjoyed getting Sophie out of her computer cave and out into the field. When I began writing this book, I had an idea that I wanted more action, and a less "tech-heavy" plot (because, let's face it, computers are not my area.) I was toying with the idea of getting her out of the FBI and working for a private firm...but I had NO IDEA Jake Dunn would show up on the page, that he'd be such a powerful character and shake things up so much. Nor did I know that with the threat of her ex removed in Book 1, that Sophie would go into such an identity tailspin...but the twist at the end with the Ghost? Yeah, that was planned from book 1, and there are more surprises ahead!

Some days I wake up and pinch myself. I have the best job in the world, creating characters that take on a life of their own and capture the hearts and minds of readers, taking them on a journey to amazing places they may never see—like the Waipio Valley, on the Big Island.

Until next time, I'll be in my "writing cave," working on *Wired Hard*, book 3 in the Paradise Crime Series. Pop in and say hi on social media. I'm on Facebook, Twitter, Pinterest and Instagram!

Much aloha, Toby Neal

I hope you enjoyed *Wired Rogue*! If you think other readers will enjoy it too, please leave an honest review on Barnes and Noble, iBooks, Goodreads, or KOBO. Your thoughts matter so much, and I read them all!

Much aloha,

# FREE BOOKS

Join my mystery and romance lists and receive free, full-length, award-winning ebooks of *Torch Ginger* & *Somewhere on St. Thomas* as welcome gifts: tobyneal.net/TNNews

# TOBY'S BOOKSHELF

## PARADISE CRIME SERIES

### Paradise Crime Mysteries
Blood Orchids
Torch Ginger
Black Jasmine
Broken Ferns
Twisted Vine
Shattered Palms
Dark Lava
Fire Beach
Rip Tides
Bone Hook
Red Rain
Bitter Feast
Razor Rocks
Wrong Turn
Shark Cove
*Coming 2021*

## Paradise Crime Mysteries Novella
Clipped Wings

## Paradise Crime Mystery
**Special Agent Marcella Scott**
Stolen in Paradise

## Paradise Crime Suspense Mysteries
Unsound

## Paradise Crime Thrillers
Wired In
Wired Rogue
Wired Hard
Wired Dark
Wired Dawn
Wired Justice
Wired Secret
Wired Fear
Wired Courage
Wired Truth
Wired Ghost
Wired Strong
Wired Revenge
*Coming 2021*

## ROMANCES
**Toby Jane**

## The Somewhere Series
Somewhere on St. Thomas
Somewhere in the City
Somewhere in California

**The Somewhere Series**
**Secret Billionaire Romance**
Somewhere in Wine Country
Somewhere in Montana
*Date TBA*
Somewhere in San Francisco
*Date TBA*

**A Second Chance Hawaii Romance**
Somewhere on Maui

**Co-Authored Romance Thrillers**
**The Scorch Series**
Scorch Road
Cinder Road
Smoke Road
Burnt Road
Flame Road
Smolder Road

**YOUNG ADULT**

**Standalone**
Island Fire

**NONFICTION**
**TW Neal**

**Memoir**
Freckled
Open Road

# ABOUT THE AUTHOR

Kirkus Reviews calls Neal's writing, *"persistently riveting. Masterly."*

Award-winning, USA Today bestselling social worker turned author Toby Neal grew up on the island of Kaua`i in Hawaii. Neal is a mental health therapist, a career that has informed the depth and complexity of the characters in her stories. Neal's mysteries and thrillers explore the crimes and issues of Hawaii from the bottom of the ocean to the top of volcanoes. Fans call her stories, *"Immersive, addicting, and the next best thing to being there."*

Neal also pens romance, romantic thrillers, and writes memoir/nonfiction under TW Neal.

Visit tobyneal.net for more ways to stay in touch!
or
Join my Facebook readers group, *Friends Who Like Toby Neal Books,* for special giveaways and perks.

www.ingramcontent.com/pod-product-compliance
Lightning Source LLC
Chambersburg PA
CBHW052046240626
47153CB00006B/2240